THE MEDAL: BOOK SIX—JACK IRON

Kit McQueen—Daniel's warrior son would ally himself with a pirate and risk a firing squad to pursue vengeance . . . and a woman. For love, he becomes an outlaw. For survival, he must choose his pirate companions with care.

Raven O'Keefe—The half-breed beauty inherited her mother's gifts of prophecy and healing. Yet in Kit McQueen she found a man whose love would heal her heart—and ignite it.

Cesar Obregon—The Hawk of the Antilles ruled with a dapper mien and a devastating sword. With General Jackson's chest of gold and the sensuous Raven O'Keefe in his hold, the pirate sailed to his island fortress, primed with the spoils of war.

Captain Orturo "the Cayman" Navarre—A cannibal in gentleman's dress, he took Natividad by storm and awaited the return of its pirate prince, only to find his greatest challenge in Raven, the captive who turned his savage blood to ice.

Jean Laffite—An honorable pirate, he fought by Jackson's side until betrayal drove him to desert with an unlikely ally in Kit McQueen. His enemy Obregon was within his sights—until an even greater foe made him hold his fire. . . .

★ THE MEDAL ★
Book 6

JACK
IRON

Kerry Newcomb

BANTAM BOOKS
NEW YORK · TORONTO · LONDON · SYDNEY · AUCKLAND

JACK IRON

A Bantam Domain Book / September 1993

ISBN 0-553-29446-6

Published simultaneously in the United States and Canada

Bantam Books are published by Bantam Books, a division of Bantam Doubleday Dell Publishing Group, Inc. Its trademark, consisting of the words "Bantam Books" and the portrayal of a rooster, is Registered in U.S. Patent and Trademark Office and in other countries. Marca Registrada. Bantam Books, 1540 Broadway, New York, New York 10036.

PRINTED IN THE UNITED STATES OF AMERICA

RAD   0 9 8 7 6 5 4 3 2 1

For Patty, Amy Rose, P.J., and Emily Anabel
All captains of my ship

Thanks to some special people: my wife, Patricia, for her tireless research; Ann and Paul Newcomb, who first taught me the power of love; my agent, Aaron Priest, without whom the Mc-Queens might never have lived; thanks to Bantam Books and most especially Greg Tobin and Don D'Auria for your belief and support. Thanks, brother Jim, for being there when the system crashed and retrieve didn't work. I must also humbly acknowledge my "local color" experts, Doctor Bob Bain of Grenada and Eilene Bain, daughter Mel, and the rest of the Bainsters for "good stuff" on local customs and a proper recipe for "oil-down."

Prologue

December 17, 1814.

After sailing his three-masted brig into the harbor of Natividad and unleashing his two-hundred-and-thirteen-man crew on the inhabitants of Morgan Town, Captain Orturo "the Cayman" Navarre promptly captured the island's governor—Josiah Morgan—and ate him. Navarre neatly prepared his midday meal, flavoring cuts of the governor with peppers, wild onions, garlic, plantain, and chunks of guava. Then, in front of the subdued people gathered in the public square, the Cayman proceeded to dine.

The product of a Spanish father and a Carib mistress, Navarre had been raised by his mother's people to be strong, to suffer pain without flinching, to be cruel and merciless to his enemies, and ruthless in battle. The Caribs were cannibals; however, Orturo took his ritualistic meals of human flesh more for the effect they had on others than to appease his own gruesome appetites.

Orturo Navarre finished off the governor and washed him down with a tankard of rum, then slowly but succinctly explained to a council of the port's stunned inhabitants just exactly what he expected from them in return for his protection. The Cayman made his point, gesturing with a rib bone while he spoke, then afterward offered the Cabilde, the town council, a place at his table. Navarre laughed heartily as the merchants politely refused and hurried off to their houses, leaving the pirate and his henchmen a tentative promise of their cooperation. No one wanted to end up as the next day's "sumptuous feast."

Orturo Navarre rose from the table in the middle of the town square and, followed by a dozen of his crewmen, retraced his path up the winding street toward the governor's palace, a walled hacienda that had once belonged to the late Josiah Morgan. The palace was a small fortress with ten-foot-high stone battlements surrounding a two-story stone house. A battery of four 24-pounder cannons were nestled in a redoubt below the hacienda's walls and guarded the bay and harbor. Swivel guns loaded with grapeshot dominated the walls of the governor's palace. The island's steeply sided volcanic mountains swept up from the harbor and formed a natural barrier against any attack except from the sea. The palace's fortifications, though formidable, had been undermanned— still, the defenders might have put up quite a struggle had not Navarre brought his black-rigged ship into port under cover of night and captured the governor enjoying himself at a local tavern. (It had been Morgan, trusting to the mercy of his captors, who had surrendered the meager garrison and talked his men out from behind the palace's limestone walls only to see his guardsmen shot down and thrown to the sharks.)

On reaching the hacienda, Orturo Navarre walked to the edge of the cliff overlooking the harbor. The maw of a cannon peered over his shoulder like some baleful black eye. The wind from the bay swept up to ruffle the hem of his dark green brocade cloth coat. He was aptly nicknamed, for his features were mottled and as leathery looking as an alligator's. And his teeth, like those of the Carib, were filed into points. He stood six feet tall. His head, shaved smooth, was like the rest of his torso, burned dark from the sun by a life spent on the high seas. In contrast to his savage habits, Navarre wore finery befitting a European nobleman. A silk waistcoat, lighter green than his coat, sported mother-of-pearl buttons. He had a fondness for ruffled white shirts with lace cuffs. His skintight trousers matched his coat and were tucked into thigh-high boots. A bandolier drapped across his chest held a matched set of flintlock pistols with bone handle-grips. A cutlass dangled at his left side. He folded his arms and looked out across the bay, fringed with soft white sand and coconut palms. A hundred yards inland, the steep ridges of volcanic rock swept up toward the azure sky. The only other protected bay lay on the opposite side of the island in a place called Obregon's Cove. But it was dotted by reefs and required repeated tacking to reach the shore, a difficult task even for a brig like the *Scourge,* which was gaffe-rigged and could sail close to the wind. But Navarre had a use for Obregon's Cove as he did for Morgan Town.

He turned toward the collection of shops and taverns and stone houses comprising the port settlement. The town even boasted a church, a squat, thick-walled structure with a bell tower rising above the entrance. The church faced one side of the town square and seemed solid and impervious to the grog halls with which it shared the center of town. These were his people now; every rum runner, farmer, and wharf rat.

His second-in-command, a massive-looking African named NKenai, approached his captain and spoke in a deep, resonant voice.

"Captain Navarre, the priest would speak with you." He gestured with a wave of a broad hand toward a reed-thin, rum-soaked–looking individual in black robes and broad-brimmed straw hat that the breeze kept trying to lift from his head. Tiny red veins were etched on his cheeks and nose. His bony hands betrayed the beginnings of arthritis, his joints swollen and the knuckles enlarged. Father Albert Bernal nervously awaited permission to approach the fierce-some pirate.

Orturo Navarre nodded to his subordinate. The big African grinned, revealing a row of yellow teeth set in the tattooed ebony mask of his face. Sweat glistened on the black man's cheeks and soaked the edges of the cobalt blue fez the man wore atop his coarsely braided hair. NKenai kept a scimitar in his belt and throwing knives tucked in sheaths at the small of his back. The priest was ringed by several grim-looking men who took care to block Father Bernal's path should he try to retreat from Captain Navarre and return to the village below.

One of the pirates, a grizzled, wire-haired man with broken teeth and rope burns on his neck, jabbed the muzzle of his rifled musket into the priest's side. "The name is Quince, Bible thumper. Malachi Quince be my name, and I've sinned from Maine to Hispaniola. There ain't be nothin' I ain't done. What say you to that?" The swarthy little man spat in the dirt at Bernal's feet.

"Ask for forgiveness and the Lord will grant it, my son," the good priest said.

"Only thing I ask for is another twenty good years o' sinning. I want to earn my place in hell," Quince slapped the basket hilt of the cutlass at his side, tossed back his head, and belly-laughed.

Orturo the Cayman turned and gestured for the priest to approach. The pirate captain stood with legs splayed wide and arms folded. Indeed the man radiated a kind of cruel royalty. He had stolen Natividad right out from under its defenders and hadn't lost a single member of his crew. He could hear the songs already praising his daring feat.

"What is it you want, Priest?"

Bernal gulped and stared down at his trembling hands, then looked up at the pirate. "The Cabilde has promised the cooperation of the town and you have offered protection from . . . uh . . . others. But we wish to know what you have in mind. Why have you come?"

"Why, to make your people rich, Padre. To put coins in their pockets. What say you to that? Maybe even coins in your pocket, too, eh."

"I don't understand."

The Cayman glanced at the men standing a few feet away and grinned. "Men will come to this port to spend their money on women and grog. They will come to buy what we have to sell. Ships will flock to us."

"But the island is mostly mountainous. We have some coconut groves near the water, and inland, there are a few valleys where crops grow, but not enough to bring so many ships." Bernal knew he was treading dangerous ground, yet he intended to press the matter. The Cayman had come to Natividad for a reason and the priest was determined to learn the truth.

"Slaves . . . the black gold of high commerce. I will bring them from Africa and keep them in Obregon's Cove. They can work themselves to good health harvesting sugar cane until the slavers arrive. Natividad shall be the hub of a wheel, and along the spokes, ships will come eager to buy slaves, but not wishing to voyage all the way to Africa. They will come to me. And their crews will spend their money in the whore cribs and rum houses I will build in Morgan Town."

Father Bernal shuddered and his heart was filled with dismay. True, there were many of his flock who had been freebooters and sailed beneath the black flag. But these poor souls had mended their ways and married and lived, brought families to Natividad and made of it a sanctuary. Perhaps such people weren't as civilized as the inhabitants of the mainland. Indeed they were a rough lot, but they were honest and loyal to one another, and Albert Bernal, with all his vices, had fit right in. He was one of them. And he had helped them build a community and make something of themselves, and it didn't matter who among them was wanted for thievery or piracy or who had escaped the hangman's rope, Natividad was a place for a second chance and the priest wasn't going to see it corrupted by the Cayman.

"Slavers," Bernal muttered with contempt. "You would turn us into slavers! The devil's own!" He summoned all his courage. "Perhaps you have made a wrong choice of island," he said, hoping to reason with the pirate. "The people here are frightened, but they are all rebels. They do not give in quite so simply as you may think. And you will have Cesar Obregon to deal with."

"Ah, the Hawk of the Antilles," Navarre said in a mocking tone of voice. "I can handle him—but as for your rebellious flock, you must counsel them to obey me."

"No!" the priest blurted out. "I am not much. But the pulpit is sacred. They have built me a church. I shall not desecrate the holy ground by aiding you to destroy my flock."

NKenai started forward. He did not like the priest's tone of voice. The black robe was being disrespectful. And for the African warrior whose sole allegiance was to the Cayman, disrespect could not be tolerated. He drew a dagger from his belt and started forward. The Cayman read his henchman's intent and shook his head. The simple gesture stopped NKenai in his tracks. Navarre stroked his chin and studied the priest. He leaned against one of the twenty-four-pounder cannons below the walls of the governor's palace and looked out over the bay. Below him, mangle-blanc trees clung to the rugged rocky slope. Among those twisted branches nested a variety of lizards, darting dragonflies, and yellow-throated parakeets. There was a constant breeze here, cool and refreshing in the warm glare of sunlight. Orturo the Cayman might be a cannibal, but he was not without an eye for beauty.

Navarre considered the priest's remarks. The last thing he wanted was to deal with some constant and tedious insurrection. He needed Bernal to use his influence to bend the people to Navarre's will. The death of the governor might not be enough after all.

Inspiration struck him. Navarre called to one of his men, a gnarled-looking freebooter with thinning hair, a full brown beard, and pockmarked features. He wore a loose-fitting shirt and baggy cotton breeches and carried a musket. A pistol and cutlass were tucked in a wide leather belt circling his waist.

The pirate hurried forward, certain Navarre was no doubt sending him out for something important.

"Aye, Cap'n Navarre," the pirate called. Tom Bragg was eager to take his place among Navarre's inner circle of cutthroats.

"How long have you faithfully served me, old friend?" asked Navarre.

"Ever since you fished me out of the sea, Cap'n, and kept my hide from becoming shark bait. Must be nigh on to six years now since the *Magnus* went down." The pirate scratched at his pitted cheek and tried to tabulate the months that had passed since he'd been accepted into the *Scourge*'s crew.

"No man has been more reliable. No man has shown more courage."

"Thankee, Cap'n Navarre," Bragg said, beaming.

The Cayman drew a pistol and fired. Blood spurted from Bragg's left calf and the pirate howled and crumpled to earth. He groaned and clutched at his wounded leg. NKenai moved quickly to disarm his comrade to prevent him from doing anything rash.

"Oh, sweet mother of God," Bragg groaned through clenched teeth. A lizard darted out from under rock and across a patch of blood on the earth.

Navarre turned and held the smoking gun up to Father Bernal's face. The priest grew pale. He had never in his life confronted such raw evil. It left him speechless. The groaning from poor Tom Bragg punctuated the priest's silence. Finally Father Bernal spoke out in indignation.

"This man is your trusted comrade. How could you treat him in so base a manner. What kind of monster are you?"

"Precisely," Navarre said, drawing close to Bernal and placing his hand on the smaller man's shoulder. "Hear me, Priest. This man was like my brother. Look at him and think to yourself what course my wrath might take toward the men, women, and children of Natividad who mean no more to me than what I leave in my chamber pot."

Bernal grew pale and his rail-thin frame shuddered at the thought of the endless possibilities, each one more gruesome than the one before.

"In the name of God . . ." he muttered.

"I leave you your God," said Navarre. "But Natividad is mine." He returned the gun to his belt. The Cayman waved a hand, and NKenai took the priest by the arm and started him back down the shell-paved road to town. Bragg was carried away to the ship's surgeon to have his wound staunched and cauterized. Navarre tucked a small pouch of Spanish doubloons into Bragg's shirt as he was carried off. "The gold will ease the pain," Navarre told the African, who returned to his captain's side.

NKenai nodded. He could see the brilliance in the Cayman's scheme. "Now the Christian shaman will guide his people in the proper way. He will see they do your bidding. You are a clever man, my captain. The heart of a lion but the crafty mind of the fox has Captain Orturo Navarre. Orturo the Magnificent."

Navarre grinned and looked out across the bay dominated by his brig and guarded by the shore batteries he now commanded. The first stage of his empire. He was filled with a sense of triumph. "I will make these people my own; Natividad shall be my kingdom." He held out his arms as if to embrace the earth and sea and the limitless horizon. "This is only the beginning, NKenai. Who is there to stand against me?" His chest swelled as the wind pressed against him and with fists clenched, the Cayman shouted in exultation, "Who can stand against me!"

Chapter One

Kit McQueen wasn't laughing as the British marine clubbed him with the butt of his musket and sent the redheaded American sprawling in the dirt alongside the lightning-shattered hickory tree that served as a makeshift redoubt. The fallen timber capped a ridge of earth above Drake's Creek five miles east of the Mississippi River. It was the first day of 1815. And about to be the last for me, Kit thought as the heavyset Cornishman landed on his chest and drew a dagger from his white canvas belt. Kit could read the name stitched into the marine's leather cartridge box. TREGONING.

"Now, you Yankee bastard, I'll lift that red scalp of yours the same as your heathen friends would do me," Tregoning snarled. White spittle clung to his lower lip. His brown eyes widened, his nostrils flared, and his hands trembled with the bloodlust that was upon him. His breath was heavy with the rum he and his mates had been sampling when the Choctaws surprised them.

Kit worked a hand loose from underneath the man straddling him and grabbed a fistful of Tregoning's genitalia and squeezed with all his strength. The marine howled and thrust his knife, but the pain ruined his aim and the blade sank up to the hilt in the black earth inches from McQueen's throat. The marine grabbed the smaller man by the front of his loose-fitting buckskin shirt and dragged him to his feet, forcing Kit to lose his hold.

"You Brits can sing a pretty note," McQueen taunted. He felt the leather cord tear from around his neck as Tregoning staggered back, clutching a torn patch of shirt and the medal, a silver English crown sterling bearing the crudely scrawled initials of George Washington. The coin was a family keepsake, for General Washington himself had presented the makeshift medal to Kit's father, Daniel McQueen.

The English marine glanced around and saw his companions had abandoned him among his enemies. Tregoning knew when to cut his losses. He spun around and leaped over the log and started down the creekbank. He spied the rest of the skirmishers fleeing into the trees on the other side of the creek. The cowards had scattered at the first volley from the American and his Choctaw allies.

"No, you don't," Kit shouted, and vaulted the fallen hickory. He landed square on the burly Cornishman's shoulders. The impact tumbled them both down the creekbank and left the men splashing in the muddy shallows. The three remaining Choctaw warriors Kit had brought from General Jackson's camp below New Orleans stared at one another in mute amazement, then watched with alarm as another dozen English marines from General Packenham's formidable invasion force filtered through the trees. The soldiers wore faded red coats and white linen trousers and short-brimmed black hats. Their features were windburned masks of menace.

Kit and Tregoning weren't alone in the creek. They shared the mud with three dead marines and a dead Choctaw brave. The brave lay bellydown in the mud of the creekbank. His tomahawk was buried in the chest of one of the Englishmen. The rest of Tregoning's companions crouched among the trees on the other side of the creek and were feverishly reloading their rifled muskets when reinforcements arrived.

Kit counted a dozen marines rise up from the emerald shadows; a dozen muskets were aimed at him. McQueen hauled Tregoning, sputtering, out of the water and placed the half-drowned Cornishman between himself and these lethal-looking newcomers about thirty yards away.

"Kill me and you'll kill your mate," Kit shouted, figuring he had the reinforcements stymied. Tregoning would shield him all the way up the embankment to safety. The sergeant in command stepped forward, ran a hand across his neatly trimmed beard, and scowled as he recognized Tregoning.

"Shoot them down!" he shouted.

"Christ!" Kit dove to one side and Tregoning the other as this second wave of marines opened fire. Kit and Tregoning chose different routes as they scrambled up toward the Choctaw defenders. Slugs sent geysers of earth erupting from the steep bank. At five foot eight, Kit McQueen offered a smaller target than Tregoning. Kit was as nimble as a panther as he climbed the embankment. The Choctaws returned the gunfire in an attempt to cover his retreat. McQueen and Tregoning darted and leaped through a gauntlet of lead death. For all McQueen's feline grace and quickness, he reached the redoubt but a few seconds ahead of Tregoning, who lumbered across the hickory log and slumped wearily alongside the man who moments ago he'd been attempting to kill.

Tregoning's chest rose and fell as he sucked in the cold damp air. His breath clouded before his lips. He'd lost his hat, revealing a bald head ringed by a fringe of black hair. His nose had been flattened by a well-thrown punch sometime in the past and issued a faint whistling sound with each and every breath.

Kit McQueen, with his keen bronze gaze, shrewdly appraised his adversary. McQueen ran a hand through his curly mane of red hair that Tregoning had recently attempted to lift with scalping knife in hand. Slugs gouged the makeshift barricade, showering both men with splinters. One of the Choctaws, a youthful brave named Three Snakes, clutched his throat as he rose up to take aim. The brave slumped onto his side and stared with a weakening gaze at the rivulet of blood showing from his wound. Kit watched the man die and his features grew dark with fury. A waste, a damn waste.

"Your friends have won this day, Tregoning. But there will come another, mark my words."

"Friends, hell," Tregoning said. "Your heathens scattered my mates. Them behind the trees are the Chiltern Rifles. They answer only to Sergeant Tiberius, who has no use for me at all."

"So I noticed," Kit dryly observed.

"He caught me playing at "bushy park" with his dear Megan and has been trying to center me in his sights ever since. Reckon he figures to kill me and blame it on the likes of you." Tregoning wagged his bald head and scratched at his grizzled jawline. "Megan was his wife and a trollop and he's well off to know the old gal for what she is, mark my words." He glanced across at Kit, who finished reloading a matched pair of short-barreled, heavy-bore pistols he called "the Quakers." One shot from these "hand cannons" made enemies into friends or left them dead. Either result was acceptable to Kit McQueen.

"See here—what the devil?" Tregoning noted as Kit trained the pistols at him.

"You're my prisoner," Kit said. "And I'll take

that coin in your hand." Kit tucked one pistol in its buckskin holster and held out a mud-grimed palm.

Tregoning frowned, then shrugged and handed over the coin that had become a McQueen legacy. Surrender to the redheaded American squatting at his side seemed preferable to facing the outraged husband, Tiberius Smollet.

"Tregoning! Harry Tregoning!" the sergeant on the opposite creekbank called out. "Stand up so I can see that ugly face of yours."

Kit peered over the edge of the tree trunk and saw that the Chiltern Rifles were reloading and fixing bayonets. He looked back at the two remaining Choctaws. Nate Russell was a year older than McQueen, a warrior of thirty-one winters. He had long black hair and a solid muscular build and wore a blue infantryman's jacket over his buckskin shirt. Nate, like many of the Choctaw Nation, had converted to Christianity. The other warrior, Strikes With Club, was a decade younger and had no use for white men's religion. His long hair hung unbound to his shoulders. He was shivering, for he'd cast aside his blanket to free his arms for fighting. He was a handsome brave and much sought after by the maidens of his village.

"Where's Obregon?" Strikes With Club growled. "You said the others would come when they heard our guns."

Kit had no answer for his red-skinned friend. Cesar Obregon, known throughout the Caribbean as the Hawk of the Antilles and whose black flag depicted a skeleton kneeling in prayer, had taken up a position along McQueen's back trail about a hundred yards from Drake's Creek. The freebooter and his men should have come running at the sound of gunfire. It had been a cold gray afternoon and an interminable-seeming wait, yet Kit and his Choctaws had remained at their post, hoping to intercept the British soldiers who had been studying the American entrenchments below New Orleans. Kit had the disturbing feeling that Cesar and his men had tired of the wintry discomfort and returned to New Orleans without alerting their companions by the creek.

A ripple of musket fire sounded below, and another round of slugs thudded into the hickory log forcing the men behind the makeshift rampart to crouch down.

"Hey, Yankee, be a good lad and haul up that no-good soldier of the king who's with you. Prepare to meet your maker, Harry."

"Now see here, Tiberius," the Cornishman shouted back. "I didn't do nothin' to your Meg that she didn't want me to do."

"You son of a bitch!" came the reply punctuated by a pistol crack.

Harry Tregoning chuckled as shattered bark showered his chest and head.

Kit scowled. He was caught in the middle of two wars, one major and one private. *And if I live to meet up with Cesar Obregon, I'll start a third,* Kit promised himself. Maybe he ought to force Tregoning over the top and allow the marine to buy them some time as Kit and the Choctaws made good their escape. Tregoning seemed to read McQueen's thoughts.

"Now see here, I surrendered right and proper," the marine protested. He didn't like the look in Kit's hard eyes.

"Surrendered hell, you damn near put a knife in my gullet," Kit said, his bronze eyes flashed with fire.

"Well . . . we weren't friends then." Tregoning tried his most winning smile. It came out a crooked leer.

"This Meg Smollet must be blind," Kit said.

"There's something about us men of Cornwall, the women can't keep their bloody hands off us. 'Tis a cruel lot to bear. Too many women can leech a man of his strength. Suck him dry and wither him before his prime. Mistress Smollet did her part."

"Maybe I'll do Tiberius a favor and shoot you myself," Kit said, rolling his eyes and shaking his head in exasperation. What sort of character was this? Kit thought. A minute ago these two were trying to kill each other, and now Harry Tregoning was spinning tall tales of his life history as if he were sharing a campfire with the American. It was an amusing notion, an irony to stop and enjoy sometime when it wouldn't get him killed.

Kit swore that the next time he picked a human shield he'd have to be more careful. Tregoning might be more trouble than he was worth.

"You staying?" Nate asked. His pistols were loaded and his rifle cocked and primed. Strikes With Club, standing at the blue-jacketed warrior's side, looked as determined as the older brave. Kit had fought the Creeks at Horse Shoe Bend almost a year ago in the good company of these same warriors and the rest of their tribe. He counted many friends among the Choctaw and found them to be brave and crafty fighters, men not given to suicidal tactics.

"Let them come to us. Then we'll make our break for the woods over yonder," Kit said, indicating a grove of oak and hickory blocking their back trail.

"We won't have long to wait," Nate said, dusting his flashpan with a trace of black powder from his brass flask.

Kit peered over the log and saw that the Chiltern Rifles had fixed bayonets and were on the move. Sergeant Major Smollet led his men in an uncharacteristic advance. They came at a run, crouched low and howling for blood. Kit turned to Tregoning and said, "Help me." He jammed the butt of his rifle beneath the log and indicated Tregoning should do the same with the musket he had dropped during his struggles with Kit.

"Why?" the Cornishman asked, and then considered the possibilities. He'd been dodging the wrath of Tiberius Smollet ever since leaving London. Enough was enough. "Very well, then," Tregoning said, and threw his weight against the fallen tree. Using the muskets as twin levers, the two men dislodged the tree trunk, rocked it forward, and sent it tumbling over the edge of the creekbank. Like some juggernaut it crashed into the midst of the marines as they splashed through the shallows of the creek. The jagged stumps of branches wreaked havoc with British flesh and bone. A ragged fusillade from the Chiltern Rifles filled the air with lead. Kit and Tregoning broke for the trees without waiting to see the results of their handiwork. The crash of timber and the screams from the men below spoke volumes. Nate and Strikes With Club fired as they ran. Kit glanced aside and spied a patch of red uniform and squeezed off a shot from his rifled musket as he dashed for the forest.

To his amazement and relief, Kit and the others gained the protection of the thicket without incident and vanished in the gray-green gloom of the forest.

Nate took the point followed by Strikes With Club, Tregoning, and Kit McQueen, who reloaded on the move and kept a watchful eye for any telltale sign of their pursuers. The four men had the advantage now. They could move quickly and silently while the Chiltern Rifles would have to carefully pick their way along the trail and guard against ambush. Kit was satisfied to take note that Tregoning was keeping up the pace. The Cornishmen did not relish the notion of being captured by Smollet now.

"There'll be a hangman's rope waiting for poor Harry Tregoning should he ever go home again," Kit's prisoner bemoaned.

"You're alive now. No man can ask for more,"

JACK IRON ★ 19

Kit replied. But his own words sounded hollow to him. He did indeed want more. He wanted retribution. Cesar Obregon was going to pay a dear price for abandoning McQueen and the Choctaws.

The north wind began its banshee howl as the trees thinned and the four men started across the clearing where hours earlier, at midmorning, Kit had ordered Captain Cesar Obregon, the Hawk of the Antilles, and a dozen of his privateers to remain in place. Kit knew the freebooters weren't the kind to follow the commands of one who had not flown the black flag. Kit didn't trust any of them. A man like Cesar Obregon was only as loyal as the depth of the purse paying him. The empty meadow offered testament to Obregon's treachery. Kit called a halt, and knelt by a campfire and stirred the cold ashes with his fingertip. The Hawk of the Antilles had "flown the coop" hours ago. But why? He was certainly no coward.

"Looking for your mates, eh?" Tregoning asked. He scrutinized the winter-barren trees, the twisted branches dotted with nests and clumps of mistletoe, branches clacking together like old bones or drooping earthward, bowed beneath a load of moss like widow's weeds. "I don't blame them for leaving," Tregoning shivered.

"The tracks head north to New Orleans," Nate said, kneeling at the perimeter of the clearing. "He's gone on back. But why?"

"Maybe he left something there," Strikes With Club interjected, standing midway between Nate and the remains of the campfire.

"Not 'something'—'*someone*,'" Kit said, realization slowly dawning. There by the ashes a name had been scrawled in the dirt, left for McQueen to discover as if to taunt him with its implications.

The same soft green eyes, the same coppery features, and flirting smile that haunted Kit's heart had caused Cesar Obregon to abandon his inhospitable post for the drawing-room passions and scented boudoirs of New Orleans.

Kit McQueen stood and muttered, "The son of a bitch!" He bolted across the clearing and swept past Nate Russell at a dead run.

"C'mon!" McQueen shouted to the others as he plunged through the underbrush obscuring a deer trail that wound through the timbers. In the wake of his passing, remained Kit's friends, his prisoner, and a name written in the dust.

Raven.

Chapter Two

Iron Hand O'Keefe had a cold. He sneezed, and the bedroom walls seemed to expand under the force of the air pressure, then settle back to their original construction. He cursed, and the effort caused his sore throat to sting even worse, which in turn caused him to curse anew, the cycle repeating itself until he slammed his fist down on the bed linen and collapsed against the pillows propping him upright in bed. The hook that replaced his left hand darted out and spitted a wedge of pale white cheese and lifted the morsel to his mouth. The bed slats groaned beneath O'Keefe's shifting weight. Iron Hand O'Keefe was no wilting flower or mere slip of a man. He stood well over six feet tall; the heels of his large callused feet dangled over the bedboard. Silver hair hung past his shoulders, and the gray-black beard concealing his lantern-jawed features were bushy enough for a sparrow to nest in. His normally swarthy appearance gleamed a pasty white in the sallow light. The flesh around his eyes was creased and wrinkled and heavy with lack of sleep.

He sneezed again, this time like a cannon shot,

and grabbing a kerchief he dabbed at his raw red nose. Then he blinked his watery eyes and tried to focus on his daughter. Raven O'Keefe was as pretty as an autumn sunset. Her skin was a dusky copper brown and her long black hair was shiny and soft as a fine pelt; she was lithe and willowy. She glided with supple grace across the floor, soundlessly, as she moved to her father's beside. At first glance she resembled many of the fine and lovely women of her tribe. Only on closer examination could one discover the vibrant green-eyed gaze and hear the lilting Irish brogue that colored her speech when she chose to make a point. Raven was a half-breed, receiving her wise and quiet beauty from her Choctaw mother, learning, too, the magic and mystery of the world. Raven's stubborn Irish pride and fiery Irish temper were her father's gifts.

Music drifted up from below: the jangle of a tambourine, trills of a concertina, a merry duel between three fiddlers and a pair of fifes. Madame LeBeouf was hosting a party downstairs and had opened up the entire west wing of her house for the enjoyment of her guests. LeBeouf's house opened onto a neatly arranged flower garden and walled courtyard fronting Bourbon Street a stone's throw from Dumaine. The music from LeBeouf's house filled the block, and several passersby paused at the wrought-iron gate to peer longingly in at the gaily lit house. The townspeople within were obviously having a good time. The amber flow escaping through the cracks in the shutters lent a cheery counterpoint to the cold and dreary winter's eve. No matter the British were threatening to overwhelm Jackson's militia and take the port. Olivia LeBeouf was determined to offset the gloom pervading the town. So decorations were hung and special friends invited, many of them unattached gentlemen whom the widow LeBeouf considered candidates for her affections, and fires filled the hearths in every room. Musicians had been hired for the entire evening, and already, the guests had begun to arrive. Madame LeBeouf had not played favorites; there were soldiers as well as townspeople among the arrivals. And if she found no one to excite her fancies, there was always her old friend O'Keefe upstairs.

"Listen to them. How can people be so happy when others are suffering?" O'Keefe said, overcome with self-pity.

"Poor Papa, so miserable you are. And no one to soothe you with a song or the gentle stroke of a hand. But don't you be worryin'. Olivia LeBeouf would not have offered you a bed beneath her roof if she didn't have a special caring for the likes of you." Raven laughed, and tugged at his chin whiskers. "Best you regain your strength before she steals it."

"The only thing I'm worrying about is the way you been playing with Kit McQueen and Cesar Obregon. Both game lads they be, and it's wrong of ye to set them one upon the other." O'Keefe frowned, and wiped his hook clean on the quilt covering his lower extremities. His fever had broken but left a wracking cough and swollen sinuses in its wake.

"I've done no such thing, Father."

"And I say otherwise. Ever since we come to New Orleans you been sashaying about and making those shamrock-colored eyes o' yours go all moist and such every time Cesar Obregon comes to call."

"At least he takes the time, which is more than I can say for some."

"You know Kit McQueen ain't got a spare moment for himself since Jackson's had him and the Choctaws scouting Lord Packenham's lines. Would you have him endanger us all just so's you can lure him to the hayloft for a quick tumble?"

"Father!"

"Don't act so surprised. I've known since before

Horse Shoe Bend. And lucky for Kit McQueen I think the world of him, else he'd be singing high notes in a castrati choir!" O'Keefe sneezed three times in rapid succession. The force of the spasm doubled him forward and left him gasping for air. At last he settled back against the pillow and straightened his nightcap. Besides the four-poster, the room was appointed with a small table and ladder-backed rocking chair. The hearth blazed as flames greedily devoured the dry wedges of oak Raven had recently added to the fire.

She stared in speechless silence at her father. Raven and Kit had tried to remain discreet. Their moments alone had been few and far between. "Kit didn't tell me."

"Funny that. But no matter. I understand more than you think. Don't let these gray hairs fools you, lass. Your pa had the same itch below his belt for your ma, God rest her soul. You and McQueen belong together same as your ma and me. And I think you know it."

Raven shrugged, and lowered her gaze to her folded hands. She was the very picture of contrite submission. But O'Keefe knew his daughter too well to fall for such a ruse. She had as much surrender in her as a cornered cougar. But, my, oh my, she did look a pretty sight in that cream-colored dress of Spanish lace. Removed from the forest and the influence of her Choctaw friends, her Irish heritage rose to the fore and he couldn't blame any young man for being smitten with her. O'Keefe shifted in bed and coughed. Damn, he thought, if I ain't talking myself right out of my anger. She's winning after all. He glowered at his daughter.

"I suppose that be the dress Obregon give you?"

"It is."

"And I reckon you think it suits you more'n your buckskins. Or have you forgotten who you are?"

It was Raven's turn to frown. "*This is* who I am," she replied, indicating the dress with a sweep of her hand. Then she lifted the hem of the lace dress to reveal the brushed deerskin moccasins she wore in place of the slippers that had cramped her toes and made walking an agony. She had decorated her footwear with shells and tiny glass beads and laboriously double-stitched them with sinew. "And this also," she added.

"So I guess you'll be wearing the dress."

"And dancing with the man who gave it to me. And if it makes Kit McQueen sit up and take notice, then so much the better."

"Women! You spin a cunning web and wrap us men in your silken chains and hold us fast and there's nary an escape." O'Keefe leaned over and poured a measure of hot buttered rum from a clay pitcher into a pewter tankard. A look of pleasant anticipation settled his features. Was there a drink finer than hot buttered rum on a wintry night? Not by a hornpipe.

"You worry too much, Father. I'm playing a little game. Nothing more. It's one the likes of Cesar Obregon has no doubt played in a dozen ports with a dozen moonstruck lasses carried off on the tide of his charms. He knows the game, mark you."

"Aye, but is he playing by your rules?" O'Keefe countered, and having made his point, he drained the contents of the tankard without pause for breath. The bedroom door swung open and Madame Olivia LeBeouf entered, dressed in a pink cotton dress trimmed with French lace across her daring décolletage. Raven welcomed the woman's arrival, for it spared her from having to come up with a rebuttal.

Madame LeBeouf was a brash and cheerful widow whose slender figure seemed woefully off balance beneath the weight of her abundant bosom. Her cheeks were caked with rouge. A mole on her left cheekbone had been accentuated with a touch of black ink. Her head was crowned with ringlets of light brown hair piled high and dangling in thick lustrous coils along the back of her neck. The room's interior seemed to brighten as she entered bearing a tray laden with a freshly baked sweet potato pie and a tureen containing short ribs of beef floating in a broth of drippings seasoned with pepper, onions, and topped with cornbread dumplings.

Madame LeBeouf had not come alone. An eight-year-old boy stood at her side. He was tall for his age and long-limbed. His sandy brown hair was uncombed and curled to a natural cowlick at the back of his head. His eyes were pale green and pouchy from lack of sleep, for he had taken the same cold as Iron Hand O'Keefe. Despite his illness he watched O'Keefe with keen interest, for even at his young age he had heard tales of Iron Hand, the white chief of the Choctaws.

"This is Johnny Fuller," said Madame LeBeouf, indicating the young lad with a wave of her hand.

"Indeed. And when did you drop a pup?" O'Keefe asked, peering at the woman and boy over the lip of his pewter mug. He hadn't seen the widow LeBeouf for nigh onto a year, and anything was possible where Olivia was concerned.

"I'll thank you to keep a civil thought in your skull. He ain't mine." She glanced at Raven and continued. "Well, *now* he is—since his mama caught the grippe and passed away. Consumptive she was, the poor dear. Coughing all the time." The woman tousled the boy's hair and patted his shoulder. "Johnny's a good lad, ain't you?"

The boy shrugged and continued to study O'Keefe with interest from behind the protection of Madame LeBeouf's dress. He carried two stoneware bowls and a pair of spoons and two-pronged forks. He wore a sleeping gown and was barefoot. He scratched his left ankle with the toes of his right and then fell into step alongside LeBeouf as she crossed the room to O'Keefe's bedside.

"Up you go now, and try not to muss the covers and be sure not to spill any of your dinner in bed, for you'll be sleeping on these very linens." The widow placed the tray of food on the table near the bed. She took care not to meet O'Keefe's openmouthed stare.

"See here. I ain't no wet nurse!" he protested. He looked at his daughter for help, but Raven covered her smile with the back of her hand and fled the room. "Raven. We haven't settled the matter of these men . . . uh . . . Daughter!" He scowled. "Goddammit!"

Madame LeBeouf reached out and caught Iron Hand O'Keefe by his ear and gave it a terrible tweak.

"Yeow!"

"Watch your mouth—there's a child present," the widow painfully reminded her former lover. "The kind of sweet boy we might have had if only you'd been willing to surrender your heathen ways and live among your own kind." Madame LeBeouf sniffed as if to hold back her mock tears. O'Keefe wasn't fooled for a second. He glared at the eight-year-old who crawled up to take his place in bed alongside the burly Irishman.

"Any child of ours would've been full of piss and vinegar, wild as a wolf cub with twice the bite."

"I would have refined him," Madame LeBeouf flatly replied. Then she filled a plate with ribs and corn dumplings for Johnny, who silently accepted his meal. It was obvious he was as uneasy about this sleeping arrangement as the big man next to him. O'Keefe watched the widow load a plate for him and then hand it over.

"Enjoy your meal. My guests are below and it would be rude for me to tarry."

"When you coming back?" O'Keefe surreptitiously nodded in the direction of the lad who was hungrily devouring dinner.

"I can't tell. It depends on whether or not that handsome Mr. Belouche has arrived. They say he taught the Laffite brothers all they know of swordsmanship. I, too, should like to test his mettle."

"I'm under your roof but one night and already I am the cuckold," O'Keefe complained.

"Heal yourself, Peter O'Keefe, and I might change my mind—you hairy old bear." The widow winked, and tugged his beard and kissed O'Keefe on the forehead, and then left the room with a swirl of her lace-trimmed dress. A trace of rosewater and lilac lingered in the air to mark her passing.

"Hrumph!" O'Keefe grumbled, and fixed the boy in a steely stare. "I aim to eat, then drink me another hot buttered rum and then sleep. You don't interfere and we'll get along."

"I don't like this any better than you." Johnny gnawed the meat from a rib bone and dropped it back into the bowl, then sopped some juices with a corn dumpling. "I'd hardly call you a nosegay. And if we looked real close, we might find a flock of crows nesting in that briar thicket you call a beard."

O'Keefe was taken aback by the boy's outburst. Johnny Fuller was hardly the shy and quiet type. The Irishman had been deceived by the lad's show, the way Johnny had clung to the widow and hidden behind the folds of her dress.

"Smart whelp, eh?" O'Keefe scowled. "Mind you keep a civil tongue in your head or I'll cut it out and toss the meat to the widow's hound outside." The Irishman grunted in satisfaction, and spearing a particularly stringy morsel of meat, he plopped it in his mouth and wiped his lips on his sleeve.

"Too late for that," Johnny said. "You just ate him."

"Christ almighty," O'Keefe muttered, and spat

the chunk of meat halfway across the room. It landed a few feet from the hearth. Only when Johnny could no longer hold back his laughter did the Irishman realize the trick the eight-year-old had played on him. He started to scold the boy, but launched into a spasm of coughs that shook the bed. Finally, when the worst of it subsided, O'Keefe caught his breath and muttered, "You're a black-hearted ragamuffin."

"Did I do something wrong?" Johnny asked, all innocence again.

O'Keefe sat up in bed and, with his hook, skewered a chunk of meat from Johnny's bowl. The boy fell silent as the Irishman slowly nibbled at the morsel. The ominous demonstration had the desired effect. Iron Hand licked the grease from the vicious-looking barb that capped his stump.

"How'd you lose it?" the boy asked, staring at the hook.

"A shipmate of mine asked me to lend him a hand. I did. The impudent son of a bitch never brought it back." O'Keefe looked completely serious.

Johnny Fuller was a child in years, but the eight-year-old knew a tall tale when he heard it.

"I may have been born at night, Mr. O'Keefe, but it wasn't *last* night," the boy retorted.

Iron Hand O'Keefe chuckled and settled back against the pillow. The lad was as sharp as a needle and there was no denying his spunk. Reminds me of me, thought the Irishman, resolving to keep his observations to himself. Johnny Fuller was cocky enough.

Chapter Three

Cesar Obregon took his hair snips and carefully trimmed the curled tips of his blond mustache, then cleared a little of the "underbrush" from around his mouth. When he walked Raven out into the night and took his kisses, he wanted her to feel the full effect of his sensuous lips. Cesar Obregon was a fair-skinned Castilian garbed in a black waistcoat and trousers and a black silk shirt that fit loosely over his slender six-foot frame. His straight ash blond hair was brushed back from his features and hidden beneath a black silk bandanna that covered his head. His fingers were long and slender, his physique wiry and as resilient as whipcord. His brown eyes never wavered as he concentrated on trimming his mustache.

"If vanity were a virtue, you'd be a saint." Obregon shifted the mirror to the flat homely features of Honeyboy Biggs, the chief gunner aboard the *Windthrift.*

"And if I was a temperamental captain, you'd be a mute," Obregon said. With a twist of the wrist, Biggs vanished from the hand mirror, a gilt-edged trinket that had found its way into Obregon's possession during his days as a freebooter. The privateer finished his trim and then reappraised his appearance. Damn, if there was a finer-looking gentleman in all of New Orleans, Cesar Obregon didn't know the man. He sat the mirror down.

"Come outside and join us by the fire. Young Reyner Blanche has his concertina, and Angel Mendoza has cooked up a squirrel stew that's fit for King George if he were but sane enough to hoist a spoon." Biggs was a rotund seaman in beige baggy breeches, loose yellow shirt, and a heavy wool coat made of beaver pelts to ward off the cold. Biggs was bald save for a fringe of soot-colored hair that crept up from his bushy sideburns and trailed off in a shaggy growth just past his ears.

"It is a fine crew I have, *mi amigo,* but not a one of my brave *compadres* can hold a candle to the senorita that awaits me on Bourbon Street."

"A half-breed girl, eh?" Biggs snorted in disapproval. "You've enjoyed the charms of many a fair maid. What makes this girl so special?" Biggs hooked his thumbs in the wide leather belt circling his waist. At forty-six, he was old enough to be Obregon's father and tended to address his captain in a paternal manner when the two of them were alone. "Now see here, my fine Hawk, this girl brings trouble, you mark me well. A man like Kit McQueen is no trifle either. Going against him will be inviting misfortune, like a hard tack in a hurricane. I warrant McQueen's sent under his fair share of men or I'm a three-toed lizard."

"I can handle the lieutenant," Obregon replied, and for added emphasis, he reached toward his wrists and in a blur of motion freed a pair of double-edge throwing knives from the sheaths hidden beneath his sleeves. The six-inch blades glittered in the lantern light. The image of a hawk's menacing talons had been etched into the length of the watered steel. They were silent, deadly weapons in the hands of a capable man. Obregon was a master and had a powerful arm that could hurl the daggers with uncanny accuracy.

"You forget this Hawk has talons," Obregon replied.

"The girl is not worth it."

"How would you know, my fat friend? When was the last time you took a wench to your ample lap without first crossing her palm with silver?"

Biggs scowled at the Hawk of the Antilles. Obregon's words cut as deeply as the daggers hidden in the Castilian's sleeves. "Hmmm," he muttered, and "Humm" again, and glanced around the cabin that was but one of many hurriedly erected structures dotting the fallow fields of the Chalmette plantation south of New Orleans. Jackson's Tennessee Volunteers lived in damp leaky huts and drafty barns, while the Baratarians like Obregon and his crew and Laffite's freebooters had furnished their makeshift abodes with comfortable bedding, woven ground coverings, and tables and chairs brought out from their homes in town. Even the commonest privateer had a chest of belongings to make his miserable station more endurable. Manning the breastworks that guarded the southern approach to the city was onerous enough without sacrificing the pleasantries of a civilized existence, thought the Baratarians.

"It is a wise captain who curries his gunner's favor. One day you may need these sharp eyes o' mine when we pull a broadside and dance under the cannon of a war brig just waiting to blow us out of the water." Biggs's expression brightened as his gaze settled on a bottle of jack iron, raw cane rum with a bite like an alligator.

"And just what might you do, chief gunner?" asked Obregon, playing along with the older man's game.

"I might just blink," said Biggs, and with a smile

of self-satisfaction he confiscated the bottle of rum
and headed for the door.

"Where are you going with that, old thief?"

"Me and the lads thank ye for your generosity. As
you'll be warmin' your toes at the widow's tea table,
we aim to fire some jack iron to keep us from freezin'
on this damn winter's night." A bracing cold gust of
wind brushed past the man in the doorway and
blasted into the room. Obregon reached for his frock
coat, and followed his gunner and his bottle of jack
iron out into the night air.

A group of men were huddled around the leaping flame of Angel Mendoza's cookfire. The cook was
crouching over a black kettle and stirring the contents
with a long-handled wooden spoon. He lifted the
spoon to his lips and took a taste while the remaining
dozen men looked on in hopeful anticipation that
Mendoza might pronounce the stew "done" and allow the hungry crewmen to dig in. Mendoza was a
well-scrubbed privateer who served not only as the
cook but the surgeon aboard the *Windthrift*. Mendoza
had fled the Inquisition in Spain, choosing to live as
a pirate for himself rather than die a martyr for God.

Mendoza's hair was streaked with silver though
he was only thirty-four. His knowledge of medicine
was limited, but his prowess with cauterizing iron
and bone saw were unmatched. He could remove a
limb and stanch the flow of blood in a matter of
minutes, no mean feat under fire. And he could cook,
too.

"The man has a way with squirrel," Biggs re-
marked.

Obregon kept the cabin between him and the
north wind that had ceased its swirling gusts and was
coming straight on as the sun set behind the eight-
foot-tall breastworks built a hundred yards from the
Mississippi. A makeshift palisade of mud and cypress logs protected Andrew Jackson's beleaguered

forces while the British continued to mass their troops, gathering strength, feinting against the far perimeters to test the mettle of their American adversaries. Well, it appeared the British wouldn't attack today—a fact for which Obregon was profoundly grateful. With Kit McQueen pitching a cold camp somewhere in the woods south of town, Cesar Obregon, the Hawk of the Antilles, would have Raven O'Keefe all to himself. Obregon doubted the rumors of English patrols. The Choctaws were not the most reliable military observers, as far as Cesar Obregon was concerned. The last laugh was on McQueen. Obregon grinned. He noticed Biggs studying him.

"I'd give your weight in gold," Obregon said, patting his gunner's rounded paunch, "to see the look on McQueen's face when he discovers the name I wrote in the dirt by the fire."

Biggs shook his head. But he resisted the temptation to upbraid his youthful captain for such brash conduct. He was filled with misgivings. But what was the use of talking common sense to such a man as Obregon? Like the mythical sirens that lured ancient mariners to destruction, the Hawk of the Antilles was a prisoner of his own passions. Biggs, the loyal chief gunner, quietly resolved to save Cesar Obregon from himself—if such a thing were possible.

Black-haired handsome Reynor Blanche began to play a merry jig upon his concertina. A lithe and nimble lad, he leaped and kicked his heels while his shipmates sang. The privateers' rough voices warmed their souls against the cold creeping in on darkening wings of dusk.

Obregon dug down into his coat and stepped out of the windbreak and headed for the dun-colored mare he had ridden out from town. The Hawk could feel the chief gunner's eyes boring into him as he tried to leave. Obregon decided to take Biggs into his confidence and turned to face the older man, leaning in close and keeping his voice low.

"It is not for beauty alone that I attend the widow's party," Obregon said. "Jean Laffite has learned that Jackson's Tennessee reinforcements brought a pay chest with them for the general to use at his discretion."

"Gold!" Biggs exclaimed, and then continued in a hushed tone. "Where?"

"The war chest is hidden aboard a surgeon's wagon. And to keep from calling attention to it, the general has hidden the wagon in the widow LeBeouf's carriage shed."

"Why doesn't he just issue us our pay and settle with his Tennesseans and Kentuckians?" Biggs was skeptical, but anything was possible.

"Jackson's a shrewd one," Obregon said. "By the time we've driven off the British, there's bound to be a lot less of us."

"And more profit for himself, the clever rogue," the gunner finished. "Is it well guarded?"

"That is what I intend to find out tonight," Obregon grinned.

"Then you have my blessing, *Captain Romeo,* and God speed you on your way," Biggs said, handing him the reins.

Cesar Obregon swung a leg over the saddle and mounted up astride the patient dun. Reins in hand, the Hawk of the Antilles pointed the animal north to New Orleans and tonight's passion—and tomorrow's profit.

Chapter Four

Private Dell Hitner rubbed a hand across his weathered features and tried to focus his red-rimmed eyes on the darkness. Guarding the south road was a wearisome chore that he resented being assigned to. No one ever came down the road; certainly no one expected the British to, because the road itself only continued on for another mile or so before petering out in a labyrinth of forests and swamps. There were a couple of plantations up this way, nothing more. Certainly no redcoats, unless one counted the occasional red wolf that could still be glimpsed on moonlit nights stealing out of the black forest in search of its four-legged dinner.

"What's that!" said the man pulling picket duty with Hitner. He was a skittish lad with an active imagination, who seemed to hear something almost every hour on the hour. Private Francis Pelliere grabbed for his rifled musket and accidentally discharged the weapon as he scrambled clear of the small cookfire that had supplied the two near-frozen soldiers with their only warmth on this winter's night.

Hitner was older and wiser, but his back hurt and he was out of patience. He dodged the lead slug as it whined past his ear. Inches to the left and he'd have been a casualty. Hitner grabbed the cap from Pelliere's head and proceeded to slap the nervous youth across the cheeks and shoulders.

"Enough I say! Enough! I've lost a lifetime of sleep with you on guard and you've scared me nigh on to death with your imaginary patrols, but I'll not have my lights shot out just because you hear redcoats behind every hedge and bush."

Pelliere shielded his face with his hands and forearms as he retreated from his companion's on-slaught. He was a thin and clumsy youth with little stomach for the military career that he'd unwittingly undertaken for the love of a cobbler's daughter who had an all-consuming passion for young men in uni-form. Hitner's would-be assassin pleaded for clem-ency. "It was an accident!" *It was always an accident.*

Dell Hitner relented and tossed Pelliere's cap down on his chest. Hitner could afford to be merciful to the youngster. Anyway, his back hurt too damn much to continue the lad's punishment.

"Listen you well, my edgy friend," said Hitner, leaning forward on his musket, propping himself up to catch his breath. He rubbed a work-roughened hand across his dry mouth, exhaled sharply to clear his throat and nose, and then continued his admon-ishment. "From now on, you stand your guard with your musket unprimed. That way, if you must awaken me at least I won't get shot betwixt the eyes for my trouble."

"But what if the redcoats come a-charging out of the woods?"

"Why, then they'll kill you, dear boy. And more's the pity they don't come on right now." Hitner chuck-led, and sighed, then held out his callused hand. He was a farmer by trade whose own plot of land was nestled between two large plantations upriver. He and his wife held no slaves but worked their soil with the help of two trusty mules and a cantankerous coon hound.

Pelliere hesitated before taking the farmer's offered hand. But Hitner hauled the youth to his feet and even helped to dust him off. Suddenly Pelliere's eyes widened, and he gasped and pointed past Hitner and then grabbed for his powder horn.

"Oh, no, you don't!" the farmer exclaimed, and batted the powder horn from Pelliere's grasp. "You got wood chips for brains, I swear. Now see here, we just come to an understanding . . ." Hitner turned and froze as four figures materialized out of the gloom. "Sonovabitch!" He tried to bring his own musket to bear on the shadowy intruders.

"Uh—halt. Who be you? Stand and deliver."

"I'll deliver your teeth if you point that musket at me," Kit growled. An aura of sheer menace preceded him as McQueen slogged out of the underbrush and onto the wheel-rutted road. They had gotten lost in the dark and were soaked to the knees from wandering through a cypress bog. He was cold and hungry and mad as hell and wasn't about to pause for the formalities of a password. His hard bronze eyes were fixed on an image that no one else could see. Cesar Obregon drifted before him, mocking him, and leading him down the road to town.

"It's the lieutenant . . . why, bless my soul. Lieutenant McQueen," the older sentry exclaimed.

"Thank God," said Private Pelliere, but his voice trailed off as he added "I think . . ." for McQueen wasn't alone. Two fierce-looking Choctaws and bull-necked Henry Tregoning brushed past, chasing the redheaded lieutenant.

"Good evening, gents," said Tregoning, hoping to pass unnoticed. The deeper he went behind the American lines, the more like a target he felt. "Bloody awful weather, ain't it?'' The three men melted into the night before the sentries had a chance to protest. Pelliere was thankful to be rid of them all. He did not trust these heathen redskins any further than he could toss one. As for Dell Hitner, the crusty farmer stood between the wheel ruts and peered down the road. He scratched his skull and wondered if he was losing his senses. Damn if one of Lieutenant McQueen's howling savages hadn't looked and sounded like a blasted Englishman.

In New Orleans on Dumaine Street, Cesar Obregon stood as still as a statue while his mind wrestled with a problem. He could approach Widow LeBeouf's house from Bourbon Street or turn here and proceed up the alley to the rear of the house and the small but stoutly built barn that housed her carriage, a pair of gray mares, and, most recently, a wagon of ''medicines'' and supplies. Well, the ruse wasn't completely a lie. Gold was a sure cure for most wounds.

Obregon grinned and proceeded down the alley. Though he was in a hurry to join LeBeouf's party and feast his eyes on Iron Hand's delectable half-breed daughter, gold was a mistress whose charms he had never been able to resist. A wind gust pressed the hem of his greatcoat against his legs as he led his horse toward the rear of the brightest house on the block. Music drifted toward him, borne on the night air and the darkness that seemed to part before him. The buccaneer took note that the entrance to the alley had been unguarded. Obviously Jackson was relying on the ruse of the medical supplies. Old Hickory had no concept of the elaborate network of informers used by the Baratarian smugglers. Jean Laffite, his brothers, and fellow freebooters like Obregon had a thousand eyes and ears along the coast and upriver for a hundred miles. Nothing and no one entered the lower delta country without the sea rovers knowing who and where and why.

Obregon reached the barn unchallenged, his cheeks and ears benumbed from the cold. He'd kept his hands tucked in his coat pockets and was able to reach for the latch with limber fingers. That's when he heard a musket being cocked and saw a gun barrel poke from between the shutters of a hayloft window directly overhead.

"Who the blazes are you?" a gravelly disembodied voice drifted down from above.

"Cesar Obregon," the Castilian replied. "At your service, my friend."

"I ain't friend to no pirate."

"A pirate. You discredit me, sir. I am a privateer in the service of these United States," Obregon said with a disingenuous smile and courtly bow.

"Callin' sowbelly . . . uh, turkey and trimmings don't make it anything but sowbelly," said Gravel Voice. "Pirates is pirates, now just you stand clear."

"I am a guest of the Madam LeBeouf and have ridden in from Chalmette. I do not intend to leave my poor mount untended and without shelter."

"Hell and biscuits, just wait a minute," said Gravel Voice. "I'll need to check a moment."

Obregon nodded. So the guard wasn't alone. He obviously had someone of superior rank to contend with. But how many companions in all? He stamped his feet to get the blood going and blew in his cupped hands. At last the hayloft shutters opened a crack.

"All right. Leave your horse. We'll bring it inside."

"See here. This is a game animal and one I like to care for proper."

"Your horse will be well looked after."

"How do I know that?"

"Because the men of the Nashville Mounted Rifles pride themselves on the quality of their stock. Ain't no finer horses or horsemen in all the state. Just hitch it up and we'll bring her in after you're gone."

Nashville Mounted Rifles, thought Obregon. Another morsel of information and one he hoped to put to good use. Off to the left of the barn doors, a pair of black iron rings dangled from the barn wall. Obregon looped his reins through the ring closest him. He had discovered all he could, for now.

"As you wish, *mi amigo*," said the buccaneer. "You have been most helpful."

"Ain't no '*amigo*,' neither. The name is Whipple. Emory Whipple. I'll give your nag a combing and straw and bid you a good night." Gravel Voice closed the shutter and ended the conversation. But Obregon was satisfied. He was convinced the medicine wagon carried gold. And with the alley unguarded, the men in the barn were left virtually blind. General Jackson was clever, but no match for the Hawk of the Antilles. The Castilian smiled, satisfied with his evening's efforts. He felt like celebrating. And he intended to do just that, with Raven's help, of course.

A massive gray-bearded figure filled the window overlooking the alley and the widow's barn. Iron Hand O'Keefe had crept from the bedroom and abandoned the slumbering boy to his dreams.

The music from downstairs was louder in the dark hallway between the bedrooms. All the better to conceal the big man's rasping cough. Spend a night with that black-hearted lad—not hardly. O'Keefe had outlasted the youth and exited the room in triumph. He knew the way to the widow's bedroom, but the well-placed window that offered him a view of the barn caught his attention.

O'Keefe's breath clouded the window. He dabbed a finger and drew a line through the moisture and followed Obregon as the buccaneer crossed the alley and vanished beneath the windowsill, following a stone walkway around the house to the front courtyard.

"Hmmm," O'Keefe muttered to himself. "Wonder what that Spaniard's up to." Kit had entrusted O'Keefe with news of the gold's arrival. The Irishman had kept the news to himself. "He might know something. When a freebooter smells gold, trouble's sure to follow." It was General Jackson's intention to keep the wagon under a token guard, hoping to avoid suspicion and free more of the Tennessee militia for the breastworks where those eagle-eyed riflemen would do the most good. Kit had suggested to O'Keefe that a couple of Choctaw warriors stationed at either end of the alley might be a wise precaution. However, O'Keefe had yet to choose the braves.

"Well, Captain Obregon, I have my eye on you," the Irishman grumbled. "It'll take a better man than you to catch Iron Hand O'Keefe off guard." He turned from the window and collided with Johnny Fuller, who had stolen up behind the Irishman while his attention was centered on the events in the alley.

O'Keefe gave such a start he crashed back against the window and cracked a glass pane with the back of his head. Being cautious by nature, the Irishman immediately took the small shadowy figure for a threat.

"Ah!" he bellowed, and hand and hook shot up to block a blow that never fell. Seconds later he realized the identity of the intruder who had crept up on him in the hall. "Gawd strike ye, or has ol' Scratch sent you to end my days!"

"Did I do something wrong?" Johnny Fuller asked, feigning innocence. He enjoyed giving the big man a scare. "You told me you had the keenest ear in the woods."

"Well, sure and by golly I ain't in the woods!" O'Keefe said bringing his lantern-jawed, leathery face close to Fuller's. "Now why don't you be a good lad and toddle off to bed and leave a man to a man's business."

"You mean a widow's business," the boy corrected, and retraced his steps down the dark hall to his room. He paused by a tall narrow table on which an oil lamp was precipitously balanced alongside a little wooden figure, a keel boatman carved of cypress wood. "Of course, it won't do you no good. She's got her sights set on a Frenchman. So it's best you bring your poor old bones to bed."

O'Keefe blinked and stared in disbelief at the boy. Little Johnny Fuller sounded almost motherly. The Irish-born Choctaw chieftain strode purposefully up to the widow's bedroom and tried the knob. By damn, it was locked. No doubt she anticipated he might try to wait for the widow in her room and ambush any would-be consort who tried to follow her through the door.

He scowled and scratched at his silvery beard, gave his predicament some thought, then shrugged and lumbered off to his bedroom.

Johnny Fuller sat propped up in bed, O'Keefe's clay pipe clenched between his teeth, tobacco smoke curled from the bowl. The boy puffed merrily and watched himself in a hand mirror to see how grown-up he looked.

"Not my pipe, you little varlet," O'Keefe growled. "Enough is enough!" He swept down on the boy with all the fury of a spring squall. Thunder filled the big man's voice; lightning crackled in his red-rimmed eyes. "I'd sooner run a gauntlet of howling redsticks than abide ye one moment longer. I'll—"

Johnny Fuller reached inside his nightshirt and retrieved a leaden bit of metal that he held out toward Iron Hand O'Keefe, stopping him in his tracks.

"I'll trade your pipe for this."

O'Keefe's bluster subsided and he squinted at the

youth's outstretched hand. A lesser spirit would have been reduced to tears before the Irishman's terrible onslaught. But here was Johnny Fuller trying to work a bargain.

"A man's tobacco pipe can be a real comfort on a cold night," O'Keefe scoffed. "What's a lad like you got to offer in trade."

Fuller opened his hand. "The key to the widow's bedroom door. I snuck it off'n her dressing table before she brung me over."

O'Keefe stared at the key. A slow grin crawled across his grizzled countenance. "Hmmm. Stealing don't make a man special," he soberly pronounced, as if preparing to give the lad a stern lecture. "But knowing what to steal . . ." The grin broadened. "Younker, there may be hope for you yet."

The widow LeBeouf knew how to host a party. A cordial temptress, always deferring to the needs and the wants of her guests, she flitted from one acquaintance to the next. She danced a quadrille with Major DuClerc of the Louisiana Battalion and another with Wainright Vasquez, a local plantation owner whose warehouses languished empty thanks to the British blockade at the entrance to the Mississippi. The Spaniard Vasquez had lent his slaves to the effort of fortifying the port with a series of breastworks and ramparts guarding the approaches to the town from both the river and landward sides.

More than forty townspeople were crowded into the west wing of the house, and Raven O'Keefe had long since given up trying to remember names. It didn't really matter. The ladies all seemed so beautiful in their finery and the gentlemen as chivalrous as knights. She found herself a woman of two worlds and made this observation while standing off to the side, leaning against the dining room wall while Negro servants hurried past her bearing trays of cus-

tards, petits four, and honey-glazed tea cakes filled
with wild plum jelly. Zenon and Marie Raux introduced themselves. The woman was a sweet-natured
soul with an inviting smile and dimpled cheeks and a
round full figure barely constrained by the pale pink
cotton confines of her festive gown. Zenon, her husband, was a quiet unassuming individual of forty, an
umbrella maker by trade. He had avoided service in
the Louisiana Battalion by purchasing horses for a
contingent of dragoons and outfitting the men with
uniforms, rifled muskets, and an umbrella for their
commander, Major DuClerc.

Raven listened and smiled and glanced around
as discreetly as possible for some sign of Kit or the
dashing buccaneer Cesar Obregon, who had presented her with the dress. Her father's warnings nibbled at her conscience. But she was enjoying herself.
The room was filled with music and light and gaiety.
She did not pretend for a minute that such a life was
for her, although she didn't mind teasing her father to
the contrary. But for all the excitement of the evening
and the delights to be found in walking a different
path for a few days, Raven knew where her heart lay.
The eternal hills had worked their special magic on
her, the spirits had whispered her name in the wind.
No quadrille could match the great forests awash
with the music of bubbling spring-fed brooks and the
rustle of leaves in the passing breeze. The voice of an
umbrella maker ended her reverie.

"You must come by my shop," said Zenon after
describing in detail how his parasols had become the
rage of New Orleans society. "I have a shipment
bound for Mobile if this dreadful fellow Packenham
will ever see fit to allow us the use of the Gulf again."

"Rest assured he shall get his comeuppance,"
Marie Raux spoke up. Her belief in the inevitable
triumph of the Americans was unflagging. "General

Jackson will send the British on their way in good order."

"My wife is a champion of Old Hickory," Zenon added.

"As well she should be," Olivia LeBeouf interjected, coming toward them with the uniformed Major DuClerc following her like an obedient pet. The commander of the Louisiana Battalion had fallen under the widow's spell. Although Raven genuinely like the widow, she did not pity her father, who would be sleeping alone this night. Better he should rest than attempt to satisfy the widow LeBeouf, whose sexual appetites could exhaust a man half her age, if rumors were to be believed.

"Andrew Jackson is going to be an important man one day. Just you wait and see," the widow added. "Too bad he's so sickly. I'm told he can't keep anything on his stomach but cornbread and buttermilk." She sighed and shook her head.

"Now, there's a lonely gentleman I wouldn't mind keeping on *my* stomach." Madame LeBeouf chuckled as she looked toward the front of the house. Cesar Obregon had just entered the room. He cut a dashing figure, all dressed in black with his blond locks trailing out from under his black bandanna. He bowed to every lady as the dancers swept past him in the arms of their escorts. Bootheels rap-tapped upon the wooden floor, and ladies' dresses swirled and brushed against one another, underscoring the music with a sound like hushed whispers.

"Olivia LeBeouf—how you do carry on," Marie Raux exclaimed. But it was her husband, the umbrella maker, who blushed at the widow's risqué remark. "Best you save your flattery for Major DuClerc," Marie continued. "It's plain as spring flowers who the Hawk fancies."

Raven felt color creep to her own cheeks as both women gave her their undivided attention. They made no attempt to conceal their envy as Obregon skirted the dance floor and made his way to the side of the dark-haired half-breed in her dress of Spanish lace.

"And I thought this dismal evening was shorn of stars but now I find your radiance has illumined the night," Obregon said with a sweeping bow. Off to the side, Olivia LeBeouf and the umbrella maker's wife nearly swooned. Obregon straightened, he nodded in their direction, and, eyes twinkling, grinned.

"Why, ladies, never have I seen such lovely creatures. I say, Zenon, take heed lest someone come a-creeping to your wife's bedroom window and spirit her away."

"Well, I never . . ." Zenon stammered. "Indeed, the very notion, I mean—sir, do you take me for a fool?"

"Take you? No, *compadre*. I much prefer the company of ladies," Obregon slyly replied with a wink and a shake of his handsome head. Like a stallion among his herd, he moved across the crowded dance floor with Raven on his arm. She was in step beside him before she even had time to resist. Not that the bemused woman intended to pull away. Obregon was charming and in his own way irresistible. He led her out into the quadrille and proceeded to dance with all the grace of a gentleman bred to the salons of Paris or the boudoirs of Castille. Poor Raven stumbled from time to time and her cheeks reddened as she attempted to keep in step with the couples around them. She managed to bluff her way through the experience; however, she did not regret when the music ended. Obregon was perceptive enough to offer his arm and escort Raven from the floor.

"I enjoy watching everyone," Raven said. She wasn't the type to remain embarrassed for long. "Oh, I could learn to move with as much grace, but . . ."

Then she grinned and sighed good-naturedly. "No, I couldn't."

That was one of the qualities Obregon most liked about Raven O'Keefe: her self-effacing honesty was wholly refreshing. The half-breed probably glided through the forests as soundless as a cat at home with the wilderness and unfettered by the constraints of civilized men and women.

"I will teach you," Obregon said, "my savage flower." He bowed courteously and kissed her hand. The buccaneer had started to say "tame" but caught himself in time. Yet that was what he desired, to tame this Irish-Choctaw maiden and make her his own. By God she set his blood afire.

The west wing of the house was warm from the press of bodies and the cheerful blaze consuming the logs in the fireplace. Iron screening had been placed before the hearth to prevent some woman from trailing the hem of her dress too near the flames.

"Walk with me into the night, Raven O'Keefe," said the buccaneer. He thought about the barn. A man and a woman might not be perceived as a threat and manage to get inside.

"But you just arrived," the woman replied.

"I did not come to drink the widow's punch or taste her tea cakes or brush elbows with the aristocracy of New Orleans."

"Then, why are you here?" Raven's long lashes fluttered as she lowered her gaze.

"Because you are here, *mi querida*. You are the light. Look, and you will see my shadow."

Raven managed to suppress a laugh. Cesar Obregon certainly had the gift. His poetry of passion was nigh overwhelming, especially when spoken in such silken tones. Looking out the window, she saw, through her own reflection, nothing but the dark outline of a courtyard wall that belonged to an adjoining house. The whitewashed wood frame surrounding the panes of glass rattled at the touch of the wind's unseen hand.

"It would seem uncomfortably chilly," she commented.

"I will keep you warm," Obregon said, his soft brown eyes daring her to chance his company, alone in the night.

Raven toyed with the notion. There was no denying the effect he had on her. She had experienced the feelings before, and even more intensely, with another who had captured her heart.

Cesar Obregon stepped closer to the woman and lifted her hand to his lips. His kiss was slight, warm as a spring breeze, inviting . . . no, daring. Ah yes, there was the word again. Daring. And in another time and place, Raven might have succumbed. For they were kindred spirits, these two.

"I am almost tempted, my dashing friend." Raven gently freed her hand from his grasp.

"Surrender to your temptations. I always do," Obregon said, curling the tip of his blond mustache. The chattering guests all seemed to blend together, becoming a single droning noise that only served to underscore the rush of sound he realized was his own breathing. His passions were aroused. And so was his curiosity. The Hawk of the Antilles was unaccustomed to having a woman resist his charms.

"I think it would be for the best if we remain inside," Raven replied.

"As you wish, *mi querida*." He lifted his sleepy gaze to the musicians as Major DuClerc called out to the performers that enough time had passed for the music makers to refresh themselves with cups of sangria and rum punch. The gallant Louisianan offered his arm to Olivia LeBeouf and walked her to the center of the room, and as the musicians struck up another quadrille, the guests followed suit and escorted their ladies to the floor. The oil lanterns in the

chandelier overhead flickered and gleamed. Wall
lanterns hung from brass armatures cast a cheerful
glow. The servants continued to feed the crackling
flames in the hearth with oaken logs whose crumbly
bark instantly caught fire as soon as the logs were
lowered to the existing pyre.

"Perhaps I can learn something from these people after all," Obregon said with a nod to the dancers.
"At least when the musicians play, the gentleman
embraces his lady; then anything is possible."

He was hardly the forlorn cavalier he pretended
to be. But Raven found his performance amusing. She
had never in her life met anyone quite like the black-
garbed buccaneer. And as Kit was off somewhere
serving General Jackson, what was the harm in allowing the Hawk of the Antilles his moment in her sky?

"Well, sir, if anything is possible, then teach me
to walk the trails of the widow's dance floor." Raven
opened her arms to him. "That is, if your toes can
withstand the punishment."

Obregon smiled. It appeared he would get no
closer to the barn tonight. But there was always tomorrow. At least he had learned something of the
way the wagon was being guarded. So much for
future profits. Tonight he embraced a treasure of
another sort. One he did not intend to allow to escape
his grasp.

"Follow my lead, senorita. And I will take you
places and show you sights the like of which you
have not dreamed."

"I'll be happy if I learn the quadrille," Raven
replied, hoping to defuse his intensity. She remembered her father's advice. She heard O'Keefe's cautioning voice replay his warning in the back of her
mind. But then the music began and Obregon swept
her away into the heart of the gaiety, into the innocent
temptations of the dance.

Chapter Five

"Good evenin', suh," said the widow's manservant, a mulatto with salt-and-pepper hair combed flat
against his skull. "Lieutenant McQueen, isn't it,
suh?" The mulatto spoke in a low melodic voice,
deeply resonant and bearing a sense of authority as
befitting the manager of Olivia LeBeouf's household.

"Yeah, Mr. Flatt, it's me," Kit said, stepping
through the doorway, where he paused a moment
and stood still and listened to the music and took his
bearings, surveying the few people in the foyer of the
house to see if any of them were Obregon or his crew.

Kit was soaked to the waist. His buckskin
breeches were caked with dried mud, and his blue
regulation-issue coat was spattered from his recent
trek through the bayous to the south. His cheeks were
flushed and stubbled with the red beginnings of a
beard. The manservant shivered before McQueen's
smoldering gaze.

"Is Obregon . . ." McQueen began. His voice
cracked and he started again. "Is Captain Obregon
here?"

"Why, yessuh. He preceded you by half an hour

ago. Maybe more. I believe I saw him enjoying the company of Miss O'Keefe. Yessuh, they made a dashing couple, if I do say so myself." Flatt made a valiant effort to block Kit's path. "Mr. McQueen, you aren't properly attired . . ."

But the servant was summarily brushed aside by the soldier, who headed straight for the dining room. Ladies gasped at the sight of him and hastily grabbed the hems of their dresses to avoid contact with such a disheveled character as this latest arrival to the party.

Kit ignored the women. He did not care a whit for their hushed remarks of disdain. A gambler in a frock coat and ruffled shirt stepped forward to intercept him, but Kit halted the man in his tracks with a single malevolent glance in the fellow's direction. There was death in McQueen's hollow gaze and a fury that his genteel New England upbringing barely managed to contain. The gambler retreated to the arms of his lady standing near a table laden with cakes and cobblers and platters of tea biscuits.

The couples on the dance floor paid him no mind. They were lost in the music and gay conversation and the excitement of being arm in arm. Olivia LeBeouf swept past, this time in the embrace of a young Creole merchant. The merry widow was twenty years his senior, which made his attentions all the more flattering. Another couple of dancers whirled past and then Raven in her dress of Spanish lace. She was laughing at her partner's remark and concentrating so hard on her footwork that she was completely oblivious to the arrival of Kit McQueen.

The lieutenant scowled at the sight of Cesar Obregon. The buccaneer had abandoned his post and disobeyed orders. His negligence had nearly gotten them all killed, and here he was enjoying the widow's hospitality and the charms of the woman Kit loved. Dark was his fury. His fists clenched and unclenched as he struggled to contain the anger that demanded to be unleashed.

"The hell with it," Kit muttered, and skirted the dance floor as he made his way to a long low table topped with a lace coverlet and three crystal bowls of punch de crème, an island drink favored by the widow. It consisted of sweet cream, eggs, nutmeg and cinnamon, sugar, and lime peel, which she had stored in stoneware crocks two days before the party and then laced with a liberal portion of rum for the festivities.

The guests parted as the spattered man approached, giving him all the room he needed to hoist the nearest punch bowl in his brawny arms. He winked at a powdery-white-haired matron seated in a curved-back chair like a queen on her throne. She was the mother of William D. D. Pentwell, a personal aide to the governor of the state. She was a fragile-looking woman with a lively smile and a twinkle in her eyes, and though age had curved her back and plagued her with aches, Kit, during his stay in New Orleans, had never known the elderly woman to complain. Jackson had introduced him to Letitia Pentwell a few weeks ago. The charming lady had trounced Kit at chess three times in a row, but he had proved himself a good loser, at least at chess. Love was an entirely different matter.

"Mud and tatters, now that is a novel formality for a ball," she said, appraising Kit as he lifted the punch bowl.

"I created the wardrobe myself," Kit replied. He had confided in the woman on more than one occasion. She had taken a motherly interest in him. Letitia well knew how confusing life could be, especially when matters of the heart were concerned. He had confided in her about his feelings for Raven O'Keefe.

"And given yourself quite a thirst for your efforts," she observed, dabbing at her lips with a silk handkerchief.

"Not I," said Kit. "But Cesar Obregon looks a might parched, don't you think?"

"Thirsty as General Jackson is for a victory over Packenham's royal troops."

Kit nodded, and with the punch bowl firmly clasped in an iron grip he broke through the circling couples and headed straight for the black-clad freebooter, who had just finished his dance and stood with his back turned to the approaching soldier. Kit managed to traverse the spacious dining-room floor without spilling but a few frothy drops of the punch de crème. He swung the bowl to the side and called out, "Obregon!" and hurled its contents.

What followed seemed to play itself out in slow motion, and, rooted in place, Kit would have given anything to call back his rash behavior. He saw Obregon spin around, sensing a threat. He ducked as the punch drew a milky arc in the air and, spreading, passed over the buccaneer and caught Raven full in the face and chest.

"Oh!" she managed to scream as the punch exploded over her bosom and drenched the dress of Spanish lace, soaked her hair, and left her gasping and sputtering for breath. She staggered back a few steps off balance and then tripped on the hem of her gown and landed on her rounded derriere in the corner of the room.

"Christ," Kit muttered beneath his breath. His outstretched hands lost their grip on the punch bowl and it clattered to the floor. The bowl was made of thick crystal and did not shatter. Horror-struck at the results of his handiwork, Kit was rooted in place. He wanted to run to her side, but his limbs refused to obey him. It took Cesar Obregon to knock this statue from its pedestal.

The man in black straightened and loosed a

roundhouse left that Kit saw coming but was unable to duck. He was staring past the oncoming fist at Raven, who had managed to wipe the milky liquid from her eyes and behold the identity of her inadvertent attacker.

"Raven, I didn't—" Kit never finished. Obregon's fist caught him full in the face and knocked him backward into the center of the dining room. McQueen hit hard and lay momentarily stunned, watching a display of swirling stars become the chandelier overhead. Obregon reached down and caught the soldier by the front of his mud-spattered coat and began to drag him toward the foyer.

"You come in here reeking of rum, sir. And assault a lady, the hem of whose garment you are not fit to kiss!" Obregon spoke loud enough for the guests in the room to hear. The more damage he did to Kit's reputation, the better. Let them think him a drunken lout and the Hawk of the Antilles a gentleman of principles. The buccaneer had indeed been caught completely by surprise. What on earth had brought the lieutenant back from patrol? Well, McQueen's behavior could not have been better. This night's action had no doubt finished McQueen in the eyes of Raven.

Showing an impressive display of strength, Obregon reached the foyer, where he ordered Mr. Flatt to open the front door. "Be quick about it and I will rid your household of the likes of this boor."

The manservant hurried to obey the privateer's command. He swung the door open. The cold of night gusted into the house. Obregon reached down to haul McQueen to his feet and propel him through the doorway with a well-placed bootheel. Kit came to his senses as the man lifted him up. He caught Obregon by the wrists and, lunging upward, drove the top of his head to the base of the Spaniard's jaw. Obregon staggered and saw a constellation of his own creation as he fell back against Mr. Flatt.

The manservant recognized a deteriorating situation when it presented itself and beat a hasty retreat. Or at least he tried to, but Obregon snared the mulatto and flung the man at Kit, then dove in low. Kit shoved the manservant aside and was struck by Obregon. The momentum of the assault carried both men through the entrance and out into the walled courtyard of the widow's house. Kit managed to twist so that he landed on the privateer. He heard the man in black grunt as the wind was forced from him by the impact. Still, both men crawled to their feet and faced one another on the stone walk.

"What shall it be?" Obregon gasped. "Tomorrow? Pistols at ten paces? We can meet out in the cotton fields."

"How about here and now," Kit said.

"Ordinarily I make it a habit never to kill a man over a woman. It's bad luck." Obregon winced and rubbed his bruised jaw. "And what will it prove? After you showered her with punch de crème, I doubt Raven will have little to say to you but 'get thee hence.'"

"This isn't about Raven O'Keefe, you bastard," Kit retorted. "You abandoned us out there."

"I wasn't about to freeze to death waiting for some imaginary British patrol."

"Imaginary? Tell that to the men I lost fighting them! We could have all been killed waiting for you to bring your men up!" Kit fixed the man in a murderous stare. "Maybe that is exactly what you wanted."

"Now see here . . ." Cesar Obregon was taken aback at McQueen's outburst. He had never believed in the reliability of the Choctaw scouts and had convinced himself that the British were nowhere around. By heaven, McQueen was in the right. But right or wrong, Cesar Obregon wasn't about to take a beating from any man. "Perhaps I have been mistaken. But do not think to shame me in front of the widow and her guests." He nodded toward the front of the house, where men crowded the doorway and faces jammed the windows.

"I cannot dishonor a man who has no honor to begin with," said Kit.

Obregon scowled and reached to his cuffs. It was an odd gesture, one that prompted Kit to take warning. He dropped his hands to the gun butt of the flintlock pistol tucked in the belt on his right side. It was an unnecessary precaution. He had two buckskin-clad guardian angels watching over him. Obregon froze in midmotion as Nate Russell and Strikes With Club materialized out of the shadows beneath the courtyard wall. Their rifled muskets were leveled and cocked and trained on the freebooter. A squeeze of the trigger and he'd be blown in half by the big-bore flintlocks. Obregon grinned and for a moment considered hurling his daggers at the braves and then making a try for Kit. The buccaneer crouched and his whole body seemed to tense, his muscles coiling like a spring. In another second Madame LeBeouf's courtyard was going to be filled with powder smoke and there'd be blood flowing amongst the barren flower mounds.

At that precise moment, fate intervened in the form of a distinguished but uninvited guest to the widow's festivities. The courtyard gate creaked open and a tall gaunt officer led a half-dozen other soldiers into the garden. A tremor of excitement coursed through the onlookers at the door. After all, General Andrew Jackson was a busy man these days and had little time for socializing.

Old Hickory hadn't come to party. It was obvious from his demeanor he was in a grim mood. At a glance from the commander of the American forces protecting New Orleans, Kit dropped his hand from the gun at his waist and his Choctaw allies lowered their rifles. Even Obregon, who felt no allegiance to the general, straightened and left his hidden daggers up his sleeves.

"I sent you men out on patrol. You're my eyes, watching what the British are up to north of Chalmette. Then reports come in that you both have returned—and not so much as a whisper what you've found out." He ran a hand across his cheeks, then fixed his fierce gray eyes on the widow's guests. "You gentlemen better see to your ladies, else I may need to press a few of you into service this night to man the breastworks."

The crowd at the front door vanished as hastily as they had gathered. No man wanted to trade Madame LeBeouf's hospitality for that of Jackson's. The general continued down the stone walk between rows of mulched earth where the widow intended to plant her tulip bulbs when the weather permitted. Jackson wore a small leather cap, and his long-limbed frame, emaciated from a bout of dysentery, was wrapped in an old blue Spanish coat trimmed with bullet buttons and a high collar he had pulled up to protect his neck.

"I don't know what's between you two—and I don't care, as long as it doesn't interfere with my own plans. I've had lesser men flogged for such dereliction of duty."

"No man takes a whip to me," Obregon replied.

"Do not tempt me, Spaniard." Jackson dismissed Obregon with a single glance. "I did not expect such behavior from you, Lieutenant."

"I am sorry, General." Kit dabbed at his swollen lip. Blood had begun to dry at the corner of his mouth. He took satisfaction in Obregon's swollen jaw. At least I've given the freebooter something to remember me by, Kit thought.

"Then, I will have your report back at my house," Jackson said.

Kit looked dismayed. He needed to find Raven and apologize and somehow explain his actions. He desperately wanted to make her understand.

"General Jackson, if you'll permit me just a brief moment . . ."

"It would seem you already have taken several moments to yourself and placed your affairs above the importance of my defenses," Jackson replied. He had a sneaking suspicion as to the nature of McQueen's unfinished business. Damn it all, if he didn't like the mettle of this headstrong officer despite the younger man's mistakes. Kit McQueen had put his life in peril more than once over the past few months. Jackson could attribute his recent victory over the Creek Indians at Horse Shoe Bend to the courage displayed by McQueen and his Choctaw allies. The general had almost talked himself into allowing Kit to reenter the widow's house when he noticed the third man standing between Nate Russell and Strikes With Club. He recognized the uniform even at night.

"By heaven, a spy." He pointed toward Harry Tregoning, who cringed as Jackson's armed escort turned their weapons on him.

"I ain't no spy, General, sir. Blimey, it would be a poor show if the only disguise I could come up with was a uniform of the King's royal marines."

"Arrest him at once!" Jackson curtly ordered. Harry cast an imploring look in Kit's direction. Hanging was the punishment for a spy. The thought of dancing a dead man's jig from the nearest tree branch made the Cornishman go sick inside.

"I don't know how in the name of Jehovah you made it through our lines—" Jackson began.

"I brought him through," Kit interrupted.

Jackson sputtered, and turned on McQueen as if

the lieutenant had physically struck him. "You what!"

"He's my prisoner."

"Indeed, then why isn't he in irons?" Jackson was scowling now, and his normally bad temper grew worse. "He's seen our defenses."

"We sort of had an agreement, Your Generalship," Harry said, flashing his most winning smile. "You see, I promised not to try and escape, and that way I figured Mr. McQueen . . . uh . . . the lieutenant . . . might visit his lady fair. I mean, I ain't in no hurry to taste the prison bread, if you catch my drift." Harry moved into the moonlight to reveal he was unarmed. Bluffing was the only course open to him. He scratched beneath his arm and continued his explanation, much to Kit's chagrin. "Let no one say that Harry Tregoning lacks respect for true love. Why, a good woman is worth her weight in gold, don't you agree, General, sir? What do you say?"

Andrew Jackson seemed to swell in size. Color came to his cheeks and lightning flashed in his eyes. "What do I say . . . ?" He grabbed the cap from his head and wadded it up in his fist. The stone-faced men of the Tennessee Volunteers flanked their commander. With guns leveled, they awaited his orders. Old Hickory's iron gray hair stuck out from his head in wild disarray. "What do I say?" He looked from Harry to Kit, his gaze darting back and forth from one man to the other. "Arrest them both!"

Chapter Six

"You can't arrest me," said Kit McQueen, standing at attention in the middle of Jackson's study. The general had taken an apartment at 106 Royal Street and had commandeered a spacious suite on the second floor of a three-story building whose balconies were trimmed with wrought-iron railing forged to resemble a swirl of black vines across the face of both the second and third stories. "Come on, now, General," Kit continued. "I was placed under your command to aid in routing the Creeks and destroying their confederacy. My presence here is of my own choosing and beyond my assigned duties. I am an officer in the army of the United States. Your ranking originated in the militia. You're a volunteer like the Tennesseans manning the breastworks."

"And you, sir, by your own admission were not posted to New Orleans and are therefore also a volunteer and subsequently under my authority." Jackson chuckled at his own cleverness and eased back in the chair behind the desk. He clasped his hands beneath his chin and allowed his gaze to drift over the shelves of books and, in the corner, a what-not carved of cherry wood and displaying a collection of stoneware tankards with pewter caps. On a nearby table, a silver tray was set with a dark green bottle of sherry and another of elderberry cordial and three short-stemmed glasses, one of which still held traces of a reddish brown liquid. "However, this argument is meaningless. You see, Lieutenant, a few months ago the secretary of war appointed me the commander of Military District Number Seven, which includes Tennessee, Louisiana, and the Mississippi Territory." The general was taking obvious pleasure at McQueen's discomfort. He had pointedly avoided telling Kit McQueen of the appointment, saving the news for just such a moment when the upstart lieutenant attempted to avoid Jackson's orders. "Any way you slice it, Lieutenant, it's still humble pie. You are under my jurisdiction and I can have you stand post, flogged, or dance naked in a briar patch."

Kit inwardly groaned. He'd been able to pick and choose his orders up to now, allowing himself the freedom to act in a way he thought was best for himself and Iron Hand's Choctaws. But the game had changed and a new one begun and General Andrew Jackson was writing the rules.

An orderly entered the room and saluted Jackson, who promptly instructed the man to refill the general's glass. Willem Brookey lost no time in obeying Old Hickory's command. The orderly was a portly fellow in a tight-fitting dark blue coat with red facing, white breeches, and calf-high black boots. His round pale cheeks were pitted from a childhood bout with the pox. He had a perpetually cheerful demeanor, which Kit found in welcome contrast to the often-dour Andrew Jackson.

"Thank you, Brookey. You can leave us now."

"Yessir, General. But you wanted to know when Captain Laffite arrived."

"Well, then, show him in. Immediately. And pour a sherry for him."

"That won't be necessary. I prefer a less refined drink," said Jean Laffite as he stepped into the room. The buccaneer stood about five feet ten, the same as Kit. He was built slim and carried himself erect and proud. His hazel eyes met Kit's bronze stare and the two men silently appraised one another.

Kit had become acquainted with the notorious pirate a few weeks back, but their introduction had been hastily made in the company of a host of other officers. Kit knew the man by reputation, one that had prepared him to encounter a vile and treacherous individual. Instead, McQueen found Laffite to be both elegant and cordial. Scandalous stories to the contrary, Kit sensed there was more to the man than the stuff of rumor and conjecture. These were hard and difficult times. Men and women survived by their wits and their courage. The frontier had a habit of culling the weak and burying them in the dust of their unattainable dreams.

Laffite's hair, eyebrows, and mustache were a curious rust red. It was the topic of some conjecture that the pirate frequently washed his head with a mixture of potash and gunpowder to achieve his peculiar hair coloring. It was all considered part of a disguise. In truth, all the Laffite brothers—Jean, Pierre, and Alexander—kept the true nature of their appearances hidden beneath beards and mustaches.

Pierre had been known to wear oversized clothes and pad them to make himself seem larger than he actually was. Alexander on the other hand had even changed his name and sailed under the black flag as the merciless freebooter called Dominique You.

"So this is the lieutenant my friend Cesar Obregon so colorfully described." Laffite bowed toward Kit. "Ah, and I can hear your thoughts. This one is thinking, *Mon Dieu*, we have allied ourselves with pirates." Laffite chuckled, and walked to the French doors that opened onto the balcony.

"I'd fight alongside the devil himself to drive the British from American soil." Kit folded his arms across his chest. The two men shared the same height but Kit's upper torso was corded with muscle. His father, Dan McQueen, had been a blacksmith by trade and Kit had often worked alongside the man at his forge. With fire and anvil and hammer, they had shaped iron to their will. Kit McQueen's powerful physique was a legacy of those earlier halcyon days.

"You will. Mark my words, my young patriot. In fact, there are many 'devils' among us Baratarians."

"I marked one tonight," Kit replied.

"Yes. I saw Captain Obregon's jaw." Laffite stepped closer and peered at Kit's swollen lip. "It seems he left his signature on you as well."

"Devils . . . patriots . . . I don't care what they're called," Jackson said. "Just so long as they can fight." He raised a glass of sherry in toast to Laffite. "Finer cannoneers I have never seen in all my days. My only regret is that we have so few pieces of artillery for your lads to put to good use." Jackson rose from his desk and crossed to the French doors and peered through his own reflection at the city. The streets were devoid of life. The north wind had chased the inhabitants indoors. "Three of the six-pounders will hardly deter a British attack."

"I've placed a pair of twenty-four-pounders at the breastworks just this day. And fortified their redoubts with timber," said Laffite. "We'll get a few licks in before the British gunners can train their artillery on us."

"Well done, Captain Laffite. I'll be moving my headquarters out to the McCarty farm. I want to be able to overlook the center of our defenses. With the river to his left and marshes and swampland to the right Packenham is going to have to meet us head on. The twenty-fours loaded with grape will be a nasty surprise."

"Would that I had some lengths of pig iron to strengthen the redoubts and provide my cannoneers with some protection."

"What about cotton?" Kit suggested. "There's plenty of bales in the warehouses. We can make the defenses as thick as we want. And I haven't seen a man yet injured by splintered cotton."

"Bien," Laffite exclaimed. "The bales would absorb the British shells. Every shot that strikes would only add to the strength of the redoubt."

"I believe you have a warehouse of prime bales near Chalmette," Jackson added with a wink in Kit's direction. Laffite paled at the general's unspoken suggestion.

"Surely you are not suggesting we use my stores. My cotton is some of the finest in the Delta."

"Then, you won't find any hardship in defending it," Jackson said. "I'll dispatch a work detail of my Kentuckians and set them to the task. Might as well put them to use. They showed up at this fight expecting me to arm them." Jackson scowled, and slapped his fist into the palm of his hand. "Never seen a Kentuckian without a gun, good whiskey, and a plug of tobacco. Not until now."

Laffite sighed and shrugged, resigned to the fact that his fine cotton was to be turned into battlements. "I must compliment you on your suggestion, Lieutenant." The buccaneer took in both men as he bowed. "I bid you good-night, my friends. Tomorrow is another day, and one that promises no small sacrifice on my part. *Oui?"*

"One for which we shall all remain truly grateful," Jackson said. He reached out and the two men shook hands. Kit could not help but note that had the British never invaded American soil, General Andrew Jackson might well have mounted an expedition to drive the Baratarians out of their bayous. But a common enemy had forged an alliance between them. It was anyone's guess, though, just how long the bonds of friendship would last.

Laffite turned to leave, then paused by Kit. "The Hawk of the Antilles is not to be taken lightly. His prowess with pistol and cutlass is without equal." The buccaneer hesitated as if in thought, then he decided to say no more.

"I don't frighten easily," Kit said.

"Obregon is accustomed to having his way. What doesn't stand aside, he walks over or through."

"Not this time," Kit matter-of-factly replied. It was no brag, just a simply stated fact.

A hint of a smile touched the corners of Laffite's mouth. He said no more but sauntered from the room, a man wholly confident of himself and one who perhaps possessed secrets other men could only guess. *Barataria*, taken from the book *Don Quixote*, in which it was the name of an unattainable island-kingdom, a place of dreams and fulfillment. There was magic in the name and a sense of pathos for one's impossible desires. Laffite's way of life was coming to an end whether the British were repulsed or not.

"And as for you, my insubordinate young rap-scallion," Jackson said when the two were alone again, "keep clear of Captain Obregon. I want your word on that. We need these Baratarians. And though I hate to admit it, I need the likes of you, too. So if I must imprison you to keep you from getting your fool throat slit, then by heaven I shall." Jackson strode to the French windows and stared out at the night-shrouded streets of the Crescent City.

"You have my word, sir," said Kit.

"Then be off with you. Place a mark on Brookey's map just where you encountered the British patrol. And do me a favor. Don't go showing off our defenses to just any old English marine who wanders over behind our lines."

"Yessir." Kit saluted and started to leave. Again Jackson halted him with a final word.

"Oh, and give my regards to Raven O'Keefe."

"General?"

"I know the hour is late, but dammit, man, I was a young stag myself . . . a hundred years ago." Jackson never looked around. He continued to study the city he had sworn to protect.

Kit slipped through the doorway and departed the house. Come morning he would turn his thoughts to war. The fortifications could wait until sunup. Tonight he had business elsewhere.

Chapter Seven

A winter fog crept up from the river and sent ghostly tendrils to explore the silent waterfront where only the listless current lapped and a three-masted gaffe-rigged schooner rode close to the dock alongside a sidewheel paddleboat christened the *Hannah Louise.*

The schooner had recently been repaired and its name yet to be painted on the bow by its owner. But it was a sleek tight ship, devoid of life and left to the rolling gray fog, to keep its lonely vigil against the silent terrors of such a night as this.

Kit unerringly made his way through the city. He could have found Madame LeBeouf's house blind-folded. The lieutenant's moccasins padded softly on the cobblestone street as he rounded Dumaine and headed down Bourbon. An inner sense, the legacy of his Highland forbearers, made him cautious as he approached the wrought-iron gate that opened onto the courtyard from which Kit had been taken under guard a couple of hours ago. Poor Tregoning was condemned to languish in the town jail on Magazine Street by order of General Jackson. At least he wasn't destined for the hangman's noose. Kit had convinced Old Hickory to spare the British marine's life. However, Jackson intended to turn the man over to the proper British authorities once the question of hostilities was settled . . . a fate that did not sit well with Tregoning. After all, he was a deserter now, and British officers were meticulously devoid of mercy when it came to such a crime, no matter the extenuating circumstances.

Kit pulled up his collar and eased out of the mist's damp breath and stood for a moment in the lee of an entrance to the office of Doctor Yves DeCologne. The doorway was set in a shallow alcove and provided some relief from the cold. He waited and then heard the sound again. Yes, a boot scraping against stone. The sound was followed by a cough, then silence. Someone coughed again and spat.

"This here's a fool's voyage you've sailed into, mark my words, Robert Bonabel," a voice softly spoke. A man was apparently talking to himself, for there came no reply. The same man sighed and repeated, "A fool's voyage, and curse Cesar Obregon for it. McQueen ain't coming back here, not after Jackson hauled him off. But here I stand, stiff as a pine board and nary a drop of rum to warm my blood." Another cough followed as the unseen man struggled to endure the watch he'd been assigned.

Kit settled back against the door behind him and gave the situation some thought. The fog left him blind to the dangers ahead. He turned around and discovered he was able to read the name on the physician's door. It gave him his bearing. He remembered that the widow's courtyard lay just across the street and a few steps further along. It bothered him that Obregon had placed a guard to watch the approaches to the widow's house. Perhaps the buccaneer was already inside, making love to Raven

O'Keefe. The very notion brought a scowl to Kit's unshaven features.

Something brushed against his leg and Kit nearly leaped into the street before he realized it was a cat come wandering up out of the mist. Kit had noticed the little female calico riding in Doctor DeCologne's lap as the good-natured physician made his rounds, tending to the needs of his private patients before seeing to the wounds incurred on the skirmish lines around Chalmette plantation. Kit reached down, scooped up the feline in his right hand, and shifted the animal to his left while he stroked the creature until a deep-throated purr rumbled in his throat. Kit began to devise a plan to rid himself of Obregon's troublesome shipmate. It involved the friendly tabby.

McQueen continued petting the cat as he eased out of the doorway. He announced himself by moaning in a low pitiful voice just loud enough for the pirate up ahead to hear.

"What the hell is that!"

Kit continued to moan and slowly advance on Obregon's startled henchman. Kit estimated the distance and adjusted his pace. He took his time for maximum effect. There was a second door in an alcove just up ahead marking the entrance to an accountant's office, and Kit guessed that Bonabel had chosen the alcove for his post.

"Who the devil are you?" From the tremor in the pirate's voice, Bonabel was obviously unnerved by the fiend without a face approaching him from out of the ghastly mist. "Saints preserve me. Jesus, Mary and Joseph . . . I say stand or suffer the consequences." Kit heard the telltale click of a gun being cocked. He doubted that Bonabel could see well enough to hit him. A wound would be plain dumb luck. Kit searched the fog and found he could just discern the dark patch of doorway in which Bonabel had taken refuge from the night. Kit moaned again, sounding for all the world like some tormented soul risen on this shrouded eve to haunt the living with its dreadful presence.

"Devil or not, you'll taste the lead in my brace of pistols, so get you back to perdition and leave all good Christians alone!" Bonabel had backed himself against the door. Suddenly his protection from the elements had become a trap. "Blast your dead man's eyes," the superstitious ruffian called out. "Why do you haunt these streets. Who do you seek"

"Yoooouuuu!" Kit wailed. "I've come for yoooouuuu!" He punctuated his horrid summons by twisting the cat's tail and giving a vicious tug that elicited an angry inhuman cry from the feline. As the animal screeched and hissed in pain and bared its fangs, Kit tossed the frightened furious creature at the black expanse of doorway. Airborne and howling, its claws outstretched, the cat must have seemed like an agent of the netherworld, cast in fire and brimstone and summoned to drag the pirate into the inferno. Bonabel shrieked and dropped his pistols and took off running down Bourbon Street for all he was worth, hounded by the unleashed monsters of his own imagination.

Kit McQueen chuckled softly and listened to the buccaneer beat a hasty retreat into the mist. Then with the coast clear, he sauntered across the street and slipped through the courtyard gate and found himself once more in the widow's garden. The windows were dark and the house appeared devoid of life. Evidently the widow's party had ended earlier than expected. Kit muttered a silent prayer of thanks. He wasted no time in heading straight for an oak tree at the right front corner of the house. A bench swing dangled from one of the tree's stout branches. Kit tramped through the freshly turned earth and reaching the tree swung up into the branches, climbing hand over hand until he reached the balcony railing.

The iron railing was showing rust on the few bare spots that weren't covered by a lush tangle of leafy green vines. Kit had no problem in reaching the balcony and alighting quietly outside twin French doors that he knew from a previous visit opened onto the bedroom Olivia LeBeouf had provided for the half-breed daughter of Iron Hand O'Keefe.

Kit tried the door. The latch turned under pressure and the door gave way. Kit eased it open and slipped into the room, pausing to allow himself to become accustomed to the room's dark interior. After a few moments he felt confident to move away from the doors.

The bedroom was comfortably appointed with padded chairs and japanned end tables to either side of the bed. And the bed . . . an ornate piece of furniture that looked as heavy as a trireme. The frame was of solid mahogany, with tapered posts at each corner that supported a ruffed canopy of amber-colored cotton panels trimmed with embroidered roses and daffodils and magnolia blossoms.

Kit glimpsed a huddled form wrapped in blankets and sheet and burrowed in a nest beneath the quilt that Olivia LeBeouf had herself sewn from a box of cloth scraps she stored beneath her bed and guarded as a miser would his gold. Quilting was another of the widow's passions.

Kit stole quietly to the bedside and then, leaning down, reached around the sleeping form to take Raven in his arms. Behind him a shape detached itself from the dark side of a chiffonnier and darted toward the unwary intruder. And as Kit discovered he had embraced nothing more than a pillow and a rolled-up blanket, the point of a knife dug into his side.

"I saw you in the garden," Raven whispered in his ear.

"I never made a sound."

"No matter. I knew you would be coming. I saw it in a dream."

Kit sighed. Raven and her dreams were an inexplicable phenomenon. Her mother, the woman Iron Hand had taken to wife, had been a revered medicine woman among the Choctaw. Great powers had been attributed to her. She had been a seer and healer among the tribe, who had held her in great esteem and mourned her untimely death. Despite the mix of bloodlines that flowed through Raven's veins, it was said, she had inherited the gifts of her mother. Kit was a firm realist, but from time to time, Raven's skills and knowledge left him completely baffled. There was a part of her world he would never understand or be one with which made his longing for her even more poignant. Whatever part of her life she could give him was enough for Kit McQueen.

"You ruined my dress," Raven said. "And you embarrassed me in front of Olivia's guests." She increased the pressure on the knife. The man winced but did not move. "What do you think your punishment ought to be?"

"A good flogging might be in order," Kit suggested.

"Too public."

"You could press home on the knife and carve out my liver."

"Not painful enough."

"Ah . . . you want to cause me pain."

"Right you are, dear lad. Now you've said it."

"Well, then, tell me to leave and never return. Tell me you will never forgive me for being a jealous fool." Kit turned and sat on the bed. Raven wore a flannel robe and her long black tresses flowed down across her shoulders and fell to her waist. She smelled of lilac and rosewater. Kit ached to take her in his arms and lose himself in the wild abandonment of their lovemaking.

"I thought of that. Only one thing stopped me," said Raven.

"What?"

"I couldn't bear the pain." She sighed. "I suppose I should be grateful you were finally paying attention even if you nearly drowned me in the process."

"Then I am forgiven?"

Raven pushed him back onto the bed and straddled his lower limbs with her tawny thighs. "I'll let you know." She bowed forward and a cascade of her soft black hair spilled over him. "Come morning." She kissed him and lost herself to the fire in his flesh and the magic in her heart.

Chapter Eight

"Where the devil is he?" Iron Hand O'Keefe growled, looking over his shoulder and checking their back trail. Kit turned in the saddle and checked the surrounding woods for some sign of the eight-year-old rascal whose mission in life had something to do with being a thorn in O'Keefe's side. Neither McQueen nor Raven could spy any movement among the oak trees. It was a cold sunny day, and the forest was a patchwork of slanting shadows that could have provided concealment for an entire war party, much less a tan and sandy will-o'-the-wisp named Johnny Fuller.

O'Keefe scowled and rubbed the back of his neck. "Curse it, even when he ain't with me, he's with me."

"Grumble all you want, but the lad's adulation pleases you no end." Raven grinned and winked at Kit, who rode at her side ahead of her disgruntled father.

"Adulation . . . why, girl, it's a plague. The scamp pops up when I least expect it. Every time I turn around or strike out on my own, there he comes, sure as the sunrise. Never seen a pup move so quiet-like. I swear he's got Choctaw blood in his veins, or worse, Creek. Now, them redsticks can sneak up on a man and slit his throat while he's clearing to spit. But we took their measure at Horse Shoe Bend.''

O'Keefe chuckled, and straightened his great girth in the saddle. He glanced up at the cloudless sky that looked blue as ice and thought to himself how good it was to be alive. His gaze settled on the couple riding a few yards ahead of him on the way to the Choctaw encampment north of New Orleans. His heart swelled with affection. Look at them, Star Basket, he said to himself, carrying on an internal dialogue with the medicine woman he had taken to wife and who had borne him a special daughter. Raven had filled his days with joy and given him a reason to go on living after the untimely death of his Choctaw bride. She's as pretty as a morning star and got your courage. Aye, and I'm thinking there's more here than I can see. She has the gift. These dreams and such. The way she seems to be able to see the spirit in things like some I seen in the old country, them who were blessed by the little people and given a second sight. O'Keefe shook his head in wonderment at the turns of his life, and he felt a twinge as Kit leaned to the right and spoke in a hushed tone and Raven laughed clear and sweet. He was losing his daughter to the lieutenant. Kiss the Blarney stone, what was he saying? He had *already* lost her to McQueen, and it was time to face that fact once and for all. She was gone, and there was no returning to the way things used to be. Times had changed. The daughter of yesterday had become a woman in love today. By God, it left him in awe, the way his life had unfolded from the emerald hills of County Kerry to the American wilderness with its savage beauty and dangerous days. A man was always on the edge here. But he wouldn't have it any other way. O'Keefe never felt more alive than when he walked the wild places.

He knew Kit felt the same way. Perhaps that was the reason he had taken a liking to McQueen, sensing a kinship in the lieutenant whose Yankee upbringing had not quelled his fierce thirst for adventure. God bless his Highland blood, he'd make a good husband for Raven and she a good wife to him. Ah, there it was again, a tug at his heartstring for the child who had blossomed into a woman. A father's sense of loss indeed, but a father's pride.

The back of his neck began to itch and he began to scratch it with his good right hand while gripping the rein in his teeth. Then, out of a naturally cautious nature, he craned his head around and discovered who he had been looking for since leaving the crescent city almost an hour ago. Johnny Fuller sat astride a mule in the middle of the wheel-rutted road about a hundred yards behind O'Keefe, his daughter, and her lover.

"There's the young scalawag. I knew he'd followed us." O'Keefe reined in his mount. Kit and Raven followed her father's example.

"He certainly wasn't born with any 'quit' in him," Kit noted. He crossed his hands on the rounded pommel of his Spanish saddle and glanced at Raven. She had forsaken her finery for a cream-colored smock of brushed buckskin and leggings of the same. Butter soft moccasins encased her feet. The "Belle of the Ball" had been replaced by a dark-haired Choctaw maiden with flashing green eyes. As much as he was enamored of the former, this was the Raven he loved.

In his mind's eye he relived the first moment he had glimpsed her. About a year and a half ago, the first of September, she had been surrounded by Creek warriors anxious to capture the daughter of Iron Hand. Armed with nothing more than her own bare hands, she had defied her enemies who circled her like a pack of wolves and held them at bay. It had been clear Raven wasn't about to be taken prisoner. The Creeks would have to kill her. And that was just what they had been about to do when Kit interfered and saved her life. A few moments later and she had saved his, shoving him out of the path of a lead slug fired at his back by one of her attackers. In a single afternoon they had managed to save each other's lives.

Memories gave way to the present, and Kit watched as Johnny Fuller rode toward them for a few moments, then halted his mount and watched for O'Keefe's reaction.

A cloth cap with a crumpled leather brim covered the boy's unkempt hair. He wore a loose-fitting cotton shirt and an oversized coat that hung below his knees. His woolen pants were coarsely woven but in good shape. The widow LeBeouf had patched the knees on his trousers herself.

"I ought to cut me a switch and drive him off," O'Keefe muttered.

"Oh, Father, let him come along. He's been wanting to see the camp," Raven said.

"We ain't riding into no picnic, Daughter. Nate sent word that Strikes With Club is stirring the waters again and riling up the young blades. He's as much trouble as Spring lightning, mark my words."

"The lightning comes with the nourishing rains. If we are to have the one, then we must endure the other." She had grown up with Strikes With Club and knew that although he was a firebrand, he only had the good of the Choctaw people at heart.

"Since when did you start sounding so all-fired wise?"

"Since you started to listen," she replied. "I think the boy's place is with us."

"If you drive him off, then you'll wear out your neck watching our back trail and you'll be chewing horseshoes wondering where the lad has gone and seeing him in every shadow and behind every bush," said Kit.

He sat easy in the saddle. He wore a blue service coat and buckskin breeches tucked into his boots and carried the Quakers loaded and primed and caught in the belt at his waist. A rifled musket hung by a sling across his back. The bone-handle grip of a broad-bladed Arkansas toothpick jutted from a buckskin sheath at the small of his back. He could snake a hand around and have it in his grip in the blink of an eye.

"That's straight talk," O'Keefe sighed. He made a soft clucking sound and ran his tongue over his teeth as he considered his choices, and then with a shrug he waved the eight-year-old to come on. Johnny Fuller grinned and, removing his cap, slapped the mule across the rump. The animal broke into a trot and bellowed indignantly at the treatment he had so far endured. The last place the stable-bound animal wanted to be was outside in the wintry air where the sunlight held nothing but the illusion of warmth.

"You can tag along. But you stay close and do what I tell you or I'll let the Turtle Clan string your hair to their war belts."

"You won't regret this," Johnny excitedly said as he drew abreast of the burly Irishman known along the length and breadth of the Mississippi as Iron Hand, war chief of the Choctaw Nation. "My eyes are sharp and keen. Ain't nothing I miss. A man your age needs someone to watch out for him."

"A man my age!" O'Keefe snapped. He noticed Kit and Raven quickly looked away. "Well, see if you can keep up with Methuselah." O'Keefe reared his mount and charged down the trail, forcing Kit and Raven to leap their horses out of harm's way as he barreled past.

Johnny Fuller walked his mule up to the lieutenant and O'Keefe's daughter. "Did I do something wrong?"

Kit chuckled and guided his mare back onto the north road. "No, younker. It's just that some men fly to the truth, and others . . . well . . . they see it coming and run like hell."

Nathan Russell did not consider himself any less of a Choctaw than the volatile young men ringing the council fire. But Strikes With Club had given them other ideas. He strutted before the warriors and circled the blazing pyre of logs and pressed home his point that the white soldiers were playing them all for fools. The Choctaw were not equal in the eyes of General Jackson, and once the British were driven off, then the one called Old Hickory would forget the red men who had allied themselves with him and spilled their blood on the common battlefield. What made things even worse was the fact that Nathan Russell, who had once been called Blue Feather, now used a Christian name and spoke of the white man's God as the one spirit.

Nathan had heard these arguments before and did not doubt he would again. But Strikes With Club was getting under his skin. He allowed the younger man his moment before the elders, as was the way of the Choctaw, for each man had the right to make himself heard. And besides, Nate was buying time, permitting the members of the Snake Clan to gather in support of one of their own. Nate had also sent word to Iron Hand about the unrest in the Choctaw camp. Strikes With Club was attempting to add verbal tinder to an already-volatile situation.

The Choctaws had chosen their campsite well. Iron Hand had found a relatively solid patch of ground north of New Orleans. The glade was ringed by oak and shagbark hickory. Further out, the ground became spongy and eventually marshlike and virtually impassable for most men, although the Choctaw had long since adapted to the conditions and often traversed the bayous on logs cut and hidden in the underbrush for just such purposes. The woods were silent and still near the camp although a flock of geese had chosen nearby Muggat's Bayou for their winter haven. Several of the birds had been trapped by the men in the camp and roasted over a dozen smaller cookfires where the hundred and thirty-eight warriors took their meals and awaited orders from the general whose sincerity many of them had begun to doubt.

"You wear the soldier coat," said Strikes With Club. "You follow their orders rather than the council of your elders. It is true you are no longer Blue Feather. The soldiers have given you a new name, one you share with all the Snake Clan. Now you are called White Man Runs Him."

"Enough!" Nate Russell said, rising up and walking across the clearing to stand before the younger man. Though the same height, Nate was much more solid. He was a farmer and his physique reflected the kind of life he had lived, toiling in the fields, planting crops, and uprooting tree stumps to clear more land. He had built a large blockhouse in the Choctaw village several miles upriver of New Orleans where his wife and children yet lived, awaiting his return. "It is true I have chosen to work the earth and plant the same crops as the white man. My cotton is the equal of any I have seen on the plantations around here. And I have taken a white man's name. But I am still Blue Feather as I am also Nathan Russell." Nathan studied the faces of the men surrounding him. The entire camp was present. He could see the restlessness and suspicion in the countenances of the young braves and the sympathetic glances of those warriors who, like him, had changed their names and striven to live in a fashion that was wholly incompatible with the old ways. He noticed the arrival of Iron Hand and Kit McQueen, but did not call attention to them. He wanted to make his own point without the aid of the Irish chieftain.

"You have seen the white men. Their numbers are great. We must learn to live as they do or we will surely be buried by them. "He raised his right arm, holding aloft a war club. "Today we fight alongside the Americans. General Jackson will not forget what we do. By making our stand with him, we will earn his gratitude and use it to protect our way of life."

"General Jackson does not even know we are here."

"You're wrong about that!" Kit called out. Most of the Choctaw braves in the center of the camp turned to watch Kit and Iron Hand ride up to the council fire and dismount. Raven and Johnny Fuller were only a few paces behind. Several of the younger men instantly took note of Raven. She was the only woman who had accompanied the war party south to meet with the Tennesseans and Kentucky militia outside the city. The half-breed sensed their hungry glances and tried to ignore the undue attention many of the lonely men were giving her.

Raven had refused to remain in the Choctaw village with the other women and children and had cautioned her father that she sensed her place was in New Orleans. O'Keefe was superstitious and loath to doubt his daughter's intuitive skills, but he exacted a promise from Raven that she would remain well away from any fighting and keep out of harm's way.

Actually, Raven had stretched the truth. Kit had been her real reason for tagging along with the war party—not to mention a desire to enjoy Olivia Le-Beouf's hospitality once again. But as the days of siege wore on, she began to suspect there was more at work than her own harmless ruse. A premonition began to nag at her thoughts. Perhaps fate indeed had a role for her to play in the outcome of these unfolding events. But as to the nature of her part, she could only guess.

Kit dismounted from horseback, winked at the eight-year-old who had ridden out from New Orleans with them, and strode purposefully up to the council fire, taking care to see that Iron Hand O'Keefe preceded him into the circle of warmth cast by the blazing logs.

"You have no place at this council," Strikes With Club cautioned, and flanked by a pair of braves, Spotted Owl and Yellow Leaper, he moved to block Kit McQueen's entry into the camp. Despite his imposing size, O'Keefe moved quicker than the three men and intercepted them.

"Let him have his say. Kit fought alongside us against the Creeks and killed Wolf Jacket in hand-to-hand fighting. I reckon the lieutenant has earned a listen or two from us." O'Keefe glanced at the men around the fire. He knew almost all of them by name. Long ago he had come among them as an outcast, but his courage had won their respect and his cunning had gained him a place among the chiefs. "Or am I no longer welcome?" He centered his gaze on Strikes With Club as if silently daring the younger man to commit himself and chance repudiation for his boldness from the tribal elders who continued to hold O'Keefe in high esteem.

Strikes With Club wavered and lowered his gaze. He tried to capture support from his companions, but they had business elsewhere and were already in retreat. "We will hear the soldier." He followed his companions to the perimeter of the circle where he stood shoulder to shoulder with the Turtle Clan, all of whom seemed to be noticeably lacking in firearms. O'Keefe happened to glance over his shoulder and saw Johnny Fuller watching him with renewed respect. The Irishman's chest swelled with pride. The lad was seeing O'Keefe in his element, as the war chief of his adopted people.

Kit didn't begrudge Strikes With Club his displeasure. The unhappy brave had lost a friend on his last sojourn with McQueen when they had narrowly escaped capture by British marines. Kit knew what it meant to lose a friend.

"I have spoken to General Jackson, and in his own words he has said that there is not a man who can match the courage of the Choctaw," said Kit. His words rang out across the clearing. They rode the cold air above the crackling flames. "He has said the United States owes the Choctaw a debt he can never repay. But when the British are driven back into the sea, your chiefs and I will sit down with the general and help him find a way."

Nate Russell beamed triumphantly, vindicated by the lieutenant's words and the murmur of approval he heard rippling through the crowd.

"How do we know the British will not destroy us? They have more cannons, more soldiers, more everything." said Yellow Leaper. He was an earnest-looking man of nineteen who had fought at Horse Shoe Bend when the Choctaw and Cherokee had destroyed the Creek Confederation. But the British were something else entirely, and the rumble of their cannons and whooshing rockets filled him with dread.

"Not everything," Kit corrected. "They do not have the Choctaw."

"Yet they are like a great storm that sweeps up from the Great Water and tears down the trees and floods the land and is our destroyer," said Yellow Leaper. His voice betrayed his deep pessimism at the inevitable disastrous outcome.

"The British will not conquer us," Raven said from the edge of the clearing. It was unthinkable that a woman should address the council, for this was war talk and obviously a man's work. Defying tradition, Raven left Johnny Fuller's side and joined her father and Kit by the fire.

"Go on back to your lodge, woman," Strikes With Club called out. Many of the men around him shared his feeling. But an old warrior with stringy gray hair and skin like worn leather held up a hand for the complaining to cease. His name was New Moon Fox and he had joined the tribe after their victory over the Creeks. His people lived further north, between the Mississippi and the Yazoo rivers. O'Keefe knew him from earlier times and held him in respect.

"Let her speak," said New Moon Fox. His grainy voice was barely audible, yet everyone heard him. "She is the daughter of Star Basket, the medicine woman. The Great Spirit often whispered in her ear, taking the shape of smoke or a mourning dove and giving her that sight which is beyond seeing."

His hand lowered and the gathering grew silent. Even Kit and O'Keefe stepped aside for the woman, amazed at her conduct and awed by her sudden mantle of authority as she addressed the gathering.

"Last night I walked in a dream. All around me there were the dead and dying. The cannons sounded like thunder. The sky was streaked with smoke and fire. The ground ran red with blood. And then the veils of powder smoke drifted apart and I beheld the might and strength of the British army broken and scattered like leaves in the time of the harvest moon. And the air was filled with the stench of death and the sound of weeping from the camp of the redcoats while among the Choctaw there was chanting and celebration and we stood among the soldiers and the Baratarians as equals, like a strong cord woven of many strands from which it takes its strength. These things have I seen. And I know them to be true." Raven finished, and without so much as a "by your leave" she returned to the horses where Johnny Fuller, his jaw slack, handed her back the reins to her mare.

"How can such a thing be?" Strikes With Club finally spoke out, though he was obviously affected by Raven's words. "Of what use are we to General Jackson? How can we stand as equals when he does not even give us the guns he promised?"

"Perhaps he wants us to kill the redcoats with our war clubs while they butcher us with their rifles and cannon," said Yellow Leaper. Raven's dream to the contrary, he still had his doubts. "If General Jackson does not trust us with the rifles he promised, then we will never be equal to his soldiers and we can expect nothing from our alliance with the white man but our own destruction."

"You will have guns," Kit said, defusing the man's argument in a single stroke. O'Keefe appeared startled by McQueen's pronouncement and drew close to the lieutenant and caught him by the arm.

"Boy-o, what the devil are you up to? We've nary a spare musket between us. And Old Hickory has even less to offer."

"Jean Laffite and Cesar Obregon have a warehouse hidden in the bayous south of the city," Kit said. "They often cache their smuggled goods outside of New Orleans. Madam LeBeouf knew the location and drew a map for me. We'll take Nate Russell and some of the others and help ourselves to the Baratarian's stores. I should imagine we'll find rifled muskets aplenty the way Laffite continues to trickle the supply to Jackson. The freebooter raises the price for each load of flints and gunpowder."

"Laffite? Obregon? It's Jackson's own orders you'll be disobeying. He told you to keep clear of Cesar Obregon. There's enough bad blood between you two that the next time you meet you're bound to spill more'n a drop, mark my words."

Kit pulled free of O'Keefe's grasp, and faced the council of elders. He was determined to keep the Choctaw in the alliance. They were the eyes and ears of Jackson's army, constantly ranging the woods and the bayous and probing the perimeters of the British lines without ever attracting the attention of the redcoats.

"The lieutenant promises us guns," said Strikes With Club in a derisive tone of voice that momentarily captured the attention of his companions. "When?"

The question was a gauntlet hurled in McQueen's face, a challenge he refused to allow to go unanswered. Kit ignored O'Keefe's cautioning glances and attempts to dissuade the lieutenant from committing himself to a course that courted disaster. Kit knew what had to be done, no matter what the price.

"Today!" he said.

Behind the soldier in buckskins, O'Keefe groaned and wiped a hand across his grizzled features. "Stealing guns ain't exactly the army's way," he grumbled, knowing full well his warning would go unheeded.

"No, it's my way," Kit replied.

He knew Old Hickory was probably going to be furious and Obregon and Laffite even more so. Raven's father was just looking out for him, and Kit was grateful for the big man's concern. But O'Keefe ought to give it up. Some things just naturally went together, like powder and flint, thunder and lightning, winter and cold . . . or a McQueen and trouble.

Chapter Nine

"Now what?" said Iron Hand O'Keefe in a scolding tone of voice. "I could have told you something like this was bound to happen." The Irish-born war chief waited on horseback in the shadow of the woods about seventy-five yards from the solid-looking warehouse that dominated the clearing. The Baratarians had concealed their smuggled goods within a veritable blockhouse built of heavy oak logs laid one upon the other and chinked with mud. The walls were dotted with gun slits, and what few windows allowed sunlight into the interior could be closed and shielded by heavy-looking shutters that like the walls sported cross-slit gunports. Under siege, the warehouse would afford its defenders ample protection.

Today, however, the clearing in the forest was the scene of much activity as Cesar Obregon had his crew in the process of loading a couple of wagons with rifled muskets and gunpowder liberated from a Spanish frigate by the privateers and hidden for just such an occasion. Jackson was desperate to arm his recently arrived Kentuckians, and a handsome profit awaited the entrepreneur who arrived in the American camp with a shipment of firearms.

Kit McQueen sat astride his mare alongside O'Keefe and counted the crewmen milling about the two mule-drawn wagons arranged in front of the warehouse. There were at least a dozen privateers as best he could estimate. He glanced behind him at the seven Choctaws—Nate Russell on a farm wagon and Strikes With Club included—who had accompanied Kit and O'Keefe from their encampment to the north. Nine men in all and among them rode the boy, Johnny Fuller, and Raven O'Keefe. The medicine woman edged past the warriors to see for herself just exactly what had upset her father.

"You need to stay back," Kit complained. "Your 'dreams' aren't going to protect you if the lead begins to fly."

"Which will certainly happen if I don't ride with you." Raven spoke with surprising certainty. Kit was intrigued.

"What do you mean by that?"

"Meaning . . . my brick-top Highland lad . . . I doubt that Cesar Obregon will surrender a single flintlock. He'll never deal with you. But he might with me."

"I don't like it," Kit scowled.

"Of course." Raven's green eyes flashed and she patted his arms. "You aren't supposed to. However, if you want the guns . . ."

"Come on, then," Kit replied. Her logic was sound. And he needed everything in his favor he could get.

"Whoa! Hold it now, the both of you," O'Keefe protested. "Don't I have a say in the matter?"

Kit and Raven turned as one. "No," they said, and walked their mounts out of the shadows across a stretch of marshlike earth and onto the narrow winding wheel-rutted path that wound between patches of quicksand and led right to the warehouse.

It was a quarter past noon and the freebooters had paused in their efforts to reward themselves with a swallow or two of rum before resuming work. Despite the cold, the crew of the *Windthrift* had worked up a sweat. Their respite came to an abrupt end as the party of intruders appeared on the trail.

Honeyboy Biggs had just shouldered a barrel of black powder onto the wagon bed when Angel Mendoza, standing by the mules, bounced a pebble off the gunner's bald head. Biggs came up glaring and began to curse the ship's physician, but the white-haired man arched his eyebrows and jabbed a thumb in the direction of the newly arrived visitors.

"Hey, Biggs!" Reyner Blanche exclaimed as he approached with an arm full of muskets.

"Looks like we have company," a third crewman by the name of Keel Longley spoke up. A man of average height and build, Longley's scarred features bespoke a violent and quarrelsome man. Years ago he had decided St. Peter would slam the pearly gates smack dab in his face for the crimes of his youth. At thirty-two years of age, Longley expected to spend eternity with the devil and could see no reason to repent or change his ways.

"I see 'em," Biggs muttered. "Reyner . . . you run and fetch Captain Obregon. Tell him we got trouble." The youngest of the crewmen instantly obeyed and took off at a dead run. In a matter of seconds he had reached the open double doors and vanished inside the warehouse. "All right, pretty bastards, you've had your rum, now let's see you stand by your guns." Biggs tugged a pair of flintlocks from the waist of his striped breeches.

"Oh my . . . I'm a healer of men. Not someone who would stoop to taking a life." Angel Mendoza was indignant at the mere suggestion he ought to arm himself. He preferred to remain as far from the fighting as possible.

"Those Choctaws are gonna sure take a liking to that fine head of hair of yours," Biggs said. "They plumb fancy white scalps as being sort of special."

A look of alarm crossed Mendoza's aquiline countenance. He did not appreciate any talk of scalping. He was certain that Biggs was bluffing, but just to be on the safe side the physician worked his way back toward his companions, taking care to keep the wagon between himself and the oncoming Choctaw warriors.

Biggs and Longley shared a moment of unspoken amusement at Mendoza's expense. Behind them, another eleven men exploded from the barn and hurried to form a skirmish line using the wagons as cover. Cesar Obregon was the last to arrive. He strolled leisurely from the warehouse and walked across the soft earth to stand alongside his chief gunner.

"Choctaw." Biggs was nervous. It made him abrupt.

"I have eyes," Obregon purred. "And I recognize who is leading them." The buccaneer was delighted at seeing Raven O'Keefe again, but one look at McQueen made the captain's jaw ache.

"Shall we rattle them with a volley?" Longley asked, cocking his rifled musket and training his sights on the brave driving the wagon. The privateer braced his elbow on the side of the freight wagon to steady his aim.

"Not with the girl in the lead, you idiot," Obregon growled.

"These redsticks can't be trusted," another man contested. The Hawk of the Antilles silenced the crewman with a single glance from his hard blue eyes.

"I'll keelhaul the first man who opens fire without my say-so," Obregon called out. Then, before Biggs could offer a protest, the captain of the *Windthrift* climbed up into the wagon bed in full view of the oncoming warriors. He made a perfect target garbed in his black shirt and breeches, his sun-bleached blond hair held back from his aristocratic features by his ever-present black silk scarf.

As she reined her mare to a stop a few feet from Captain Obregon, Raven felt her own heart stir at the sight of him, for he cut a grand and glorious figure, this Castilian. He was like the wind blowing over the ocean and churning the waves, the constantly changing sea breezes, gentle one moment and raging the next and always unpredictable. She chanced a peek at the man alongside her. Kit was like the land, there was a permanence to him, and yet the land in its own way was as full of mystery as the wind.

"You are either a very brave man or a fool to come here," Obregon said to Kit. Then he bowed with a flourish to Raven. "Senora, it is a pleasure to see you again. A pity you have not chosen better company for your sojourn in the forest."

"I am with my friends, Senor Obregon," Raven replied.

"And why have you come, Senora? Perhaps it is I you seek, no?"

"We've come for the guns," Kit spoke out. He had wearied of Obregon's arrogance and sure as hell did not care for the way the buccaneer seemed to be undressing Raven with his eyes. Confrontation was one way of diverting the captain's attention. Raven had called for subtlety, but Kit wasn't about to put up with the Castilian's conduct.

A ripple of tension went a-coursing along the ranks of the privateers. Guns were cocked and leveled on both sides, but Obregon, despite being caught off guard by McQueen's pronouncement, had the calmness to raise his hand as a signal to remind his men to hold their fire.

"Now I have the answer," said Obregon. "You are indeed a fool."

"Not all the muskets. A hundred and twenty will do. And powder and shot," Kit continued, ignoring the captain's remark.

"These wagons are intended for General Jackson's troops," Obregon flatly explained. He twirled the tips of his mustache while he tried, and failed, to stare the lieutenant down.

"The Choctaw are Jackson's troops," Kit said. "But many of them have been facing British bayonets with little more than tomahawks and spears."

"Just think of us as sparing you lads a trip," O'Keefe interjected, trying to remain at his jovial best. Winning the buccaneer over was certainly better than fighting him, especially as the Choctaw were outnumbered and outgunned. "We brought our own wagon. Just point out the rifles and we'll be on our way." The Irishman started forward. Reyner Blanche, standing near the singletree, swung his rifle to bear on the big man.

"You be holding it right there, you tub of guts."

Iron Hand O'Keefe gave the young privateer a hard look and proceeded to grumble about the insolence of youth. Then he shrugged and nodded to Blanche. "As you say, me bucko. You have the musket. But one day I mean to take you aside and have a *pointed* conversation with you." He held up the black iron hook jutting from his left sleeve and wiped the sharpened tip on his broad buckskin-covered chest.

"I had hopes of making you understand our predicament," Raven said, walking her mount another step closer to Obregon.

"If you had come alone," Obregon said with a shrug. "*Mi querida.* Still, there is a chance. Bartering is an honored custom among the Baratarians. Now let me see, I have the guns and now what do you have to offer in trade? Hmmm. Perhaps together we might come up with something."

His meaning was as clear as the fiery passion

smoldering in his eyes. He did not care how he wound up with this raven-haired senorita whom he perceived as a lady one moment and then, in the next, as a wanton savage, elemental and untamed.

"I will trade you for the guns," Kit said. "I offer you that which you and your men no doubt prize above all other goods."

Obregon was intrigued. He was always ready to make a profit. Love could wait. He returned his attention to McQueen and carefully scrutinized the soldier in army-issue coat and beaded buckskin breeches. What manner of soldier was this McQueen who was as much at home among the savages as his own kind? "I have no use for trade beads." Behind him, the crew of the *Windthrift* laughed at the lieutenant's expense.

"Do you have any use for your lives?" Kit asked.

In a matter of seconds the air had thickened with tension, and the silence that followed was as loud as the roar of a cyclone.

"Do you think we came alone?" Kit called out. "There are more warriors in the forest, three times your number hiding behind every tree and bush along the trail to New Orleans. You've more than an hour's ride to Chalmette through dense thickets and stands of timber in which the entire Choctaw Nation could hide. Your crew is no doubt a brave bunch of lads, Obregon. But they'll never see the faces of their killers. And in the end, the Choctaw will have all your muskets and all your powder and shot." Kit swept the line of buccaneers in a single contemptuous glance as if he were counting so many graves. It had the desired effect. The privateers were obviously unnerved by McQueen's revelation and even Obregon shifted his gaze to the surrounding forest.

The Castilian was at a loss to explain how McQueen had discovered the warehouse. However disconcerting, it paled alongside the prospect of being plagued by unseen assailants all the way back to the breastworks.

"You are bluffing, Lieutenant McQueen," said Obregon.

"So be it," Kit replied. He tugged on the reins of his mare to turn the animal about.

"Seems a waste of good men," O'Keefe said, playing along with the ruse. He looked back toward the forest and lifted a bugle to his lips. It was a battered instrument that dangled from the Irishman's neck like Roland's horn. O'Keefe never went into battle without trumpeting his defiance. He split the air with a blast loud enough to wake the dead. But to Obregon's thinking, the Irishman had just signaled the Choctaws concealed in the depths of the woods.

"Wait!" Obregon called out. Kit and Iron Hand O'Keefe faced him again. "These are General Jackson's guns. I will not lose a man for them. Load what you need. But be quick, for you have tried my patience this day." Obregon bowed to Raven. "I will see you again, senorita." He leaped down from the wagon and started back up the path to the warehouse, pausing only once to bark an order to his men to assist the Choctaw in obtaining the muskets and ammunition they desired.

With all the men working, it only took half an hour for Nate Russell's wagon to be loaded. Kit was as anxious as anyone to be on his way. O'Keefe spent the time regaling everyone within earshot with orders and swaggering around the clearing. He cut quite a picture with Johnny Fuller tagging along in Iron Hand's shadow. When the Choctaw had started back down the trail, Obregon emerged from the doorway of the warehouse and dispatched a man to bring more wagons. He intended to remove all the stores and burn the warehouse to the ground now that its location had been discovered. He straightened as Kit left the departing Choctaw column and rode back across the clearing, and the buccaneer's hands drifted to his concealed daggers, for he was unsure of the lieutenant's intentions.

"We've only taken enough to adequately arm each of O'Keefe's men. I'll clear it with Jackson."

"That is not what you rode back to tell me."

"No," Kit said. "I want you to leave Raven alone. She is not for you."

"Oh. And why?"

"Because you don't love her . . . and I do."

"And she loves you?"

"Yes."

"*Love* . . . A man can love a good ship, a sail full of wind, the temptress sea. But a woman . . . you sail dangerous waters, Lieutenant McQueen. Go and sail them alone and trouble me no more. I am done with you both!" Kit studied the privateer for a moment longer, then whirled his mount and left the Hawk of the Antilles in the settling dust.

Honeyboy Biggs had watched what transpired, trying not to appear obvious as he strained to overhear the brief conversation between the two antagonists. After Kit had departed, Biggs stepped out of the shadowy interior of the barn.

The gunner wiped beads of sweat from his bald plate. Loading wagons was work for younger muscles, but he was too stubborn to stand aside and not lend his back to the efforts of the other men of the *Windthrift*. Nor was the gunner about to subject himself to their jibes about his encroaching age. Honeyboy Biggs was determined to prove he was the match for any of the crewmen.

Obregon's remarks to Kit McQueen had been music to the older man's ears. Biggs had been worried sick over the Castilian's obsession with the half-breed daughter of Iron Hand O'Keefe. It was time to put an end to such fancies and concentrate on the tasks at hand.

"Wisely put, Captain. You are well rid of the woman. Her kind bring nothing but misfortune." Biggs was fairly beaming as if a great weight had been lifted from his soul. But his happiness was short-lived.

"You old rum pot," said Obregon with a mirthless chuckle. "I lied."

Chapter Ten

"Poor Harry Tregoning," the marine muttered to himself, and kicked at a cockroach crawling sluggishly across the straw-littered floor of the storage shed that served as his jail. It was the eighth of January, a gray and dreary dawn. Daybreak had brought not only echoes of distant thunder but another bone-chilling mist from the river. It blanketed the shoreline and wound along the apartment and tavern-lined streets of the French Quarter and drifted past the shuttered windows of Tregoning's prison. He reached over and scooped up the cockroach and tossed it through the black grate of the Franklin stove, where the hapless insect exploded with a pop and melted into an oily black glob among the chunks of firewood.

He immediately regretted the act. It wasn't like Harry Tregoning to punish a helpless creature. He shook his head and sighed. "What's to become of this poor Cornishman?" The thunder had yet to abate. The marine listened carefully to what he had taken to be a most peculiar storm. Spring thunderheads in the dead of winter? "Harry Tregoning, you deaf fool.

Have you been locked in this damn storeroom so long you've forgotten the roar of cannons when you hear 'em?" His blood turned icy in his veins. Unless he missed his guess, the battle for New Orleans had begun.

A rattle of the door warned him that someone was about to enter. He tensed. Had General Jackson changed his mind about hanging the British marine? It had been over a week since his capture, but Tregoning was still suspicious of the general's intentions.

He heard the bolt slide back. The door creaked open on its rusted iron hinges, metal ground against metal, then, to Tregoning's surprise, a young woman in a pale blue woolen dress and wrapped in a heavy shawl entered the storeroom. She carried a woven reed basket whose contents were hidden beneath a beige cloth. Tregoning relaxed his grip on the three-legged stool with which he intended to fight off the imagined lynching party.

"By heaven, what do we have here?" he exclaimed, completely taken aback by the gender of his visitor. Harry Tregoning had a weakness for the fairer sex. And this was a comely young maiden indeed. Why, she looked part injun despite her attire.

"Well, if this ain't a grand thing. Dear missy, but you are a welcome sight. Already my damp and miserable abode seems brighter." Tregoning stepped aside and turned up the flame in one of his lanterns and then gestured to the room's spare furnishings, which consisted of a cot, a rather rickety looking table, and two stools. "You have a seat right here." He dipped his hands in a nearby bucket of water and smoothed down the fringe of black hair that wreathed his skull.

He sniffed the air and caught the aroma of the fresh-baked biscuits still warm from the oven. Tregoning's eyes grew wide as the woman unloaded the contents of her basket: a platter of biscuits, several thick slices of honey-cured ham, and a bottle of sherry Raven O'Keefe had personally selected from Madam LeBeouf's wine cabinet.

"By all the saints, you're an angel of mercy," Tregoning exclaimed, and dug into the food. Half a minute into his meal he glanced up sharply, crumbs spilling from his mouth and cheeks bulging. "This ain't poor Harry's last meal, is it? They ain't planning to hang me for a spy what with the commence of fighting?"

"Kit . . . uh . . . Lieutenant McQueen thought you might be hungry and asked if I would bring you something to eat," Raven said.

Tregoning nodded in understanding. "A decent sort for an officer. In truth, he's the best man I ever tried to kill. I'm right glad I let him get away." He proceeded to wolf down his food.

"Kit gave me a different version of your encounter," Raven said. Hers was a hollow smile. She, too, had heard the faint rumble of a distant cannonade and knew that if the British had begun their attack, the two men she loved most in this world, her father and Kit McQueen, would be right in the thick of things. Raven took in the storeroom at a glance. It was a bleak place but a sight warmer than any of the city's drafty jails.

"First names, is it?" Tregoning noted. "You must be the lieutenant's lady. He mentioned you the last time he paid me a visit." The marine tilted the bottle of sherry to his lips and washed down a mouthful of biscuits and bacon. "I'm surprised the lads outside the door let pass a mere slip of a girl like you."

"The guards have left. The entire Louisiana Battalion has moved on down to the breastworks south of the city. Something's happening." Raven looked toward the open door. "Packenham has begun his final assault." She remembered good-byes and a farewell kiss that was much too short and the pressure of

Kit's embrace when she thought he might squeeze the life out of her.

Three days had passed since the afternoon when he came to tell her that the British forays had increased and British troops were massing on the opposite bank of the Mississippi and it was obvious to one and all that British patience had worn thin. The city must fall or the British army abandon its attempts to take the city. Provisions were low, and as Kit had said, it was time for the might of the British force to "root hog or die a poor pig." Kit McQueen would remain at the breastworks until the issue had been resolved.

Raven understood, but she wanted to be at his side. She could handle a gun as well as any man. Yet down deep inside, she knew her place was back in the city. Had she joined the Choctaw, Kit might well get himself killed worrying for her safety. It was an all-too-real possibility.

"You came here alone, then?" Tregoning asked, intrigued. His gaze drifted to the doorway. No guards, she had said. None at all. "You weren't fearful for your safety?"

"I can take care of myself," Raven said.

"You've more than your share of grit, dear missy. But what's to stop me from tossing you aside and running out of here right this very minute?" Tregoning started toward her. He meant the half-breed no harm, especially as she was McQueen's consort, but there was a battle raging in the distance and he needed to look after his own welfare. "Being as you are all that's between me and freedom."

"Not all," Raven said. "There's me. And this." She pulled a short-barreled flintlock pistol from the basket and leveled it at the marine's chest. The look in her eyes and the steady hand gripping the gun gave the marine fair warning Raven was not to be trifled with. Tregoning slumped on one of the stools, his homely features sour and dejected-looking.

"You make a fair point, missy. I'll not be the fool who argues with you."

"Good. Then finish your meal and come along. My friend, the Madame Olivia LeBeouf has a bath and a change of clothes waiting for you. Nothing grand, but a simple woolen coat, a shirt, and breeches."

"I don't understand," Tregoning said.

"Kit told us you were a man without a country. Once hostilities have ceased, Jackson will either toss you in prison or hand you over to some English officer. Kit figured you'd find either situation intolerable."

"English justice will see a noose around my neck. Alas, poor Harry," the marine muttered.

"But a change of clothes could see you on your way."

Tregoning scratched his scalp and considered the young woman's offer. The storeroom prison was hardly the kind of place a man grew attached to. As for soldiering, Harry Tregoning had loved well but not wisely, and it was for the best that he distance himself from the wrath of irate husbands.

Tregoning cocked his head to one side and studied his visitor, searching her expression for any hint of duplicity. What he found was a woman of honest virtue, a woman who was as strong as she was lovely. He envied the lieutenant.

"Don't try and question his motives, Mr. Tregoning. You will fare no better than I," Raven added. "Kit believes you are a good man. And as you were his prisoner, he insisted he had the right to offer you parole." She turned and started toward the unbarred door. "I have a carriage outside," O'Keefe's daughter added. "And the streets are thick with mist." She paused in the doorway and returned the pistol to the basket. Tregoning raised the bottle of sherry and drank deep, emptying a measure of liquid courage down his gullet. Then he corked the bottle and tucked it under his arm. He crossed the storeroom and followed Raven into the gray-shrouded street.

The carriage had been left in front of the storeroom a few paces from the doorway. Tregoning clambered up and Raven took a place alongside him. She flicked the reins and the mare in its traces broke into a trot that took them through the city at a crisp pace. Twenty minutes later, Raven pulled the mare to a halt before the courtyard gate of Madame Lebeouf's house. Tregoning jumped out of the wagon and glanced worriedly up and down the street, searching the fog for a glimpse of betrayal.

Raven joined him at the gate that creaked open at her touch. Rust was everywhere, she thought as she led the way into the garden where Harry Tregoning had been arrested.

"I ought to warn you about Olivia. She is a widow . . ."

"Ah. Some of my very best friends have been widows," Tregoning chuckled. His smile faded, for the distant cannon fire had yet to abate. It was a low rumble, muffled by the mist. But it had underscored the trip through the deserted streets and it was present now. Men were dying with every step through the widow's barren garden. *But you've been given a second chance, Harry Tregoning. The rest of your life is up to you.*

A window exploded in the front of the house and a china pitcher crashed out in the courtyard.

"Raven! Run! It's—" The outcry was cut short, but Raven recognized the voice of Johnny Fuller as he shouted his warning through the window he had shattered. A trio of rough-looking men rounded the corner of the house and trampled the dry brittle leaves littering the courtyard.

A woman's scream. A succession of gunshots.

Tregoning snatched the pistol from it's place of concealment in the basket. His eyes blazed with anger.

"Jezebel!" he cursed beneath his breath, and then charged his attackers.

"No!" Raven called after him. Too late. Tregoning was among them. More gunfire and the sound of fists thudding against flesh and the groans of wounded men and the dull flash of a cutlass blade.

Help. They needed help. She had to find Kit and tell him what had happened. Raven turned on her heels, lifted the hem of her dress, and bolted down the garden walk. The moccasins she wore in place of slippers padded soundlessly on the loose cobblestones. She braced herself for a struggle in case another set of brigands rose out of the mist to block her escape.

Her heart leapt with joy as she cleared the front gate and entered the street. The dress hampered her movement, but she still managed to vault into the carriage with most-unladylike grace.

In a single fluid gesture she reached for the reins. A hand reached out and caught her wrist in a grip of iron. The man in black sat beside her in the carriage and lifted her fingers to his lips and kissed her hand. Kit McQueen, General Jackson, and their ragtag army were occupied with the British attack. There was no one to stop Cesar Obregon. The city was his.

"Mi querida," purred the buccaneer in his silken voice. Treasures. A chest of gold coins and this tempestuous half-breed now both belonged to the Hawk of the Antilles. "I have been waiting for you . . ."

Chapter Eleven

The Congreve rocket made a horrid swoosh as it spiraled toward the American breastworks. The weapon was an eight-foot stick, as thick as a man's wrist and capped with a pointed iron head encasing enough black powder to blow a man to doll rags and shower his companions with shrapnel in the process.

"Never you mind em', lads. They're nought but English toys," Kit McQueen shouted above the din of cannon fire. The Kentuckians cowering nearby did not appear convinced. From behind breastworks of timber and cotton bales and mounded earth, these "rabbit hunters," as the British called their adversaries, watched the sputtering weapon arc out of the mist. It was but one of many the British had hurled against General Jackson's makeshift army of volunteers.

Further along the line, the Choctaw fared no better than the wary Kentuckians. To their eyes the rockets were demons unleashed by the British to kill the Americans and their allies. Fortunately men like Strikes With Club and Nate Russell were too proud to run and set an example for many of the others.

Suddenly the iron tip on this latest projectile nosed down. The rocket fell short, about a hundred feet from the breastworks. The menacing weapon continued to sputter and shoot flame as it writhed like a maddened serpent across the grassland toward the unnerved Kentuckians. There was simply no way to predict the rocket's point of impact or when the fuse within the device would burn its course and explode the powder charge. All along the breastworks the defenders watched with morbid fascination as the rocket bounced and zigzagged over the terrain. Then the weapon hit a clump of dirt and became airborne again, spiraling straight on course about six feet above the meadow.

Kit joined the others as they ducked down. The rocket struck about thirteen feet from his position, near a redoubt where one of the six-pounders valiantly returned fire. The explosion shook the ground, and one of the men by the cannon arched and rose up on his toes, then dropped to his knees. He continued to clutch at his lower back as his companions dragged him from the redoubt and hurried back to load the cannon.

Kit estimated they'd endured about forty minutes of bombardment. To the credit of Jean Laffite and his Baratarians, the artillerymen were according themselves with honor. Each redoubt was manned by cannoneers who had seen plenty of action on the high seas. One by one the American cannons aimed and fired by these former corsairs silenced the British rocket launchers.

Kit heard his name called, and he glanced around to see O'Keefe crawling toward him. The big man was dressed for battle. His chest was crisscrossed with two broad leather belts sporting three flintlock pistols to a belt. Another pair of pistols were tucked in his waistband along with a tomahawk. He did not intend to reload once battle was joined.

Kit wore the garb he usually favored, his military coat, a loose-fitting shirt of homespun cotton, and buckskin breeches. His Quakers, a Pennsylvania rifle, and an Arkansas "toothpick" with a double-edged twelve-inch steel blade were his weapons of choice.

"What is it?" Kit said.

"Yellow Leaper just come at a run from the woods. He said the British have sent their Haitians into the bayou to flank us."

"Damn!" Kit muttered beneath his breath. Such an assault was the last thing they needed. The American fortifications stretched from the river to the woods where the ground turned soft and became treacherous with pools of water and quicksand. The approach to the city was successfully blocked as long as the American troops held the breastworks and redoubts. However, if the Haitian troops managed to flank McQueen's command, then General Jackson's entire line of defense could be jeopardized. The men at the breastworks were already outnumbered and could never repulse a frontal assault and a flank attack simultaneously.

"Give Nate Russell fifty men and he'll stop them." O'Keefe knew his adopted people and what they were capable of doing.

"Have him take every third man," Kit suggested. "That will give him about sixty braves."

"More'n enough." O'Keefe grinned. "I ain't seen the day that a Choctaw warrior wasn't worth three of them West Indians in a tussle."

O'Keefe turned and crawled on hands and knees back to his position. The breastworks were built high enough that the big man could have stood and simply run at a crouch, but the rockets streaking overhead made a man want to hug mother earth. Kit returned his attention to the battlefield and the curtains of mist and powder smoke behind which the British were no doubt advancing, marshaling their forces, and preparing to attack. He had heard rumors that the Black Watch might lead the way. Kit McQueen came from Highland stock, and he could not fail to note the irony that today he might well be responsible for the death of a blood relative, perhaps a distant cousin. Who could tell? He forced the speculation from his mind.

Suddenly the English cannons fell silent. And the American gunners quickly followed suit, reading a dread purpose in the British actions. Even the rockets ceased to fall. A silence settled on the smoldering landscape that seemed more horrible than the thunderous exchange that preceded it.

"Never heard anything so loud," a Kentuckian named Kemp Howard said, peering over the breastworks. He was a good-natured, even-tempered soul with a ready smile and a helping hand for any man. Kit had become acquainted with the trapper only this morning, but he had taken an instant liking to the man. Howard leaned on his long-barreled rifle and fished a pouch of tobacco from his possibles bag and tucked a plug in his cheek. "Reckon they quit and went on back to their boats." He scratched at his week-old growth of chin whiskers.

"Don't count on it," Kit replied. He liked these Kentuckians. They were men with the bark on. Lord Packenham was a fool to hold this rough lot in contempt. The English general had made it plain that he considered the American forces arrayed against him nothing but pirates, savages, "dirty shirts," and drunkards. The British were about to discover the truth. Maybe there wasn't a pretty uniform to be seen behind the American lines, but Kit McQueen would not have traded this command for any other in the world.

These volunteers had come to fight for their country. They were determined to drive the British army from America's shores. Its diversity was its strength, men from every walk of life, physicians, farmers, barristers and frontiersmen, keelboat men and umbrella makers, soldiers and Indians and pirates standing shoulder to shoulder against a common foe. What would history say of these events? What tales would the children hear of those who sacrificed today? A hundred years from now, would the country still remember?

Kit reached inside his shirt and cupped the makeshift medal in his hand. George Washington's initials gleamed as if with a life of their own. Kit's father, Dan McQueen, had worn the coin throughout the long dark days of the Revolution when the fate of the thirteen colonies hung in the balance and a valiant colonial army had triumphed over the might of the English military.

"Here we are again, Father," Kit said beneath his breath. He tucked the keepsake inside his shirt and began to walk the length of the breastworks under his command. Jackson had suffered a shortage of senior officers and entrusted the lieutenant with holding the left flank. McQueen cast no shadow on this cold gray January morning. And his footsteps made no sound as he trod the moist earth. Kentuckians and men of the Louisiana Battalion glanced at him as he walked past. Kit had become a familiar figure. He came by his authority honestly; it rested in his bearing. These volunteers were not the type of men to give allegiance to a uniform. But they would follow a man they respected to hell and back.

"Reckon today's the day, Lieutenant," a man called out.

Another of the defenders, a Cajun, raised a jug of corn "likker" and took a swallow, then offered the jug to Kit as he approached. "Here you be, Loo-tenant. This'll put some fire in your belly I gar-antee." Jean Baptiste Benard was a grizzled-looking sort with thick features and a bulbous red nose and a track of liver spots that ran the length of his hands and arms.

This lean hard man who looked as if he could have used a month of meals kept a rifle at his side that showed loving care. Its walnut stock had been recently polished, the frizzen and hammer oiled and the old flint replaced. He carried a cutlass at his waist and wore the blousy shirt, patched cotton pants, and stocking hat of a veteran seaman. The only man Benard owed allegiance to was Jean Laffite.

"I'll drink with you and be proud of it." Kit grinned, and took the jug. "Just so long as I'll be able to see the redcoats after I've tasted your brew."

"Never fear," Benard replied in his melodious voice. "You'll be seeing them plenty good." A wail of bagpipes drifted out of the mist. He glanced up as the faint strains of a bagpipe carried to them from the mist. The Louisianans around ceased their good-natured banter and became deadly serious. Underscoring the bagpipes, men could hear the footfall of an army on the move. "And seeing them plenty soon, I think," the Cajun added, returning his attention to the trampled grassland and muddy ground stretching between the British and American redoubts.

Kit took a swallow and gasped as the Cajun's home brew went coursing through his body. It spread warmth to his limbs and left him sucking in great draughts of wintry air to cool the blaze in his gullet.

"What do you think?" said Benard.

"If the redcoats breach the wall, you just heave that jug at them and duck," Kit managed to reply in a hoarse voice. The men around Benard began to laugh at his expense. Benard chuckled good-naturedly. But his eyes never left the battlefield.

The bagpipes were a good choice, sounding unearthly behind the rolling mist. Kit started back to his position. He noticed the men at the six-pounder were preparing to reload.

"We'll let them cut their teeth on grapeshot now, Lieutenant," said one of the cannoneers. The gunners

had been handpicked by Laffite, and Kit had every
faith they would stand their ground till doomsday.
He waved to the cannoneers and paused to observe
the skill with which they prepared to receive the
enemy. It slowly dawned on Kit that he had not seen
Cesar Obregon or any of his crew the entire morning.
McQueen had misgivings about the buccaneer's ab-
sence. Lord only knew what mischief and treacheries
that Castilian rogue was capable of. Surely the Hawk
of the Antilles had alighted somewhere along the
defenses. Kit tried and failed to convince himself he
was misjudging Obregon.

"By heaven, I see them," Kemp Howard shouted.
Kit hurried back to his place behind the breastworks.
O'Keefe and his Choctaws were to the left of the
lieutenant; the Kentuckians and part of the Louisiana
Battalion waited to the right.

"Nice of Packenham to invite so many to the
dance," O'Keefe called out, resting the barrel of his
rifle in his hook while his right hand slowly thumbed
the hammer back.

The only sound from the American lines came
from rifles being primed and cocked and the rasp of
knives being honed on whetstones one last time. Kit
did not know how many of the British were advancing on the defenses where General Jackson sat astride
his charger and called out encouragement to his men.
But Kit was certain there would be enough of the
British for every man to have his fill of fighting. It
wasn't hard for the volunteers to accept that the hour
of battle was at hand. Indeed, many of the soldiers at
the breastworks greeted the unfolding events with a
measure of relief.

Kit watched the British line of attack materialize
out of the mist. The British soldiers were immacu-
lately garbed in dark red coats and black kilts and
black tufted caps upon their heads. They marched
several hundred abreast with the dull metal of their

bayonets forming a wall of steel in the damp air and the muffled *tramp tramp tramp* of their footsteps beating an ominous rhythm beneath the blaring bagpipes. The British regiments lowered their rifles at a shouted command from one of their officers on horseback. Onward they came, at a quick clipped pace, marching as if on parade to the tune of the bagpipes. This was the cream of Packenham's army: the 21st Fusileers, the 95th Rifles, and the 4th King's Own Regiment. These were men who had never tasted defeat and weren't about to start today.

But Kit McQueen and the defenders of New Orleans had other ideas. Kit sighted on one of the soldiers in the distance. A cool detachment settled round his heart. There was bloody work to be done this morning. Kit hadn't asked for the job. But like his blacksmith father, he was prepared to stand and fight because his country needed him. The British had come to reclaim their lost empire. That attempt was going to end here and now.

Kit did not exhort his men or attempt to stir their spirits. They knew what needed to be done. The enemy was visible now, row upon row of them, marching implacably forward, an oncoming, seemingly irresistible force determined to drive these ragtag volunteers to the grave or back into their precious wilderness.

A dance, O'Keefe had said. Well, thought Kit, it's time someone started the music. He squeezed the trigger. A flash in the pan as the priming charge ignited; a second later the rifle spat flame and recoiled against his shoulder, and a hundred yards away, the first Englishman to die that day clutched his chest, flung his musket from his outstretched hands, and dropped face-forward onto the sacred soil.

A swell of gunfire swept the breastworks and a bugle blared above the crash of guns. Iron Hand

O'Keefe was offering his own brand of defiance in the face of those unnerving bagpipes. Like Roland in days of old, O'Keefe rose up and blew the bugle and the Choctaw responded by unleashing a volley from their recently acquired muskets. To McQueen's right, the six-pounder roared and grapeshot reaped a harvest of death among the British ranks. The redcoats opened fire; as one line reloaded, another marched forward a few paces and fired. Then a third line stepped to the fore and loosed a volley, followed by the first rank again. One rank after another, alternating, they worked their way closer and closer to the breastworks. Soon they'd be ordered to charge. Kit knew the British mustn't be allowed to storm the fortifications and get within bayonet's length of the defenders. No matter how adept at close-in fighting these backwoods volunteers, once the battle became hand-to-hand, the superior numbers of the British would carry the day.

Musket balls slapped into the cotton-barricaded redoubts and thudded into the mounded dirt and timbers protecting the riflemen. The British had no cover. They were crossing open ground in the face of a murderous gunfire delivered by the volunteers, most of whom had cut their teeth on rifle barrels. On the frontier, men became adept with their firearms or went hungry or fell prey to their enemies. Kit had to admire the courage of these British regulars. An unending chorus of gunfire from the American lines took a murderous toll among the redcoats.

Did they think the "rabbit hunters" and "dirty shirts" would run at the first glitter of a bayonet or the first glimpse of veteran British regiments attacking in force? If so, then Packenham had made a terrible miscalculation. He wouldn't be the first English officer to underestimate his foe.

Kit swabbed the barrel of his rifle. He tore open a paper cartridge with his teeth and emptied the measured charge of black powder down the barrel. Then with the ramrod he loaded the cartridge wadding and lead shot after the gunpowder and tamped it firm. He trickled a trace of black powder onto the pan, to prime the weapon. The entire process had taken less than a minute.

Kit rose up with Kemp Howard and a dozen others as an opposing line of British fusileers opened fire. Kit ducked below a cotton bale and heard the bullets thud into the breastworks. Kemp Howard, with a foolish belief in his own invulnerability, remained standing and tried to squeeze off a shot. A British musket ball slapped him in the chest. Howard groaned and slowly spun until he had his back to the breastworks, then slid slowly to a sitting position with his legs splayed out. He reached for and caught McQueen by the leg. Kit knelt by the Kentuckian and noticed the dark stain already spreading across the front of the trapper's buckskin shirt.

"Looks like I've gone and got myself killed," Howard said with a voice filled with disgust for his own carelessness. He took Kit's hand and placed it on the long rifle the Kentuckian had carried with him since boyhood. "Old Sting's loaded. I'd appreciate you not waste the shot. Fire her one last time for me."

Kit nodded, and setting his own rifle aside, he raised up and snapped off a shot at the British ranks, about seventy yards from the breastworks. Kit immediately crouched down and set the rifle across the trapper's legs.

"Obliged," said the trapper.

"She shoots true," Kit said, and patted the man on the shoulder. "I can carry you back to the physician's tent."

Kemp Howard shook his head no. He coughed and a trickle of crimson phlegm formed at the corner of his mouth. "You do your job," he said, "and I'll do mine."

Kit took up his own rifle and peered over the cotton bales. The six-pounder roared again, to be echoed by the heavier field pieces along the fortifications. The bagpipes continued to play, but not as loudly as before. The marksmanship of the volunteers had taken a deadly toll. The ground was littered with the dead and dying. For every five yards the British regiments advanced, they left a carpet of corpses in their wake.

"Our Father . . . who art in heaven . . ." Howard's voice drifted up from below. Kit shouldered his rifle and brought the gun to bear on a soldier in the process of advancing forward to fire. Here was a brawny, black-haired fusileer who refused to break ranks and flee. Although his comrades were dropping all around him, this fusileer seemed impervious to harm. He reached his position and knelt to fire. His bullet ricocheted off a chunk of timber a yard from Kit. The fusileer fell face-forward as the six-pounder roared and sent a load of grapeshot plowing into the soldiers forming behind him. Then the clever fusileer sat up and started to feverishly reload.

Kit shifted his aim as an officer on a white charger trotted past his field of vision. The officer was exhorting the battered ranks who had just received the grapeshot to press on. Press on. The officer waved his saber and stabbed the curved blade toward the American lines. The British officer was a hatless, handsome-looking individual who sat erect in the saddle, disdainful of the bullets that fanned the air around him.

Kit exhaled and squeezed the trigger. The rifle's report was lost in the din, but Kit felt the characteristic shove against his shoulder. An acrid cloud of black smoke spewed from the muzzle. The officer clapped a hand to his throat and toppled from horseback into the arms of one of the bagpipers. A trio of soldiers instantly bore the officer from the battlefield.

"Thy will be done on earth . . ." poor Howard prayed with his back to the fray.

Kit reloaded and fired again. Reloaded and fired. A shot went wild. Another had no effect. A third sent a soldier crumbling to his knees and left him crying out to his companions for help. And still the regiments pressed their attack. One by one the bagpipes ceased their keening cry and the men of valor became fewer, and the bravado in the eyes of the living gave way first to fear and then to numbness as the slaughter continued.

". . . on earth as it is . . . in . . . heaven."

Kit himself was dazed. His senses reeled from the stench and the din of battle and the terrible carnage as Packenham's army disintegrated on that butcher's field, that meadow of madness, the last battle of a pointless war. Kit tossed his rifle aside and tugged the Quakers from his belt and vaulted the mounded earth and cotton bales to meet the British bayonets with guns blazing. But the attack had broken and he faced but a single man, the same fusileer Kit had spared by shifting his aim to the British officer. Fate had presented him with a second chance at the fusileer.

The two enemies faced one another. The black-haired soldier held his bayonet at the ready. One good thrust and Kit would be spitted like a chunk of meat. But the lust for blood rapidly cooled in the fusileer as he looked up into the matched set of fifty-caliber pistols Kit held. The soldier realized he was a dead man depending on the whim of the red-headed lieutenant.

The gunfire trailed off as the "dirty shirts" and "rabbit hunters" allowed the straggling survivors to retreat across the fields of Chalmette, across the mangled bodies of their friends and comrades. The mist reclaimed the living. The dead remained.

"Give us this . . . this . . . day." Kemp Howard

lowered his head and died, never knowing how prophetic were his final words.

To the astonishment of the fusileer, Kit lowered his pistols, his expression hardened. "Go home," he said with grave finality. Kit turned his back on the British soldier and didn't bother to watch him start back toward the river.

Twenty-five minutes had passed since the bagpipes had sounded the attack. In twenty-five minutes, Packenham's invincible army had been mauled and its commander killed, although word of Packenham's death had yet to reach the American lines.

Kit busied himself with organizing transportation for the wounded. Casualties among the volunteers were amazingly light. Kemp Howard and a Louisianan by the name of Pelliere were the only two deaths. However, Kit had three Kentuckians with shoulder wounds and a Choctaw who needed a musket ball dug out of his thigh. Despite McQueen's efforts to prepare the volunteers to repulse a second assault, the backwoodsmen from Kentucky and Tennessee broke out their jugs of whiskey and their fiddles and began to celebrate the victory they had won this day. The lieutenant's cautious admonitions fell on deaf ears.

Lieutenant Kit McQueen with O'Keefe at his side was in the process of issuing orders for the wounded when no less a personage than Captain Jean Laffite bulled his way through the milling volunteers. The privateer's usually-fastidious attire reeked of powder smoke, and his right coat sleeve was torn about three inches below the shoulder where a British musket ball had ripped the fabric but missed the flesh beneath. "Laffite's Luck" was a distinct part of the man's mystique.

The buccaneer was followed by half a dozen of his trusted crew, Jean Baptiste Benard was among them. The Cajun cradled his precious jug of "home brew" in the crook of his left arm and a long-barreled flintlock pistol of Spanish make in the other. He looked as serious as his companions, which struck Kit as odd. He figured Benard would have drained the contents of his jug by now and started another.

Something in Laffite's eyes made the hackles rise on the back of Kit's neck. He was best with premonitions of disaster. Kit steeled himself and waited for the legendary sea rover to approach. Laffite nodded a greeting.

"We have won a great victory today, Captain Laffite. And much of the credit is due to the marksmanship of your Baratarians," Kit said.

"Not *all* my Baratarians," Laffite replied. He stood aside and waved a man forward. Kit was surprised to see an unkempt, rough-looking little man who appeared to be the spitting image of Jean Baptiste Benard maneuver his way forward.

"Avast, ye blackards. Let a man through." The ruffian glared at Jean as if the two had a history of animosity. They looked evenly matched in size. Kit would have been loath to guess the outcome if the two men began to flail away at one another.

"This wiry slab of fishbait is Francis Luc Benard," said Laffite.

"Twin brothers?" Kit said.

"Ain't my fault. An accident of birth." Jean scowled. "I make no claim to his bloodline of thieves and card cheats."

"Enough, you two. Now is not the time. You save your venom for Obregon and the crew of the *Windthrift* when we catch up to them," said Laffite. His eyebrows raised as he realized he had made a slip of the tongue. Too late he caught himself and cursed beneath his breath.

"What about Obregon?" Kit asked, unable to conceal his apprehension.

"Cap'n Laffite told me to keep an eye on the

Hawk. He's a wily one, he is. Set a trap for me and left me tied and gagged, he did. But the ropes ain't made that can hold Francis Benard. I cut free and came a-running as soon as I could borrow me a horse."

Kit turned his fierce stare toward Laffite. "What is he trying to tell me?"

"Perhaps you had better come with me," the notorious privateer stonily suggested.

"Where?"

"To the widow LeBeouf's," said Laffite.

Chapter Twelve

Kit stood in the mist-shrouded courtyard, and spying a cluster of figures by the front steps, he shouted the name of the woman he loved and received no answer save the mournful cry of a mourning dove nesting in the oak tree off to the side of the house. Less than a week ago, he had climbed that tree to Raven's bedroom and taken her in his arms . . .

What had happened here? The smell of gunsmoke clung to the still air. The once-festive house that Olivia LeBeouf kept gaily lit seemed gray and draped with sorrow. He did not run, but walked like a man in a dream to the front steps where a trio of Laffite's men had gathered around the furious widow and Harry Tregoning.

The British marine sat on the steps and cradled his bandaged head. Blood had seeped through the rags, but Olivia LeBeouf was tearing a cotton nightshirt into strips to replace the dressing. She was personally tending to the weary marine. Tregoning glanced up as Kit arrived. The widow cried out and stood to take him in her arms and press him to her ample bosom like a mother consoling her young.

"My poor boy. It is all so terrible—I tried to stop them, but what can one woman do?"

"Dear God, Olivia. What has happened?" Kit could scarcely ask the question. His surprise at finding Tregoning at the house was overshadowed by the dread he felt that Raven had somehow come to harm. "Tell me Raven is all right. For the love of heaven, tell me she is well."

"Only heaven knows," said the marine.

"Where is my daughter!" O'Keefe bellowed as he brushed aside Laffite's men near the gate and swooped down on the gathering at the steps with his overcoat flapping like the wings of a bird of prey. Laffite had to run to keep up with the Irishman. They reached the widow's house shortly after Kit.

"It was Cesar Obregon," the widow bitterly told them. "He and his crew. They came for the gold . . . and for Raven."

Kit gasped and started up the steps to the house.

"You won't find her, mate," Tregoning said. "Miss Raven brought me to the widow's, to find a change of clothing and maybe a horse and to help me on my way. The pirates were waiting. It shames me to admit I thought I'd been set up and your General Jackson was fixing to stretch my neck after all." He winced as the widow began to tenderly unwrap his skull. Her attitude and the manner in which she was caring for the marine wasn't lost on O'Keefe. But the Irishman was preoccupied with concern for his daughter's wellbeing and had no time for jealousy. "I lit into them," Tregoning continued. "That's when I saw they were cutthroats, not soldiers. I tried to give a good account of myself, but one of the devils laid me low with the hilt of his cutlass. I dropped and lay as if I were dead. Maybe I passed out. I don't know, it wasn't for long. Then I came to, but I never made a move. My cheek was stuck to the flagstones. I heard the lot of them mention their captain, Cesar Obregon, by name. And how they envied him the half-breed girl he was taking to sea."

"No!" O'Keefe roared. "The bastard . . . !"

"They took Johnny, too," the widow managed to say, her voice trembling as she spoke. "He wouldn't let them take Raven without him to aid her." She grabbed for a silk handkerchief she kept tucked in her bodice and began to weep anew. The widow clambered to her feet and rushed inside the house to shed her tears.

"What she means is, the boy insisted he come with Raven and the buccaneers decided to allow him, just to quiet the little bloke. I never seen a young one carry on so. He was all but daring those brigands to take a swipe at him with their cutlasses. Mad as hornets, them pirates. They would have run him through if Obregon hadn't sent them on with the wagons."

"The lad has a way about him," O'Keefe said, nodding. "I wanted to tan his hide on more than one occasion. Insisted on being with Raven, eh? God bless the sharp-tongued little river rat."

"Obregon left us to fight while he circled back here and kidnapped Raven and the boy," Kit softly said.

"And took my gold . . . er . . . uh . . . Jackson's gold, I mean," said Laffite. "The guards never knew what hit them. They were set upon and knocked unconscious and bound and gagged and left blindfolded in the stalls." He looked disgusted with himself and ran a hand through his unnaturally red hair and added with a sigh. "Cesar always was an impulsive son of a bitch."

"He'll be a dead son of a bitch when next we meet," said Kit McQueen. His voice was barely audible, but there was murder behind every word. "Where is he?" He focused his attention on Laffite, who wasn't in the habit of informing on the whereabouts of any of the pirate brotherhood. But in this case he resolved to make an exception.

"The *Windthrift* is hidden in a cove a couple of miles below Chalmette. Cesar is probably aboard and weighed anchor by now."

"Will he risk the British blockade at the mouth of the Mississippi?" asked O'Keefe.

"On a misty morning like this . . . no problem. Indeed, we Baratarians prefer such weather." Laffite waved a hand toward the gray fog that a gentle north breeze had begun to stir. The tendrils began to thin, revealing the courtyard in greater definition. "We call this a smuggler's dawn. No, the British will never know Obregon has passed."

"Where will he go?"

"The men of the brotherhood are by nature a closemouthed lot," said Jean Baptiste Benard. His twin brother, Francis, concurred, nodding his head as he filled a pipe with tobacco.

"Now, if you were one of us . . ." said Francis. "*Mon Dieu,* that would be different."

"But he is one of us," Laffite interjected. His crewmen stared at him in surprise. "We have fought side by side with the lieutenant. We have stood against a common foe while Obregon, our brother, betrayed us. What more must a man do to prove himself?"

"Then you'll tell me where the Hawk of the Antilles has gone to nest?" asked Kit McQueen.

"Better than that, *mon ami,*" said Laffite. "I'll take you there myself. The gaffe-rigged schooner at the dock is my own swift *Scourge.* It will take two or three days to bring a few of my cannons back aboard and load provisions for my crew. Now, what do you think your General Jackson will say when you tell him our plan, eh?"

"Leave it to me," Kit McQueen confidently replied. "I can handle Old Hickory."

Chapter Thirteen

"No!" General Jackson paced in front of the contingent of militia he had brought with him to block Conti Street and deny Kit McQueen's access to the wharf and the three-masted schooner docked at the end of the pier. Two dozen Tennesseans held their rifles at the ready while the few dockworkers and Negro slaves hurried out of harm's way, their unfinished tasks not worth dying for. Jackson's militia shifted nervously. Here was a nasty bit of business. Now that the British had pulled out, it looked as if Old Hickory was planning to set them against one another. If such was the case, none of the volunteers was anxious to confront the brawny adventurer who had fought at their side since Horse Shoe Bend. Reticence was plainly visible on the faces of the volunteers.

"I said No three days ago and I haven't changed my position," Jackson reiterated. His long, lean frame was wrapped in a charcoal gray cape. He wore his silvery white hair in wild disarray. These past days of peace and victory had done nothing to repair his temper or his health. Nor had he a moment to spare to spend worrying about his appearance.

Kit McQueen had confronted Jackson the very day of Raven's kidnapping, and although the general was appalled at Obregon's treachery, he refused to permit McQueen to pursue the pirate despite the circumstances and the identity of the woman Obregon had abducted. From that moment on, Kit had resolved to bring Obregon to justice whatever the cost to himself despite the general's orders to the contrary.

It was early morning, the eleventh of January, a cold clear dawn. Laffite, true to his word, had brought eight 12-pounders and four 24-pounders aboard the schooner. An eighty-two man crew had loaded the hold with enough food and water to last, with fair winds and weather, all the way to Natividad. Laffite had personally overseen the rigging and replacement of the mainsail. The ship's name, *Malice,* had been painted on the bow. And as its captain was under command of none but his own whims, Jackson was powerless to halt the privateer's preparations.

Kit sucked in a lungful of the brisk northwest breeze and hooked his thumbs in the broad belt circling his waist. A chill breeze ruffled his red hair. He breathed deeply yet again to help him shake off the lethargy of the restless night he had spent at the widow LeBeouf's. Ignoring the protestations of his friends, Kit had refused to sneak aboard the *Malice* under cover of night. Pride would not permit him any course but the one he now chose. So he had discarded his uniform for a simple broadcloth coat, loose-fitting shirt, a heavier cotton waistcoat whose brocaded fabric had been colored by a dye rendered from crushed pecan shells, and brown breeches tucked into jack boots. He carried his Quakers, knife, and rifle and arrived at the waterfront with only the authority of his noble purpose, his sense of mission to carry him onward in defiance of General Jackson's orders.

Laffite watched with mixed emotions the confrontation at the entrance to Conti Street. Old Hickory was a stubborn man with nary an ounce of give in him. However, Kit McQueen was not the kind to back down. It was a volatile situation at best. As for the crew of the *Malice,* Laffite's men were anxious to be off. Word had just arrived from England that the Treaty of Ghent had been signed. British ships no longer blockaded the Mississippi. The war was over. There would never be a better opportunity to reach the Gulf. Jean Laffite was no less impatient, because Obregon, that hotspur, had shamed the Baratarians by abandoning the fight, not to mention stealing Jackson's strongbox, a rash and boisterous act that Laffite had personally forbidden. The buccaneer had hoped to adopt the ways of an honest merchant and abandon his earlier calling as a pirate and smuggler. Alas, Cesar Obregon had placed a cloud of doubt over the entire arrangement. Now Laffite would have to take to sea again and prove his forthright intentions.

Natividad. That was the first place to look. Laffite was certain the Hawk was returning to his "nest." They'd reach the island in six or seven weeks with fair wind and good fortune. However, they might not reach it at all if Jackson and McQueen didn't resolve their differences.

"What say you, Cap'n?" said Jean Baptiste. "The lieutenant ain't going anywhere, you mark my words. Old Hickory's mad as a nest of hornets in a thunderstorm."

"I'll take that wager, Jean Baptiste." Laffite held out his hand for Jean Baptiste to shake and seal the bargain. The cajun chuckled and accepted the arrangement, but it was Laffite who appeared the most satisfied.

Kit McQueen had not come alone to the riverfront. Iron Hand O'Keefe stood at his side, and behind him were Nate Russell and Strikes With Club, both of

whom had insisted on accompanying O'Keefe on the
quest to rescue his daughter.

"I ain't got to obey a word of your orders, General,"
O'Keefe called out.

"And I shall make no attempt to stop you. Pass
on through," Jackson told the war chief of the Choctaw.
O'Keefe had expected more of an argument and
hesitated.

"Go on. I'll be along," Kit told his friend. If
trouble came, he did not want the big Irishman in the
line of fire. O'Keefe hesitated. "Dammit, man. She's
your daughter. Now get on that boat!"

O'Keefe shrugged, and nodded in agreement.
McQueen made sense. He motioned for the two
braves to follow him and ambled through the ranks of
the Tennesseans. With Kit alone, Jackson walked
over to the red-haired lieutenant. He had hoped it
wouldn't come to this. Andrew Jackson was a
man who liked to keep his plots to himself, a talent
that would one day serve him well as President.

"Curse it, mister. You've called my hand in this.
And left me no choice," Jackson said, keeping his
voice low. Lack of sleep and the pressure of the
command had taken its toll. However, once Laffite
and his troublemakers were out of the city, he'd
be able to relax.

"Do you mean to shoot me, General? Because
that's what you'll have to do," said Kit. He was not
turning back. And if that meant facing the guns of the
militia, then so be it.

"Hell, no. I'm trying to save your life." Jackson
pursed his lips and shook his head, trying to figure
out some way of avoiding the issue, but there seemed
nothing for it but to confide in McQueen.

"Now see here, Lieutenant . . . uh . . . Kit."
Jackson's sudden familiarity aroused caution in his
subordinate officer. "You and I both know why
Laffite's offered his assistance. He intends to recover

the gold for himself. Even if you manage to best Obregon and recover what's been lost, you'll still have Laffite to contend with. And he is apt to be in an ugly mood . . . when he discovers my . . . uh . . . little ruse."

"Sir?"

"There is no gold. Merely a chest filled with lead ingots painted to look like real treasure."

Kit paled. "I don't understand . . . the guards . . . your attempts to keep it hidden."

"I knew the Baratarians would hear of it. I suspected their loyalty and decided to give them an extra reason to fight. The promise of a reward in gold. After the battle, I planned to arrange a theft so that none of the freebooters would be the wiser."

"But Cesar Obregon beat you to it." Kit shook his head in disapproval. Jackson owed much of his victory to men like Laffite. They certainly had deserved more than his distrust. In fact, the general's trickery had been the catalyst tempting the Hawk of the Antilles to his misdeeds.

"The Castilian has no doubt discovered the truth by now. Should he in turn explain my fabrication to Laffite, then you would undoubtedly bear the brunt of his vengeance."

"I'll take that chance."

Jackson raised his hands in disgust. "Haven't you heard a word I've said? Laffite will turn on you like a rabid animal when he learns we used him."

"I will find Raven and bring her safely home." Kit remained implacable. "Three days ago I fought for you—and for my country. But this is for me. This is personal." He saluted and headed for the line of militia blocking the pier.

Jackson tried to think of some other argument, but his weary mind would not respond. He knew without a doubt that if his men attempted to place McQueen under arrest, it would lead to bloodshed.

So he lifted a hand, and at his signal the militia parted and Kit McQueen continued onto the pier and, with no small relief on his part, trotted safely up the gangplank of the *Malice*.

"Who's that?" Laffite asked, his gaze fixed on a priest in black robes and a broad-brimmed hat who was hurrying down Conti Street. "Cast off," the buccaneer ordered. "I have no pulpit aboard this ship."

The priest lowered his head and quickened his pace as he drew abreast of the general. Jackson glanced at the priest in time to receive a brief blessing from the oddly familiar individual. Jackson was certain he knew the Bible-thumper, but the priest's features were heavily shaded by the hat he wore. He was obviously a thick-set man, and he grunted with every hurried step as if his feet hurt. Jackson assumed the man had spent far too much time in prayer and not enough at hard honest work. New Orleans, with its French Catholics, had no shortage of black robes. Jackson waved a farewell greeting to the priest.

"So you're sailing with them, Father."

"Right you are, mate," said the priest, and quickened his pace. Up ahead the *Malice* was just getting under way. The priest would have to hurry or be left behind. Just as he reached the Tennesseans, Jackson recognized the priest's English accent and shouted, "Hey! Just you wait, sir!"

"Not on your bloody life," one of the riflemen heard the priest mutter as he lifted his robes and broke into a run. The militia, alerted by Jackson's outburst, attempted to give chase. A couple of them fired into the air, but the priest never looked back.

The gangplank had already been drawn in, but the priest showed uncommon ability born no doubt of desperation. He reached the edge of the pier and leapt for the side of the schooner and caught hold of a loop of loose rigging inadvertently draped over the side of the ship.

Strong arms reached out to haul the man up over the side lest he be crushed between the ship and the pier. He landed on deck somewhat shaken and gasping for breath but none the worse for wear. Harry Tregoning pulled off his robes and knuckled a salute to Laffite, then to Kit McQueen, who stared at the marine in amazement.

"Mind if I join you, Mr. McQueen? There's nothing to hold me in New Orleans."

"What about the widow LeBeouf?" O'Keefe said with a snarl. Jealousy had colored his opinion of the Cornishman.

"I leave that fair flower for you to pluck, old boy," Tregoning said. "A lifetime of the same face at breakfast is not for Harry Tregoning." He glanced at Kit. "I owe those brigands of Captain Obregon a knock or two." He pointed to the scabbed-over lump on his forehead. Then his expression lightened and settled in an earnest smile. "And I owe you, Kit McQueen. And the men of Cornwall always pay their debts. So I'll fight at your side, mate, till your lady's rescued, and here's my hand to seal the pact."

It was a fool who turned a blind eye to the workings of fate. The two former enemies were together again. Kit reached out and clasped the hand of the man who had once tried to kill him. So be it. The British marine's very presence closed the chapter on the two-year-long struggle that had engulfed both their countries and set in motion events that would irrevocably change the family McQueen.

"Welcome aboard, Mr. Tregoning," said Kit. Thoughts of Raven filled his mind and heart. He must find her. One war had ended. But on a mist-shrouded street in New Orleans, in a bleak gray courtyard, Cesar Obregon's treachery had begun another.

Kit walked to starboard and leaned his elbows on the wooden siding and watched the city recede as the ship tacked into the middle of the river. O'Keefe joined his friend's vigil and watched the shore sweep past.

"I hope you know what you're about," said O'Keefe. "Do you have a plan?"

"Sure," said Kit. "Find Obregon. Kill him. And bring Raven home."

"Simple," O'Keefe dryly commented.

"That's why I like it," Kit replied.

But Iron Hand O'Keefe was sorry he'd asked.

Chapter Fourteen

    Orturo Navarre, clad only in a loincloth, danced on the crest of the limestone bluff overlooking the governor's palace. A shower had just passed across the island, filling the shallow dimples in the patches of bare rock and leaving the short-leafed grasses slick and glistening. Even the sunlight felt fresh-scrubbed upon the pirate's muscled brown torso. Droplets of sweat beaded Navarre's shaved skull and he whirled and slashed the sun-dappled shrubbery with his cutlass. Yellow warblers and green-winged hummingbirds had abandoned the clearing on his arrival only to watch the Cayman's ritualistic gyrations from the safety of the treetops.

    Navarre leaped high and landed lightly on the balls of his feet; he spun in the air and tramped the shallow soil, his actions sudden and spontaneous, as if hearing in his mind the tribal drums of his mother's people, the fierce Caribs. He danced and became one with the sunlight and shadows surging through this Caribbean isle, one with the warmth and the stillness, one with the green force that was the life's blood of every tree and fern and flower from the crest of the

Cordillera, Natividad's mountainous spine, to the palm-shaded shoreline. The blue-green sea capped by opalescent froth lapped at the bay's sandy beaches and, further out from Morgan Town, attacked the limestone rim of the island, gradually eroding and reshaping what a volcanic upheaval had deposited centuries ago.

Navarre was surrounded by a changing world. He saw himself as an important part of that world, as elemental as a hurricane, a violent force of nature striking out to claim what he wished and leaving in his wake a time and place and people forever changed. It was a role he relished, a role he was convinced would bring him riches. He was destiny's child, and for him there simply was no other course. It seemed a lifetime ago, and yet scarcely more than a decade had passed since he had become master of his own ship and discovered his power to engender fear and command loyalty among men. He had honed those skills and risen among the brotherhood of freebooters until Orturo Navarre, the Cayman, had a reputation second to no one's.

But for all his civilized trappings, for all his pretended civility and the finery he wore, there were times when the savage in him burst forth, and he would depart from the affairs of men and in solitude enact the sacred rituals taught him by the shamans of his mother's tribe. His bare feet tramped a frantic rhythm on the hard-packed earth as the drumming in his brain reached a feverish pitch.

A twig cracked. A pebble kicked loose, rattled down the hillside. Neither sound had been particularly intrusive, but Navarre heard. He always . . . heard. In an instant he grabbed his bone-handled pistols and melted into the underbrush, abandoning the clearing on the bluff to the westerly breeze and the unseen intruders.

* * *

NKenai removed the blue fez he wore and dabbed his ebony features with a white silk cloth he had stolen off the altar in Father Bernal's church. The climb up from the hacienda had winded him. Ignoring his muscular physique, the Cayman's African lieutenant scolded himself for growing fat and lazy during the three and a half months he'd been in Morgan Town. NKenai had indulged every whim, swilling copious quantities of rum from dawn to dusk and taking a woman to bed every night.

With the arrival of the first slave ships, the supply of available women had increased on the island. Navarre had personally dispatched another half-dozen girls to the Sea Spray Tavern, a riotous establishment just off of Market Square, across the plaza from Father Bernal's church. The tavern's former owner, Josiah Morgan, was dead and digested and not around to protest when Navarre made a present of the place to Tom Bragg, whose gangrenous left leg had been amputated below the knee back in December. Navarre considered such an arrangement ample compensation for shooting Bragg in front of the priest as an example of what would happen if the island's population resisted the Cayman's control. NKenai coveted Bragg's ownership and was anxious to try out these recent arrivals, none of whom spoke English. Two were familiar with the Kiswahili dialect that was NKenai's native tongue. Ah, but the pleasure these girls had to offer must wait, for there was mischief afoot in Morgan Town.

He studied the surrounding woods, a dense thicket of West Indian cedar obscuring the inland trail. NKenai rested his hand on the hilt of his scimitar and left the hillside path to amble across the clearing. He was certain Navarre was close-by. The captain's clothes were strewn upon the ground and patches of bare rock had been branded by his muddy footprints.

"Captain Navarre. *Usini-dan-gan-ye.* Do not deceive me. I come with important news."

"Speak it," a voice said behind him.

The African whirled about and found himself staring down the gunbarrels of Navarre's pistols. He held out his hands in an attitude of mock surrender. "My life is already yours, my captain, you do not need to take it."

Navarre grinned and stepped around the African. On a whim the Cayman had rescued NKenai from a slave ship many years ago, and the black man had sworn eternal fealty to the enigmatic pirate and sealed the pact in his own blood. Navarre understood NKenai and trusted him above all the other men of his crew.

The new master of Natividad strolled over to his clothes and started to dress, pulling on a pale yellow shirt trimmed with ruffles at the wrists, white breeches, black boots, and a faded brown waistcoat decorated with a delicate pattern of finely stitched flowers, embroidered with black thread.

"Njoo-uone," said the African. "Come and see," he repeated in English. "It is the priest. He may be causing trouble again."

"It is the priest's day of prayer. Every Sunday he gathers his flock."

"Prayer to the white man's God," NKenai muttered with contempt. "This cannot hurt us. But a woman in the plaza told Malachi Quince that the priest has begun to speak of other things than the Christian God. That the white shaman speaks words of war against my captain."

"The pulpit-pounder is becoming tiresome." Navarre scowled. The last thing he needed was some foolish old drunkard of a priest preaching popular dissent against the Cayman's authority. Navarre had business to exact this afternoon. One Artemus Callaghan had arrived in port but a couple of days ago. Callaghan, a well-to-do slaver hailing from Charleston, South Carolina, had established a lucrative trade with the plantation owners throughout the southeast United States and in Cuba. Fully eight months ago, Navarre had visited Charleston and convinced Callaghan that Natividad was the proper place to conduct their transactions. Navarre would receive slaves and hold them at Obregon Cove, where the hapless captives would be worked but well cared for while they regained the health they lost due to the miserable conditions aboard the slave ships. Already two ships from Africa, one of which Navarre owned, had visited Natividad and discharged their human cargo and headed back for more.

Callaghan, once convinced the African captives from Natividad would bring a much better price on the slave docks, had agreed to enter into a partnership with Navarre. However, the slave trader from Carolina was skittish by nature. If he suspected trouble from the locals, Artemus Callaghan as well as other slavers could be counted on to bolt for safer ports.

For some time now, Navarre had suspected Father Bernal of working to undermine the slaver's control of the island. However, the Carib half-breed was reluctant to execute the troublesome padre outright. Bernal still had too many followers among the citizens of Morgan Town, although the number had decreased after the arrival of the first two slave ships, whose crews had been anxious to spend their meager wages in the taverns, crib houses, and produce markets Morgan Town had to offer. Profits had won the Cayman many converts. Navarre was convinced that if he simply exercised patience, the inhabitants of Morgan Town would revert to their old callings and be his. Then the priest's "unfortunate" demise might well go unnoticed.

"Where is Callaghan?" asked Navarre. "Is he aware of the trouble?"

"He spent his night in a room above Bragg's tavern. I think he bedded two of Bragg's mulattos. As for Callaghan's crew, they are scattered throughout the town. They know nothing but the sleep of jack iron. And when they wake, the cannons will fire broadsides within their skulls." The African's robust laugh seemed to resonate from deep in his chest.

Orturo Navarre finished dressing and tucked his bone-handled flintlock pistols in his belt along with the cutlass. "I can handle the priest. Maybe we should send him to the other side of the island to save the souls of last week's guests." The Cayman grinned, revealing his pointed teeth. He walked to the edge of the bluff overlooking the governor's palace and, further below, the horseshoe-shaped bay with its aquamarine waters where two ships rode at a quiet anchor about seventy yards offshore: Callaghan's *Homeward,* a seaworthy brig and Navarre's the *Scourge.* Work parties clambered over a third craft, a sleek, swift-looking schooner that was being washed down and painted and made ready to ply the high seas once more. The schooner had preceded the slave trader's arrival by more than a week.

"Your spyglass," Navarre said, holding out his hand. NKenai snatched a spyglass from his belt and passed it to the pirate, who raised it to his eye and studied the laborious efforts of the *Scourge*'s master shipwright, Rico Amidei, and his work detail, some of whom were scrambling up the rigging while those men skilled with hammer and saw went about repairing a patch of fire damage at the stern of the vessel. Rico Amidei, a feisty Italian-born craftsman who had gone to sea with nothing but the clothes on his back and a streak of good-natured larceny in his soul, dangled from a sling draped from the bow of the craft. He was seated on a length of one-by-twelve above the deep draft waters of the bay. As Orturo Navarre adjusted the focus on the lens, a man at the bow materialized in the eyepiece. Amidei was preparing to rechristen the ship by first chiseling off the vessel's previous name.

"It's about time," muttered Navarre. He silently mouthed the letters as they were reduced to splinters and fell into the sea.

W . . . I . . . N . . . D . . . T . . . H . . . R . . .

Chapter Fifteen

The church had no name. The citizens of Morgan Town, be they field hand, overseer, or proprietor, simply called it church. There was none other. On this the fourth Sunday in Lent, Father Albert Bernal looked down from the simple oaken pulpit he had built with his own two hands at the congregation of farmers and shopkeepers who had come for Sunday service. With Easter only two weeks away, the remaining members of Morgan Town's citizens who so far had resisted the temptation to revert to their former piratical lifestyles had gathered to hear the priest's message of hope and redemption. However, Father Bernal did not fail to notice that the church was only about two-thirds full. The members of the Cabilde, the governing committee of the town, had ceased to associate with the priest. Those who had formerly served under Josiah Morgan and had held a modicum of power were the most reluctant to antagonize Captain Navarre. The Cayman's cannibalistic excesses had made cowards of them all. At least a third of the priest's flock had followed the Cabilde's example and fallen away from the church, which left the padre deeply troubled.

So Father Bernal began the liturgy, asking the Lord's blessing on the faithful members of his congregation. In Latin he led them in the rites of contrition and then read to his flock from the Gospels, concentrating his remarks on the raising of Lazarus from the dead. As an afterthought he likened the current situation on Natividad to the death of Lazarus and extolled his flock to pray for rebirth. About halfway through his homily, the rear door of the church opened and Orturo Navarre entered and stood at the back. He came alone, leaving NKenai and a dozen men stationed outside in full view of the congregation. The windows were unshuttered to permit a cross breeze through the church. Father Bernal could sense he was losing his people's attention as the pirates strolled up one side and down the other, slowly ringing the church.

The priest abandoned his discourse and thumbed through his worn leather-bound Bible until he came to an appropriate psalm, the pages creased from a great deal of use lately.

"The Lord is nigh unto all them that call upon him, to all that call upon him in truth.
He will fulfil the desire of them that fear him: he also will hear their cry, and will save them.
The Lord preserveth all them that love him: but all the wicked he will destroy.—"

A gunshot cut the priest short and startled the congregation, causing the men to jump in their seats, the women to scream and gasp, and the few children to cry and cling to their parents. Father Bernal dropped the Bible and ducked down behind the pulpit. Then, with his ears still ringing from the flintlock's report, the priest eased up to peer over the oak pulpit. Navarre's laughter filled the silence that followed as he calmly reloaded his pistol and returned the weapon to his belt.

"I do not think your God hears you, Priest," Navarre said. "But I hear. And I see all who have come to listen to your words and it displeases me. Perhaps they have heard enough." He sauntered down the center aisle between the unnerved townsfolk in their rows of hand-carved pews. Many of the benches still showed a trace of bark. The pirate captain approached the crucifix, which Hank Pariser, a former pirate turned farmer, had donated to the church. The relic was a thing of beauty, made of silver and bearing a fine-line drawing of Christ upon the cross. The crucifix was attached to a heavily weighted silver base and had been set atop the altar, a table made of stone slabs brought from back in the hills.

With casual disregard for the deity depicted in torment upon the cross, Navarre lifted the crucifix in hand and poked a finger through the bullet hole he had just shot through the chest of the crucified God. He wiggled the finger at the townspeople and grinned, showing his pointed teeth. Then his expression changed, and his eyes grew narrow, and a growl beginning somewhere deep in his chest erupted from his throat as he rose to his full height and hurled the crucifix out into the center aisle where the relic glanced off a pew and bounced and crashed along the floor.

Spittle formed at the corner of Navarre's mouth as he gnashed his hideously pointed teeth and advanced on a family of farmers seated in the first row. The father, a lanky son of the sea who had traded in his jackboots for a mule and plow, a good wife, and a family of five boys, stumbled out of the pew and led his offspring from the church. He was the first of many. Indeed, the entire congregation, still rattled from the gunshot, rose up and headed for the rear of the church, ignoring the protests of the priest, who entreated them to stay and trust in the Lord. When the last of the townspeople had fled the church, Navarre ceased his performance and wiped the froth from his lips. The wild light in his eyes faded and reason and civility returned.

"You are a mad animal," said Father Bernal, his voice weary and spirit near broken. How did one deal with a man who growled and foamed at the mouth and ate his enemies and shot his friends. "Dear God, where art thou? Have you abandoned me?"

Navarre reached in his coat pocket and brought out a brown glass flask of rum. "Lost your God, eh, Priest? Look for him here." He tossed the bottle to Father Bernal, who caught the flask with practiced ease. "From the looks of you, I'd say you found him before. Call him Jesus Christ. Call him Jack Iron. I think, for you, they are one and the same."

Navarre stiffened as a bell began to peal from a rocky point overlooking the mouth of the harbor. He had stationed some of his men to act as lookouts and sound the alarm whenever a ship appeared on the horizon marking a course for the island. Natividad was proving to be an unexpectedly busy port. Suddenly, NKenai loomed large in the open doorway.

"I hear it," Navarre said before the African could speak.

"You want the cannoneers sent to the shore batteries?" NKenai asked.

"Until we learn the identity of the ship and its crew," Navarre said, trotting down the aisle. He paused at the church's entrance and glanced back at the crestfallen priest. "I am told you speak against me. It must stop." He leaned down and picked up the battered crucifix. NKenai's eyes lit up from where he stood, watching. The silver relic was obviously of value and could be melted into coins. But to the

African's surprise Navarre placed the crucifix on the nearest pew.

"We could use that," Navarre's black-skinned lieutenant suggested.

"No. Leave the Christian God within these walls where it cannot do us any harm," said Navarre. The pirate watched with grim satisfaction as Father Bernal slowly turned his back on the empty interior of the church he had striven to fill for the glory of God. The crestfallen man of the cloth uncorked the bottle of rum and tilted it to his lips.

NKenai, standing in the sunlight, was unable to glimpse much past the crucifix but he glimpsed movement by the altar. "Now what is he doing, my captain?"

Navarre saw the bottle of grog tilt upward yet again. "Why, he's praying," said the Cayman.

From the point of land called the Shark's Tooth, the warning bell continued to sound. A Congreve rocket shot upward, fired from behind the walls of the governor's hacienda. The rocket exploded overhead, signaling to the men at the point that their signal had been received and was being acted upon.

"Come, my friend," said Navarre. "We must prepare to greet our guests."

"Shall we welcome them with solid shot and chain?" NKenai asked.

"It all depends on who they are," said Navarre, "and if they have anything I want."

The master of Natividad hurried out into Market Square in time to see dozens of his men emerge from the Sea Spray Inn across from the church. Others followed from a variety of houses, shops, and campsites; they flooded into the square and hurried toward the shell-paved road that wound down the hillside to the waterfront where an assortment of smoothbore twelve-pounders were concealed beneath tarpaulins and made to resemble stacks of crates and barrels waiting to be loaded aboard one of the ships in the bay.

Navarre noticed that several of the farmers in the town square had begun to close up shop. "Belay that, you plow pushers!" The Cayman had standing orders that business was to proceed as usual on the island both out in the countryside and in port. Morgan Town must appear that nothing was out of the ordinary, especially with the arrival of a new ship in the harbor. Navarre did not want to alarm any friends or alert any possible enemy by showing a deserted settlement to seaward. The farmers grudgingly returned to their makeshift booths, determined if shooting started to grab their trays of mangos, guavas, cassava melons, sweet potatoes and maize, and racks of salted pork and freshly caught fish, and bolt for the hills.

Navarre and his African first mate started down to the shore. Above Morgan Town, Navarre's select crew manned the walls of the hacienda and the big twenty-four-pounder cannons in the redoubts at the base of the battlements. Before long, the commotion had ended and every man, drunk or sober, had taken his place.

A stillness settled over Natividad broken only by the eternal tides and the crying gulls and the whispering wind . . . a quiet not unlike the calm before a storm.

Kit took up his spy rifle and peered over the cotton bale, then sat another peered again, to be sure he had seen another ...

Chapter Sixteen

Natividad seemed to rise and fall in the distance as Laffite's ship, *Malice,* with all sails unfurled, rode the blue-green sea. The island itself was about twelve miles long and nine miles wide of palm-ringed shoreline and limestone ridges and narrow valleys carpeted with a lush growth of ferns and wild grasses and layered with fertile volcanic soil. The hilly interior was a patchwork of barren, cactus-dotted cliffs on the south side of the island giving way to forested slopes thick with oak and pine, cotton tree, breadfruit, and mahogany. Gulls circled one another above the entrance to the bay of Morgan Town on the west side of the island. Further inland, turkey buzzards kept a sharp lookout for the day's next meal, hovering above Natividad's interior, which teemed with a variety of animal life including wild pigs, rats, bats, birds of every conceivable plumage, and reptiles the likes of which appeared to have existed unchanged for aeons.

Kit McQueen had yet to make these discoveries as he stood near the bow of the schooner, taking in the cobalt blue sky, the rolling waves, and scudding

clouds like airborne frigates plying the currents of
heaven. The ship carried a complement of a hundred
and two now. Laffite had stopped at his encampment
on the Louisiana coast and taken aboard the remainder of his crew. Kit and Iron Hand O'Keefe, Harry
Tregoning, and the Choctaws were mere passengers
who helped when they could but for the most part
tried to remain out of the way. Nate Russell had
surprised everyone and taken a liking to sea travel.
But a week into the journey and the Choctaw was
prowling the decks with all the assuredness of a
veteran tar. Strikes With Club had fared much worse.
The seventeen-hundred-mile Caribbean crossing to
the Lesser Antilles had been a nightmarish experience. The young warrior had kept precious little food
on his stomach, what with the constant pitch and roll
of the schooner. Eventually O'Keefe suggested the
hapless brave remain behind at one of the islands.
However, Strikes With Club adamantly resisted such
an arrangement and O'Keefe did not press the matter.

"Smell the land," said Jean Laffite, moving up to
stand alongside McQueen. He turned and shielded
his eyes as he checked to see that his flag, a skeleton
dancing a jig upon crossed cutlass blades, was flut-
tering from atop the mainmast. "We'll be dropping
anchor off Morgan Town in about an hour . . . if the
wind holds."

"And then . . ." Kit said. The voyage had taken
its toll on him as well. For six weeks he had enacted
in his mind the punishment he intended for Cesar
Obregon. He had never feared for Raven's safety,
oddly enough. Deep in his heart, Kit felt he understood Obregon. The man might be a rogue and a
larcenous rascal, but his actions, however rash, were
born of the privateer's passion for the half-breed
Choctaw. He certainly meant her no harm. But that
wasn't going to keep Kit McQueen from beating the
bastard's brains out if he got the chance.

"And then I trust you will allow me the opportunity to deal with Obregon. I wish to avoid violence. He will listen to me." Laffite spoke calmly and with authority. Kit nodded. Reason overrode his quick temper. He considered Laffite's request and wondered just how far the buccaneer could be trusted. Was he hoping to get his hands on General Jackson's "gold"? If so, then Laffite was in for a rude awakening. And yet the captain of the *Malice* had been nothing but forthright and generous throughout the voyage. Maybe it was time to lay all the cards on the table and find out just where the players were sitting.

"The Hawk of the Antilles has found himself a splendid lair. The people of Morgan Town trust him. They have made decent lives for themselves. Many of the town's best families are founded by freebooters who've managed to cheat the gallows and lowered their black flags for good," said Laffite, his tone of voice uncharacteristically wistful.

"You envy them?" Kit said, turning to look at the legendary sea rover.

"That I do," said Laffite. "When a man grows older, the wandering life loses its appeal. A man wants to belong to something. To build something. America is my chance. So I serve General Jackson and I receive a pardon for my . . . illustrious past . . . and I begin to build a respectable life. I aid an American officer to recover the woman he loves and I shall return the gold to Old Hickory." Laffite hooked his thumbs in the pockets of his rust-colored waistcoat. He pursed his lips; for a moment he was lost in thought, imagining "Jean Laffite, respectable gentleman." The notion had begun to sound good to him. "Why, I might even take a wife . . ." and then added with a chuckle, "Here and there."

The aroma of fried salt pork and biscuits wafted through the doorway at the bow as Iron Hand O'Keefe, Harry Tregoning, and Nate Russell with

Strikes With Club at his side emerged from the ship's kitchen. O'Keefe held half a loaf of crusty bread in one hand and a sizzling chunk of fried pork spitted on his hook. Gorging himself was O'Keefe's way of dealing with his anxieties. The closer he came to retrieving his daughter, the more worried he became and the hungrier he seemed. It was the inability to act that drove him frantic. Now, with Obregon's island within sight, it was all the Irishman could do to keep from diving overboard and swimming for shore. He had waited long enough. The war chief of the Choctaw wanted Raven back. Now. But there was nothing he could do, at least not yet. So he kept his guns loaded and his belly filled, and waited.

Harry Tregoning nodded to McQueen and Laffite. The British marine arrived on deck with tea in hand. Kit overheard the Englishman as he continued his discourse on the nature of God and creation and the teachings of the Old Testament. Tregoning, with all the smug security of his Christian upbringing, had taken it upon himself to convert these heathen savages, thereby saving their souls. Tregoning seemed oblivious to the fact that Nate Russell had already been baptized and taken a Christian name. Poor Nate had received his share of Bible lessons from the marine. However, today, Harry Tregoning was concentrating his sanctimonious efforts on Strikes With Club, who had yet to see any merit in Tregoning's beliefs. Of course, Strikes With Club was at his weakest, and Kit wondered how long the youngest of the two Choctaw would prevail.

"Now you see, God said to Adam that he could have anything in the garden, anything at all but the fruit of one tree. This special fruit was kept special and Adam and Eve were to leave it be," the marine explained. "Now you understand so far?"

"Yes. The white man's God does not wish to share. But the All-Father gives the Choctaw everything to use. All the forest is ours and the rivers and the animals that walk the ground or fly above us or swim in the rivers," said Strikes With Club. He hurried his steps to the starboard side of the boat, putting as much distance between himself and O'Keefe's salt pork as possible.

"He's worse than having a Jesuit aboard," Laffite muttered.

"You'll note he avoids giving any lectures on the benefits of marital fidelity," Kit said with a grin. He glanced toward the quarterdeck where Francis Luc Benard manned the ship's wheel. The quarrelsome Benard brothers weren't all that difficult to tell apart. Francis Luc was by nature even-tempered and stoic, while his brother Jean Baptiste was the brawler and had the scarred and battered features to prove it. "Will Francis Luc pilot us into the bay?"

"With me at his side," Laffite said. He waved to one of his lieutenants, a sour-faced Frenchman with an autocratic bearing, who went by the name of Lesconflair. "Antoine . . . find Jean Baptiste and instruct him to see that the carronades are properly loaded and primed! Then take up position below-decks." Four carronades had been loaded aboard in Barataria. The short-barreled deck guns fired a sixty-four-pound projectile and at close range were capable of inflicting massive damage on an opponent's ship. Lesconflair nodded, brushed a trace of snuff from the front of his waistcoat, and replied with an "As you wish, Captain" before departing to carry out Laffite's orders.

"Are you expecting trouble, Captain Laffite?" Kit asked. He had assumed the *Malice* was sailing into a friendly port.

"Always . . . *mon ami.*" Laffite touched his fingers to his forehead in a casual salute and then sauntered off toward the quarterdeck. The crew of the *Malice* gave way as the buccaneer passed. The anticipation of a fight swept through the crew, and several of the men cheered as Laffite's shadow swept across them.

Kit watched with renewed respect how the cannoneers under Laffite's command speedily readied their guns. Flannel cartridges of black powder were rammed down the black iron barrels, solid shot followed the powder, and for a fuse, shortened lengths of goose quills were filled with gunpowder and inserted into the priming holes at the rear of the cannon. One man in each gun crew was assigned the task of keeping a steady supply of the quills handy in a fight.

McQueen shifted his gaze to O'Keefe, Tregoning, and the Choctaws who made their way over to join him at the bow. Watching them approach, McQueen thought back to the departure from New Orleans. As the *Malice* had begun to slip away from the dock and head out into the wide muddy waters of the mighty Mississippi, Kit had huddled with his companions and revealed Andrew Jackson's ruse, pointing out that Laffite might turn on them once he caught up with Obregon and discovered the truth about the stolen gold.

The four men refused to be put ashore. O'Keefe was determined to stay—after all, Raven was his daughter. The two Choctaw warriors were resolved to follow "Chief Iron Hand," and as for Tregoning, a look of alarm did indeed cross his blunt homely features, but the marine shrugged off his concern and restated his intention to fight alongside his former foe. After six weeks at sea, Kit wondered if the marine still felt that way.

"We'll be dropping anchor within the hour," McQueen said.

"From the way these lads are making ready, we could be sailing into a fight." Tregoning checked over his shoulder and then scratched at his bald pate. Just above the fringe of hair circling his head, the previously sunburned flesh had begun to dry and peel. The constant itching threatened to drive him to distraction.

"Then I hope you will be ready to meet your Christian God," Strikes With Club added.

"Let me baptize you and you could enter heaven," Tregoning said.

"Would my father and mother be there? Would my little sister, Star Leaf, meet me? And my warrior brothers, would they join in the hunt? No. Then why should I go?"

The marine sighed in exasperation. He studied O'Keefe and Kit with hapless wonderment. "How you managed to live among these people is beyond me."

"I learned not to argue with them." Kit chuckled.

"Does Laffite expect Obregon to be waiting for us?" asked O'Keefe. "I don't fancy running under the bastard's guns without I get a chance to put a lick in for myself."

"We'll find out when we put into Morgan Town," said Kit.

"Why not come around the island and put in at Obregon Cove?" asked Strikes With Club. To the brave's relief, O'Keefe gobbled the last of the pork from his hook. The warrior's belly was shrunk from the pitifully little amounts of food he had been able to keep down.

"Laffite needs to find someone in Morgan Town who will guide us through the reefs guarding the approach to the pirate's sugar plantation," Kit explained.

"It will please me to walk the land again," Nate interjected. He lifted his eyes to the great expanse of water.

"You, too?" said Strikes With Club. "Yet you

have not suffered as I. You have taken your meals in peace."

"Do not think because my belly is without pain that my heart is light," Nate told the young warrior. "The spirits of the dead have spoken to me in dreams. They watch us from below the Great Water and have called me by name."

"I did not know . . ." said Strikes With Club, taken aback by the older man's revelation.

"I reckon the trail to wisdom is blazed with the words 'I didn't know,'" said Kit, disconcerted by the warrior's admission. He prayed to God he hadn't led these men to their doom. "All of you should have remained behind," he concluded.

"The hell you say," O'Keefe interjected.

"Here, here," said Harry Tregoning. "Who knows? Why, there might be some rather comely ladies in Morgan Town just pining to make the acquaintance of a proper Englishman." His eyes began to twinkle at the very notion of a veritable bevy of love-starved island wenches weary of these buccaneers and their clumsy, rough-edged advances. "Never let it be said that Harry Tregoning doesn't know how to court a lady, proper."

"Bed but never wed," Kit added with a grin.

"Precisely, Lieutenant. Pre-cisely."

Kit turned to face the island. The sun warmed his face. The sea breeze fanned his unruly red hair. The motion of the ship had not affected him; Kit had been to sea before. Indeed, his heart would have soared at the prospect of adventure but for the fact that Raven was in danger.

He blamed himself in part for Raven's abduction. She had wanted to come to the breastworks and join in the battle. As a favor to Kit, she had reluctantly agreed to stay with the widow LeBeouf. He had wanted her to be safe. She had admonished her lover that the only safe people were asleep in the graveyards, and yet Raven had complied with his wishes and remained in town . . . right where Obregon could find her.

Kit resolved that whatever else happened in their lives, he and Raven would confront things together. It dawned on him what he was thinking, and yes, he refused to deny the feelings. He wanted to spend his life with Raven. Kit McQueen loved this half-breed medicine woman more than his life. The enormity of his emotions had never struck him till this moment. He must find her. He must free her and hold her in his arms and speak what was in his heart. Nothing was going to stop him, not the sea and its mysteries, not the island like a fortress in the sun, and certainly not Cesar Obregon, the Hawk of the Antilles.

Chapter Seventeen

"He isn't here," Laffite called down from the quarterdeck to Kit standing at the port side, rifle cradled in the crook of his left arm. "Obregon's ship is the *Windthrift*," the buccaneer added. The schooner they had just passed bore the name *Carib*. Laffite studied it a moment, then dismissed his suspicions.

Kit nodded, and waved his hand. "Then we'll find a pilot and head for Obregon Cove." He glanced over his shoulder at the brig lying at anchor off the starboard. "*Scourge*," he read aloud. And beyond the brig, another vessel rose and settled with the oncoming tide.

"The *Homeward* is unknown to me," Laffite shouted. "But the *Scourge* can belong to none other than Orturo Navarre. So be on your best behavior, Lieutenant, or the Cayman may have you for dinner."

"I don't understand," Kit said to Francis Luc, the Cajun-born gunner. "Is this Navarre so sociable he invites his enemies to his feast?"

"Ah, *mon ami*, in a manner of speaking. His enemies *are* the feast. Navarre favors the 'long pig,' *comprendre*?" Francis Luc made a noisy sucking sound like a man gnawing a bone and draining it of marrow. "He is a cannibal." The pirate threw back his head and cackled merrily.

"Bless my soul," Tregoning said. "If Navarre's got a missus, point her out and I'll be certain to keep my distance." The marine was convinced he was irresistible to women. It was his cross to bear. He had no doubt that a cannibal made the worst kind of jealous husband.

"If he gets in my way, I'll hand him his own liver for lunch," O'Keefe glowered. He had no desire to confront this Cayman, but he wasn't about to quake in his boots.

"Pray you don't get the chance," Francis Luc replied, and blessed himself to ward off misfortune.

"No. Let *him* pray," Kit retorted, patting the walnut stock of his rifle. The Cajun gunner studied the lieutenant as if reassessing McQueen's abilities. Kit ignored the man's scrutiny. He felt no desire to prove himself, nor was he given to foolish brags. He was simply a man who was confident of his own abilities. In his thirty years, Kit McQueen had fought the British, the Creeks, raided the Barbary Coast, and plundered a caliph's treasure, been shipwrecked, and cheated a Spanish firing squad. His torso might be scarred, but his honor was unblemished. He had never backed down from a fight, not if the cause was just, and he wasn't about to start now. "Tell me, *monsieur,* how shall I know this man Navarre?"

A buzz of amusement swept over the men of Laffite's crew who were standing within earshot and listening to the interchange between the Cajun cannoneer and McQueen. With a mischievous gleam in his eye, Francis Luc winked at the carronade's gun crew, many of whom shared his private joke. "You will recognize 'Captain Cayman,'" he said. "Of that, Lieutenant, I have no doubt."

* * *

Morgan Town was a collection of buildings erected from the natural material to be found on the island: mud, wood, reeds, and stone. An irregular pattern of streets and roads consisting of hard-packed dirt became narrow streets paved with crushed shells. As a single johnny boat bearing Kit, Laffite, O'Keefe, and ten of the crew from the *Malice* nosed out of the shallows and up onto the beach, Orturo Navarre with NKenai at his side walked down a flight of wooden steps that led from the riverfront road and moved quickly across the beach to the water's edge, a distance of less than twenty feet.

Francis Luc was right, thought Kit as he climbed out of the boat and slogged through the surf to the moist white sand mottled with patches of shade where the palm trees grew in clusters of threes and fours. The man coming to greet them was unmistakable. He was dressed as an aristocrat, but his seamed leathery features, shaved head, and crescent row of pointed teeth were the stuff of nightmares. This man could only be the infamous Orturo Navarre. Kit was grateful for Laffite's presence, for the buccaneer apparently commanded respect even from the likes of the Carib.

"Captain Jean Laffite . . . I am honored." Navarre spoke in a silken tone. He had no true affection for Jean Laffite, but the buccaneer's exploits were legendary, and he was seldom without his brothers, so that an affront to one Laffite was an affront to all three. The Cayman suspected that Dominique You and Pierre Laffite were probably in the vicinity, perhaps lying offshore where the lookouts could not see them. "When I recognized your flag, I sent word to my men to prepare a celebration. Welcome to my island . . . Natividad." Navarre bowed, and then turned and gestured toward Morgan Town with a wave of his hand. "All that I have is at your disposal."

"All that you have?" Laffite replied.

"*Si.* I know you are Obregon's good friend. Like a son is this young man to you. But he had abandoned these good people. They had not seen him in months. When I came ashore, the people of Morgan Town welcomed me with open arms." Navarre glanced aside at Kit and O'Keefe. Both men wore buckskins and were armed with rifles, flintlock pistols, long knives, and tomahawks. "These two are not with the brotherhood." His gaze narrowed, leaving Kit with the distinct impression he was being measured for a stewpot.

"We aren't against it, either," Kit replied. He introduced himself and O'Keefe. The Irishman had discarded his coonskin cap but taken the liberty of tying a couple of turkey feathers in his shaggy mane of gray. Kit made no overture, but instead allowed his eyes to wander to the collection of piled goods and tarpaulins along the waterfront. Was that the dull iron maw of a cannon beneath the oilskin? He estimated the number of Navarre's crewmen in formation along the shore road and settled on about fifty or sixty men. As for the populace of Morgan Town, they seemed oblivious to Laffite's arrival, which struck him as odd.

"If Captain Laffite has welcomed you aboard his ship, then you will be my guests tonight," Navarre magnanimously proclaimed.

"We have come for Cesar Obregon," Kit told the Carib.

"And you have not seen him?" Laffite asked.

"No," Navarre said with a glance at NKenai, who also shook his head.

"He might be on the other side of the island, anchored in his cove."

"I would know such a thing," Navarre told them. "The Hawk of the Antilles has roosted elsewhere. But to put your mind at ease, I will have one of my men take a skiff around the island and see." Navarre turned and took NKenai aside and spoke in a low voice, issuing instructions that only the African could hear. NKenai nodded and trotted off across the sand toward a skiff whose bow appeared to be wedged in the soft sand. The black man single-handedly extricated the craft from the beach and, wading into the surf, maneuvered the craft into the surf. He leapt aboard and untied the single, gaffe-rigged triangular sail, and tacking once in the westerly breeze blowing from inland, he caught the wind and headed out into the bay.

"Come with me. Rest. Bring your crew ashore," said Navarre. "There are women. And plenty of rum. Are your brothers aboard the *Malice*?"

Laffite's expression never wavered. "No, but they are around if I need them," he lied with a poker face.

Listening to Laffite and watching the way he handled himself, it was obvious to Kit that they were not among friends. Since we're still alive, I guess we aren't among enemies either, he told himself.

Navarre clapped Laffite on the shoulder and then extended his invitation to the crew of the johnny boat. "I welcome all of you. Fire some jack iron, my brothers. But beware: the oildown is hot, but the women, hotter." Laffite's crew cheered to a man and followed the two captains across the beach to the wooden stairs leading up to the waterfront.

"He does ugly proud," O'Keefe said to McQueen. "But he seems like a hospitable rascal." The Irishman, despite the grave reason he had come to Natividad, was anxious to have his feet on dry land for a spell. And a tankard of rum wouldn't hurt, either. "The way I see things, maybe we passed Obregon at sea and he'll be along if we wait for him." O'Keefe wiped the perspiration from his forehead on the sleeve of his buckskin shirt. The feathers in his hair fluttered in the breeze. He noticed that two of Laffite's crewmen were starting back toward the *Malice*. Out in the bay, about seventy yards from shore, another boat had been lowered into the water from Laffite's schooner and several men were climbing over the side. Others simply dove over the side and swam toward shore, unwilling to wait their turn and be ferried to Morgan Town.

"Come on, there is nothing we can do for now," O'Keefe said. "We'll make our war plans in town over a jug or two of white rum. I reckon it's safe enough."

Kit studied the waterfront tarpaulins. Yes, that was a cannon. His gaze swept up the hills above the town to the governor's palace nestled against the limestone bluffs. His heart began to pound; his breath came in shallow gasps, the pressure building in his chest. He stared at those sun-bleached, solid walls with the redoubt at their base and shook his head and ran a hand over his face to clear his blurring vision.

"What is it, Lieutenant?" asked the Irishman.

"I don't know," Kit said. The sensation had passed and left him cold and shivering in the Caribbean sun. He steadied himself on his rifle as his windburned features hardened, betraying the iron-hard resolve that was his heritage. His hand inadvertently closed around the medal lying against his chest. "But I intend to find out."

Chapter Eighteen

By late afternoon, Laffite's crew had come ashore and gathered in the town square along with the men from Callaghan's ship and many of Navarre's swaggering ruffians. Pity those crewmen stationed on the walls of the governor's palace. From a distance, the guards enviously watched as banquet tables made of palm wood were carried out and placed around the square. Casks of rum and sorrel were loaded on carts and placed in each corner of the square, while the tables themselves were laden to the breaking point with platters of roasted pig, boiled shellfish, codfish fritters, and molasses cakes. As the sun dipped toward the western horizon, torches were set ablaze to illuminate the periphery of the town square, while in the center, timbers were stacked head high and set ablaze.

Throughout the day, Kit McQueen had wandered among the narrow streets and alleys, up to the walls of the governor's palace, where Navarre's guards turned him back. As he meandered among the houses and shops where a turner might ply his trade with wood and lathe or a gunsmith or crockmaker labor at his craft, Kit could not help but notice that the townspeople appeared far less enthusiastic about Navarre's presence than the Cayman had led them to believe. Indeed, they tended to speak of him more out of dread than affection—that is, when they would speak at all. Still, what happened on Natividad was none of his concern. Let Obregon and Navarre fight for control of the island, let them hack each other to pieces. Kit was only interested in one person. Nothing else mattered. At least, that was what he tried to tell himself.

But there was something about the way Navarre lorded over Morgan Town's populace that made Kit uneasy and riled his innate sense of justice. Even as the Cabilde came forward to welcome Laffite's Baratarians to the port, their eyes constantly shifted to Navarre as if each man feared for his life and looked to the Cayman for approval.

Kit's mother and father had fought and sacrificed during the Revolution. The conflict had left an indelible brand, one that would become a legacy to their children like the medal itself, handed down from generation to generation. A McQueen wasn't partial to oppression.

Kit felt someone staring at him and he glanced up to see a hollow-cheeked priest in black robes and a broad-brimmed black hat watching him from across the square. The padre seemed oblivious to the revelry surrounding him: a drunken freebooter staggered up to the priest and shouted something in his face. When the man of God failed to react, the drunkard continued on his way. Kit sensed immediately that the priest wanted to speak with him. McQueen had heard of Father Bernal from Laffite's crew; indeed his first stop had been the church, only to find the doors bolted from within. No one had answered his knock. Perhaps the padre wished to reveal a different version of Navarre's arrival on the shores of Natividad.

Kit rose from the table to the right of Navarre and started to make his way through the crowd. The air was charged with the noise of the boisterous freebooters, the blaring music of fiddles and concertinas and hornpipes and drums. Men leaped and whirled and chanced injury as they flailed at one another with their cutlasses to see which man could make the other flinch.

Over by the fire and much to the delight of a group of onlookers, Iron Hand O'Keefe and Navarre's own shipmate, Malachi Quince, a grizzled little throat-slitter who had escaped the clutches of the hangman on more than one occasion, were engaged in a fierce competition. O'Keefe and Quince each held a small cask of dark rum. At a signal from the Cajun Jean Baptiste, the two men began to gulp the contents of the kegs in a race to see who could be the first to drain them dry. O'Keefe towered over his opponent; however, size had nothing to do with a man's ability to hold his jack iron. Malachi Quince, inspired by the cheers of his black-hearted brethren, was the first to empty his keg and toss it into the fire, besting O'Keefe by five seconds. Both of the rum-soaked casks exploded into flames on contact with the burning timbers.

Kit continued on across the square, working his way toward the priest. Quite unexpectedly, Father Albert Bernal spun on his heels and retreated from the square, moving quickly beyond the flickering reaches of the firelight. Quickening his pace, the priest darted up the steps and through the open doorway of his church. The darkened interior mirrored the gloom strangling his heart.

A hand caught McQueen by the arm, halted his progress, and turned him around. He started to pull free and found himself face to face with Navarre's ebony-skinned henchman, NKenai. The African's grip was like iron. His fingers dug into Kit's shirt sleeve and found only corded muscle, the arm of a blacksmith, with about as much give as an anvil. NKenai arched his brows in surprise. He looked at the smaller man with renewed respect.

"*Ngoja kidogo*. Wait a little. Captain Navarre would speak with you. Laffite is with him."

"Did you find anything at Obregon Cove?" Kit asked. The African must have navigated his return by moonlight, no mean feat.

"*Njoo*. Come."

NKenai indicated the tables where the Cayman and Jean Laffite sat side by side. Several comely young women of African, South American, and Caribbean extraction had emerged from the Sea Spray Tavern to join the celebration. A hefty-set girl of no more than fifteen years immediately took up residence on Jean Laffite's lap. The buccaneer laughed and sent the girl on her way with a swat to her ample derriere. Harry Tregoning managed to catch her on the rebound and pulled her into his embrace. He wrinkled his ugly features and made a silly face that the girl found amusing. As Kit drew nigh he heard the girl ask Harry if he was a captain and heard Tregoning reply, "Why, an admiral, my dear child. An admiral."

Artemus Callaghan, a man of ample girth and prodigious appetites, commandeered a table all to himself and was enjoying his own private feast. He wolfed down pork and pastry. Grease smeared the slave trader's wobbly jowls and spattered the broad bib tucked at his throat. He ate in a hurry. The Carolinian was anxious to return to bed with one of the Sea Spray's harlots. Kit had nothing but contempt for the "peculiar institution" of slavery. No man had the right to own another. It was as plain and simple as the nose on his face, an incontrovertible truth and an issue he worried would one day divide the country if not dealt with by the government.

Navarre rose and welcomed Kit back to the table

as if the lieutenant had been gone for days instead of a few minutes. He indicated a place on the bench to his left.

"As you can see, my dear Mr. McQueen, NKenai has returned."

"With something of value to say, I trust." Kit's mood was souring. He was in no mood for carousing. The pursuit of Cesar Obregon was wearing thin, and he was no closer than when the *Malice* had set sail from New Orleans six weeks ago.

"He saw nothing but the slaves we are keeping there on Obregon's plantation. But Artemus will take many of them with him when he leaves tomorrow."

"Eh? Perhaps the day after," Callaghan called out. He ran his tongue around the ear and along the neck of the girl on his lap. She laughed and pretended to enjoy his attentions. "Navarre tells me you are searching for a girl this Obregon has stolen."

Kit stiffened and color came to his cheeks. He did not appreciate being the subject of discussion among the likes of such brigands. "I am."

"My good fellow, look about you. Why seek a flower that is lost when you are sitting in the center of a whole garden of delightful blossoms." He held up the girl's smooth, coffee-colored hand. He inhaled her fragrance and a dreamy expression settled over his pale features.

Before Kit could make a derogatory reply, Navarre slapped the flat of his hand on the table and shouted, "At last!" A man with a wooden leg emerged from the Sea Spray Tavern bearing a black iron stewpot, which he carried straight away to the Cayman's table. "Here's Tom Bragg, a good mate and loyal seaman. There's not a man or woman in all the islands who can make a better pot of oildown."

Kit McQueen watched with deep misgivings as the pot was brought forth from the Sea Spray Tavern. Dining with a cannibal struck him as a risky business.

He was relieved when Navarre listed the ingredients. The Cayman mentioned green bananas, breadfruit, coconut, onions, shellfish, and generous chunks of pork, boiled in a broth thickened with flour and seasoned with allspice.

"Evening, gents," said Tom Bragg. He raised a knuckle to his forehead in salute to Navarre and Laffite. He glanced curiously in Kit's direction. Then he nodded and limped over to the table. His peg leg crunched the shells underfoot, and where the dirt was moist from spilled rum, Bragg's hand-carved appendage sank an extra inch or so into the ground and threw the pirate off balance.

Navarre ladled a bowl of oildown for himself, Laffite, and Kit McQueen. "Be on your best behavior, Tom," said the brigand.

"Sir?"

"Mr. McQueen here is an American lieutenant. He's come looking for someone special. A woman . . ."

Bragg appeared to be alarmed by the revelation. His cheeks flushed and he retreated a step from the officer. Navarre laughed aloud and eased the peg-legged seaman's fears and explained to the Sea Spray Tavern's unnerved proprietor the nature of Kit's presence on the island. Bragg grudgingly accepted his captain's explanation and departed, limping along at a quick if ungainly gait.

"Poor Tom," said Navarre. "You see, he once served aboard an American warship. But he found there were greater profits to be made beneath the black flag, so he deserted." Navarre spooned a mouthful of oildown from his bowl and began to chew. A trickle of juice escaped from the corner of his mouth. "You can understand his misgivings. I daresay it would be best if you slept aboard ship tonight. Bragg might not have believed your reasons for coming to Natividad."

"I'm not worried," Kit replied, trying the contents of the bowl before him. The oildown had a sweet peppery flavor that would take a little getting used to. It was not unpleasant. And Kit was hungry.

"A man of confidence. And no doubt convictions and high morals," said Navarre. He glanced at Laffite. "Strange company for one such as yourself, Jean."

"I've reformed," Laffite replied with a wink and a devilish grin. "I chart a virtuous course. I seek no riches but what I earn as an honest merchant."

"Well, now, if that is the truth, then perhaps you have knowledge of where Obregon has buried his treasure." Navarre dabbed at his mouth with a silk scarf, then leaned forward, elbows on the table. "I am told the wealth our absent 'hawk' has gathered throughout his career is buried somewhere on Natividad. Did he ever confide in you as to the whereabouts of his gold and trinkets. It would be a shame for his treasure to go to waste, eh?"

"As an honest man, I suppose I would have no use for such ill-gotten gain." Laffite stroked his chin and allowed the moment to build. Orturo Navarre wasn't the only man at this table capable of stringing a story out.

"Yes?" said Navarre, hanging on Laffite's every word.

"Unfortunately Cesar kept his secrets to himself."

Navarre scowled and returned his attention to his meal. He did not like being toyed with. In fact, he did not like Jean Laffite. But he would tolerate the man for the sake of the pirate brotherhood. And besides, Laffite's brothers no doubt knew their infamous sibling had come to Morgan Town. If any harm came to Jean Laffite, Navarre would spend the rest of his life looking over his shoulder, waiting for Pierre or Dominique to catch up to him. His slave trade was too profitable an undertaking to invite such trouble. The Cayman finished his meal and rose from the table. He bowed to Laffite and to Kit McQueen.

"Gentlemen, you are my guests. Morgan Town is yours for the night." He looked at McQueen. "I am sorry I was not able to be of more help to you, Lieutenant. I hope you find the woman you seek, but I fear the odds against you finding her are insurmountable. The sea is a cruel mistress who rarely reveals her secrets."

"Nevertheless, we shall resume our search at first light," Laffite said. "I've ordered food and victuals to be brought aboard tonight."

"Then I bid you fair wind and high tide, Captain Laffite," said the Cayman, his mottled features striving to appear earnest. "Some dreams are best abandoned, Lieutenant McQueen." And with that final discouraging word, the new master of Natividad started back to the governor's palace. NKenai immediately fell in step a few paces behind his captain. Navarre waved him forward and whispered instructions to the African. The black man immediately left Navarre's company and returned to the festivities. Kit had the distinct feeling NKenai would be keeping the Cayman's "guests" under careful observation.

Navarre was not challenged as he approached the gates to the palace. His lean brooding frame and shaved head were instantly recognizable even by moonlight. The gates swung open and a brigand in a faded linsey-woolsey shirt and brown breeches managed a salute as the Cayman entered the courtyard. His keen eyes searched the surrounding walls. Men were stationed by the swivel guns above the front gates at the corners of the north wall. Other members of his crew patrolled the perimeters of the courtyard, the walkways, and the fortified roof of the stone house that had once housed the island's former governor, Josiah Morgan.

Navarre had left the interior as he found it. The rooms were furnished with luxuriously padded chairs and settees stolen from Spanish galleons or Caribbean plantations plundered by the island's inhabitants long ago. Navarre ignored the scrutiny of the guards and hurried across the courtyard. Passing a carriage barn, he headed for the magazine built of limestone and timber. Two guards posted before the door to the powder shed straightened as Navarre drew nigh.

The Cayman greeted each man and opening the door, walked down a flight of steps and paused about ten feet belowground. He lit a lamp and instantly a rectangular room approximately thirty feet in length and twenty-five in width became filled with the sallow light. The magazine housed powder and shot of various caliber, stacked muskets and pistols, assorted cutlasses and a half-dozen Congreve rockets Navarre had removed from the burning hold of a British schooner he had sunk back in January. The chamber also held five frightened women. Two were as sleek and black as panthers, their features befitting Nubian queens. The other three women were mulattos, long-limbed and lovely to look at despite the rigors of the ocean crossing. All five women were underweight from lack of proper food and the miseries of life aboard a slave ship. But Navarre intended to correct all that. They'd be filled out and shapely when he was finished. He intended to dress them in finery and personally escort them to Cuba and perhaps even to New Orleans, where beauties such as these commanded a top price. *Five!* The women, none of whom looked older than sixteen, avoided his gaze. They were bound at the wrists and ankles with strands of leather cord. He shifted the lamp in his hand and discovered a pile of sawed-through strands in the dust near the rusty blade of a cutlass whose hilt had been wedged between two powder kegs, allowing the missing woman to saw through her bonds.

Navarre tugged one of his bone-handled pistols from his waistband. He placed his back against the door.

"Where is she?" he asked. None of the captives spoke, but one of the mulattos, the youngest and the most frightened by all that had befallen her, glanced toward a patch of darkness at the rear of the chamber. Navarre held up the lamp and raised his pistol.

"Come out," he said. Navarre stiffened at the sound of a pistol being cocked.

"Put down the lamp and your gun and turn around or I will kill you," a voice said.

"I think not," Navarre replied. "A pistol you might have. But none of the powder kegs have been stove in. To do so would have alerted my guards." He chuckled softly. "I admire your spirit." He had confined the women to the magazine in case Laffite had insisted on visiting the hacienda. It had been an instinctively cautious move. Now the pirate's instincts told him his captive was attempting to bluff her way to freedom. "Drop your pistol and I will forgive this inconvenience. Do not force me to drag you out of hiding."

"Try and take me. I would rather die than be your bondwoman." He heard a faint rasp of steel and caught a glimmer of a knife blade. She was indeed resourceful.

"*You* may be willing to die. But is she?" The Cayman shifted his aim and trained his pistol on the young mulatto who saw her death was at hand. She drew up and lowered her head to her knees, and began to softly moan in terror and rock back and forth. Navarre cocked his pistol and started to squeeze the trigger.

"No. Wait." The woman in the shadows would not be the cause of an innocent's death.

Navarre recognized the tone of defeat. He had heard it often enough in his life and times. A knife thudded to the floor. A flintlock pistol struck the hard-packed earth. Silence . . .

"Come out where I can see you," the Cayman ordered.

The woman in the shadows hesitated another brief moment, desperately seeking a way out. But Orturo Navarre had left her no alternative but surrender.

Raven O'Keefe stepped into the light.

Chapter Nineteen

"I trust the food was to your liking," said Navarre.

The fire in the hearth caused shadows to dance like rapturous souls caught in the frenzy of some hellish jubilee. His bootheels tapped across the cold stone floor of the former governor's bedroom, then became muffled as he reached the coarsely woven wool rug near the bed where Raven O'Keefe waited with her fists clenched. A couple of hours had passed since her attempted escape. Since then the women had been brought from the magazine and returned to the hacienda. Raven had been separated from the other captives and escorted to the master bedroom by a pair of swarthy freebooters who made no attempt to hide their lust for the half-breed woman. But the cutthroats had made no move against her, despite their base urges, and Raven suspected Navarre's hand in this.

Malachi Quince had arrived, close on the heels of Raven's lecherous escort, and brought her food and drink, a small platter of cassava biscuits, and a pot of aromatic bittersweet tea. Hunger and thirst overrode the captive woman's cautious nature—it would do her no good to starve herself—so she devoured the contents of the platter and washed the biscuits down with a clay cup full of the dark pungent tea. Easing her hunger pains did nothing to ameliorate the cold fury with which she greeted Navarre when at last he came to call. The defiance in her eyes was an almost-palpable force that had temporarily held him at bay.

Navarre had decided imprisoning the women in the powder magazine wasn't worth the risk. If Kit McQueen or Captain Laffite insisted on visiting the governor's palace, Navarre could always return the captives to their bleak chamber. But the Cayman preferred not to. A woman like Raven, even bound hand and foot, might find a way to set off a powder charge just for spite. He did not want to take any chances.

"I have ordered clothes to be brought for you, to replace the rags you are wearing." Navarre picked up the clay cup she had left on a table near the bed. The empty platter was nearby, but it was the cup that held his interest. He was obviously pleased she had broken her fast. "Good. You must keep up your strength." His movements were broad and magnanimous, his tone of voice surprisingly congenial. Raven found the man an enigma. A few hours ago he had threatened her life. Now he was treating her like a pampered guest. What had caused this sudden metamorphosis? She eyed him suspiciously. Even in her tattered raiment, she seemed draped in an aura of royalty befitting a princess. It was a quality worth its weight in gold and one Orturo Navarre intended to exploit to the fullest. There were rich men in these Americas willing to pay a handsome price for a woman like this.

He reached out for her, his fingers touching her shoulder. She drew away and tried to brush his hand aside, but her actions were sloppy and uncoordi-

nated and she almost lost her footing. O'Keefe's half-
breed daughter was by nature as agile as a cat. It
bothered her that she suddenly seemed so clumsy.
That was the first warning. Navarre opened the lid of
the teapot and dipped his fingers into the liquid, then
held up his hand and rubbed his thumb across his
moistened fingertips until they glistened. He sniffed
the liquid.

"The datura grows in Hispaniola," he said. "My
mother's people, the Carib, would gather the roots
and dry them and blend them with the dried stems
and pulp of the ortanique and brew them to make
what the shamans call 'dream tea.'"

Raven was trying to listen, but Navarre seemed to
be speaking to her from inside her skull. His voice
reverberated along with the rustle of his garments
and the buzzing of an insect outside her shuttered
window and the crackling hissing flames filling the
fireplace as the dried mesquite logs splintered and
burst apart. Her vision intensified even as she gradually lost control of her limbs. The whitewashed ceil-
ing became brilliant and pulsing with amber light.
The walls appeared to expand and contract as if the
bedroom were breathing. Raven lost her balance and
reached out for the four-poster behind her and managed to lower herself to the bedcovers. The pace of
her breathing increased. She felt herself sinking into
the feather mattress and heard the throbbing cadence
of her own beating heart.

Navarre chuckled softly and removed his
clothes, discarding first his shirt and then his trousers. He knelt beside her on the bed. His naked chest
was covered with a spiraling pattern of scars that
trailed down from each shoulder to form a Y in the
middle of his chest and then made a single double
line to his loins. Raven knew what was coming but
was powerless to resist the cayman-faced pirate. The
medicine woman's arms simply would not obey her.

As Navarre lowered himself atop his captive, Raven turned to stare at the logs ablaze in the fireplace. With the last ounce of her flagging strength, she poured her whole being into that heart of fire until it consumed her sense of touch and hearing and sight, until she was one with the flames, inviolable and purified.

She did not even feel his warm breath fanning her cheek.

A log split; an ember cracked and exploded like a gunshot in the square. Kit McQueen spun, crouched, and reached for one of the fifty-caliber pistols concealed beneath his waistcoat. The Quaker's walnut grip filled the palm of his hand. He recognized the source of the noise almost immediately and relaxed his stance.

Kit was standing at the mouth of an alley opposite the corner of the Sea Spray Tavern and well out of reach of the light seeping through the cracks in a shuttered window. His compact powerful physique remained hidden in the shadows while he studied Market Square, which at a quarter past midnight was already strewn with the unconscious crews of Callaghan's ship and Laffite's *Malice*. Navarre's brigands were also represented, but not in as many numbers, which Kit found highly disconcerting. He intended to voice his concerns to Laffite.

The lieutenant had remained aloof from the festivities. He had finished his bowl of oildown, and finding a place apart from the crowd, he had nursed his flagon of jack iron, sipping occasionally and taking only enough to warm his belly. A restlessness was upon him, and once Orturo Navarre departed for the governor's palace, Kit managed to escape NKenai's notice and slip away from the square undetected and, along with Nate Russell and Strikes With Club, made his way down to the waterfront.

As stealthy as his Choctaw companions, Kit had

avoided the Navarre's freebooters guarding the beach and discovered for himself the cannons concealed beneath the tarpaulins lining the road above the beach. With the help of Nate and Strikes With Club, Kit made an accurate assessment of Morgan Town's fortifications. These twelve-pounders coupled with the twenty-fours on the hillside were a lethal threat to any ship entering the harbor that Navarre might consider an enemy. Kit didn't much care for the notion that Laffite's schooner was completely at the mercy of the shore batteries.

Now, past midnight, Kit had returned to Market Square only to discover Laffite was nowhere to be found. Nate Russell moved up along the side of the building to stand abreast of Kit while Strikes With Club, keeping watch at the rear of the alley, rubbed his eyes and slumped wearily against the wall of the tavern. He needed sleep but doubted he was any closer to getting any. The warrior yawned and, propping his rifled musket against the broken remains of a nearby barrel, stretched his limbs. On the other hand, Nate Russell hid his fatigue. Sleep was the least of his concerns.

"I do not like this place," said Nate. "Neither does Strikes With Club. Evil spirits walk among the living in this village. Our deaths are here if we do not leave." Nate Russell studied the square, taking in the human detritus of the night's celebration. Men slept where jack iron dropped them, on tables and under them, propped against one another or alone, curled near the still-crackling fire or hunched in the shadows. The snoring brigands filled the air with a guttural drone that was almost deafening.

"I'd like nothing better," Kit replied. "But there's something amiss here. And I must learn the truth before I quit this island." He fell silent as the front door of the tavern creaked open and Harry Tregoning emerged from the smoky interior and stepped into the night. Kit started forward and the British marine, spying movement out of the corner of his eye, turned, startled, then breathed a sigh of relief as he recognized McQueen.

"Joshua and Jericho!" Tregoning exclaimed in a sibilant voice, and hurried across the front of the tavern. "Three times Laffite has sent me into the night looking for you. I haven't had a moment to myself to enjoy the charm of Mr. Bragg's Nubian ladies. And now they're all spoke for. Taken to bed and deprived of my company while I've been wandering Market Square looking for you."

"I deeply sympathize," Kit impatiently replied.

"You lack sincerity," Tregoning sniffed.

"You'll lack more than that if you don't bring me to Laffite," Kit growled, and patted the hilt of his Arkansas toothpick.

The marine took the hint and led the way to the tavern. Nate Russell refused to follow. The proximity of the forested slopes behind the town was his security. He did not want to be confined indoors if trouble came. Nate flatly stated his intentions and retreated down the alley to join Strikes With Club. Kit couldn't blame either of them. He was beginning to feel trapped himself.

The Sea Spray Tavern was a long, high-ceilinged space with four massive roof beams running the length of the room. Upstairs, a dimly lit hallway offered access to ten bedrooms in which sleep seldom occurred, at least during the evening hours. In the tavern below, oil lamps set in wall brackets provided most of the light. As for furniture, Bragg provided his customers with a collection of palm-wood tables flanked by bench seats. A few ladder-back chairs were strewn about the room. Despite the crowded square, the tavern itself was surprisingly free of revelers. Men were slumped forward and snoring at three of the tables. And half a dozen kittens chased a fist-sized cannonball among the tables and chairs. Every time the iron shot came to rest, one of the kittens would scamper across the floor and bat the thing and set it rolling again. Heavy-looking wine casks and barrels of ale rested on their sides in a massive frame behind a bar constructed of oak and finished with embellishments of carved driftwood inlaid with shells. Tom Bragg, the tavern's owner, walked around the bar as Tregoning reentered with McQueen at his side. Bragg did not appear as alarmed by the lieutenant's presence as he previously had been. A pockmarked, homely sort, Bragg's tender side showed in the way he cradled a kitten in the crook of his right arm. A hand-carved crutch shoved underneath his left arm helped him maintain his balance as he began to tire in the late hours of night.

"Reckon the third time was the charm," Bragg said, limping forward. His peg leg and cane rap-rap-rapped with every step. A woman's voice drifted down from the stairway off to Kit's left. It could have been a moan of pain or pleasure.

"NKenai's upstairs. I sent him Ushanga and Asali. They are new arrivals and ought to keep him occupied for the remainder of the night," Tom Bragg explained. He gestured toward a thick fold of curtains off to the right of the wine casks. "This way, Lieutenant. You know, last time I was this close to an American officer, he was trying to run me through with a pike." Bragg didn't finish the story. Obviously he had lived to tell the tale. Bragg muttered a few words of endearment to the calico kitten in his arm and set the tabby down on the bar. The animal circled and began to mew. He crumbled a fistful of hardboiled egg for the kitten, who immediately ceased complaining. Bragg continued along the length of the bar and limped over the splayed legs of Artemus Callaghan's first mate, a well-fed-looking seaman rendered unconscious by the powerful brews concocted by Bragg.

"There's some that say if the devil had my rum punch, he wouldn't need Hell," said the peg-legged tavernkeeper. He snorted and cleared his throat and swallowed some phlegm, then wiped his mouth on his apron. His loose-fitting shirt was stained with tobacco and spilled wine. Stepping up to the curtains, he lifted a fold and held it back to reveal a door the color of seaweed but faded and needing a fresh coat of paint. Kit glanced at Tregoning, who nodded reassuringly, and then tried the latch. Nothing had prepared him for the scene he found beyond the green door.

Three men were seated about a large square table dominating the center of the room. Judging by the brass-frame bed against the far wall and a rolltop writing desk off to the right, Bragg called this room home.

Jean Laffite rested his elbows on the table and clapped his hands together. "At last . . . our elusive young lieutenant!" he exclaimed. The fastidiously dressed buccaneer picked his clay pipe off the table and lit the tobacco in the bowl from a nearby candle. Soon, bluish gray clouds of aromatic smoke curled upward to the rafters.

"Lordee, Kit. Where've you been? We figured the ground must have swallowed you up," said Iron Hand O'Keefe, seated next to the Baratarian. Kit had expected to find the Irishman blind drunk by now. McQueen was happy to have misjudged him. But it was the third man that held Kit's interest. Here was a gaunt-looking individual dressed in the garb of a freebooter, baggy trousers tucked into buckled boots, and a shirt that a man twice his size could have worn. The stranger held a tankard of hot buttered rum in his veined bony hands. His eyes, both bright and alert, were set in a vaguely familiar face. It took a moment, but Kit recognized the brigand as none other than Father Bernal.

"We have not formally met. I am Father Albert Bernal," said the priest. "I must apologize for avoiding you earlier, but Navarre . . . ah . . . always Navarre. I run from him like a tody from a yellow snake." The priest lifted the tankard to his lips. "Then an angel whispered to me, in the darkness of my church, and told me that there are times when prayer is not enough. Action is called for." The priest finished the last of the rum and set the empty tankard down on the tabletop. His arthritic hands trembled as he paused, allowing Tregoning and Bragg to enter the room.

Bragg nodded to the priest, then headed for a pitcher of sorrel, a potent beverage made from cooking sorrel berries and filled a jar with both pulp and juice. The red sweet drink was usually ready for consumption after a week. Age it a month and only a fool would touch the stuff.

"I am not a brave man," Father Bernal continued, "and have been afraid of death all my life. But there are some things worse than death. So here I am. I thought the disguise would fool the Cayman's watchdogs."

"You're Navarre's man, aren't you?" Kit asked, glancing aside at Bragg.

"I was . . . till he shot my leg off," the tavernkeeper admitted. "I took a fever after they sawed my limb. The padre here nursed me back to health. I owe him my life." Bragg rapped his knuckles against the peg leg. "This here be the source of my conversion, mate, and that's the truth of it."

Kit nodded. He accepted the man's explanation at face value. If Laffite trusted him, that was good enough for McQueen. He turned to the buccaneer. "The waterfront is lined with twelve-pounders. And the guns are constantly manned. I counted ten pieces. I've also been to the governor's palace. The twenty-four-pounders are heavily protected and each boasts a six-man gun crew. Navarre is ready for trouble."

"A fact which Cesar Obregon discovered, to his dismay," said Laffite.

"Obregon has been here?" Kit's hopes soared. The news hit him like a slap in the face.

"He still is," Bragg interjected. "Like I told Cap'n Laffite, the Hawk of the Antilles came sailing into port not expecting anything but a 'Hello' and 'Welcome Home.' When the guns opened up and one of the twenty-fours put a load of shot in the *Windthrift*'s stern, Obregon hauled down his flag." Bragg winced and began to rub his left leg where the stump fit into the peg leg. The pain would be with him all his days. "We were all surprised when he did, until we saw he had a lady aboard. It was plain to one and all the shore guns had him crossed, though he might have made it out to sea. But Obregon lowered his colors rather than risk her life."

Kit hurried over to the tavernkeeper and caught him by the arm and hauled him to his feet. "Is she well? Answer me, sir, or by heaven I'll—"

"Ease up, lad," O'Keefe said in a sharp tone. His cheeks were flushed from drinking too much and the room was too damn warm, but hot or cold, drunk or sober, he was still Iron Hand, chief of the Choctaw, and Raven was still his daughter. A lost temper benefited no one, especially O'Keefe's daughter.

As Bragg pried himself free of the lieutenant's grasp, Father Bernal rose from the table and placed a hand on Kit's forearm. "I have seen her, my son. Navarre holds her prisoner in the governor's palace. As for Obregon, he and some of his shipmates are being kept in a pit a couple of hundred yards inland from the palace."

"What about a boy?" said O'Keefe. "He'd be about eight years old . . ."

"Yes." The priest nodded. "He is with Obregon.

I tried to bring them the sacraments but was turned back. There's always a number of guards stationed nearby. The rest of the *Windthrift*'s crew were taken to Obregon's cove on the east shore. Navarre is using them to build shelter to house the slaves that have been brought to the island."

"The devil take Obregon. Let's get Raven," Kit said, pulling away from the priest. Even as he spoke the words, he knew how futile they seemed. The palace was nothing less than a heavily guarded fortress. An all-out assault might breach the walls, but at a bloody expense. And the ruthless brigand called the Cayman might harm Raven if he suspected an attempted rescue. McQueen held up his hand in submission. "I know. It will take planning."

Laffite chuckled. "We'll make a freebooter of you yet."

"I thought you've given up a life of piracy."

"Oh, I have. From the day my spies reported that General Jackson was bringing a load of gold-painted lead ingots to ensure my loyalty . . . and I decided to fight at his side anyway. Yes, I'd say from that moment on, I was an honest man."

Kit lowered his gaze, finding an excuse to study the floor. Old Hickory had certainly underestimated Laffite's network of spies. No wonder the man had been such a successful smuggler.

"Lose something?" asked Laffite.

"I'm looking for a hole big enough to crawl into. Captain Laffite, I misjudged you . . . General Jackson, myself, all of us. I deeply regret it. You are a patriot. I can only offer my deepest apology." This was a night of revelations, Kit thought.

"Accepted, Lieutenant," said Laffite, shifting in his seat. Apologies made him uncomfortable. "I admire your courage. You came along even though you suspected I might turn on you and slit your gullet at any time." He laughed. "Oh, but I would like to have seen Cesar's face when he scratched those ingots and the paint came off beneath his fingernail." Laffite pursed his lips and ran a hand across his stubbled cheeks. He intended to find time to shave before encountering Navarre again. It wasn't like the buccaneer to be anything less than fastidious. "Well, now. Let's see what kind of sea rover you really are, McQueen. How would you suggest we go about dealing with the likes of Orturo Navarre and saving your fair Raven O'Keefe?"

"I'll think on it," said Kit. Much to the surprise of the men gathered in Bragg's private quarters, he turned on his heels, ambled from the back room, and quietly passed the tables and the tavern's slumbering patrons. He strode to the front door and out into the night, where he halted at the edge of Market Square and looked up at the well-fortified governor's palace on the hill overlooking the town. His mind had already begun to formulate a plan. It tore his heart to watch those moonlit walls and be powerless to reach the woman he loved.

Then an anger came upon him, and a cold fury, more terrible than ever he had experienced in his thirty years, left him trembling. First Obregon's rash misdeeds and now Orturo Navarre's foul treachery . . . one betrayal leading to another. How much was he supposed to take? Did they think him of so little consequence, these brigands of the Antilles? A plan . . . Yes, indeed. He knew how it must be done. The scheme involved fire and blood and retribution worthy of the Old Testament. To hell with getting mad. It was time to get even.

Chapter Twenty

The nightmare had him. It began soft, then parted like silken curtains, ruffled by the wind, unthreatening, at first only to reveal the horror. The horror! An explosion rocked the *Windthrift*. "We're being fired upon from shore! Another image, summoned by the dream, materialized this time without the explosions. Raven waited alone with Obregon in his cabin. For six long weeks she had been a pampered prisoner aboard the *Windthrift*. He had respected her privacy and refrained from forcing himself upon her, and had gone so far as to express his love. Her reply was always the same: "Take me back, then. Return to New Orleans." Obregon's refrain never changed. Raven would learn to love him. Natividad was her home and she would love him in time . . . The image dissolved into fire and blood and the cries of the wounded. Once more Obregon relived the shame of his surrender and watched in his mind's eye as his crew lowered the flag. He had never surrendered before, but the presence of Raven and the boy aboard his vessel left him no choice. A rogue he might be, a thief and a sea raider, yes again, but

Captain Cesar Obregon would never knowingly place a woman or child in jeopardy. So the *Windthrift* struck its colors and the Hawk became a prisoner in his island home.

Johnny Fuller nudged him awake.

"Captain Obregon . . . you been hollering something fierce," the dirty-faced eight-year-old said. There was the look of age in his green eyes. But then, he had seen things.

Cesar Obregon opened his eyes and looked directly up at the soles of Honeyboy Biggs's worn boots. The irascible old cannoneer dangled from the stout limb of an oak tree that overhung the pit in which Obregon and the boy were imprisoned. Obregon struggled to his feet, dusted off his ragged shirt, and lowered his gaze. The sight of poor Biggs made him sick at heart and yearn for vengeance. He slammed his fist into the walls of the pit. Sixteen feet above him, none other than the Cayman himself peered over the lip and down at his prisoners. A stormy-looking sunrise provided a drab backdrop for Navarre as he grinned at Obregon.

"You slept well, my friend," said the Carib half-breed.

"Go to hell," Obregon snapped. His voice was a dry rasp. Navarre had ordered his pit guards to withhold water from the Cayman's captives. If hanging Biggs hadn't loosened the Castilian's tongue, perhaps watching the boy die of thirst would inspire Obregon to reveal the whereabouts of his ill-gotten gains. Rumor had it that Navarre had a fortune hidden somewhere on the island, and Obregon intended to have it.

"You do not sound cooperative today. How unfortunate," Navarre replied. He drew his cutlass and poked Biggs's corpse and set it swinging to and fro over the pit. The rope creaked where it came in contact with the gray bark. Biggs's hands had been

tied behind his back. His head was twisted now at a
garish angle, his features mottled, eyes blank with
death's sightless stare. He was beyond harm and
pain, but the indignity of his death and the treatment
he continued to receive cut Obregon to the quick.
Navarre sensed this and chuckled. "We had visitors.
None other than Captain Jean Laffite. He brought
some American lieutenant with him. They were looking for you."

Obregon fought back any display of emotion.
Laffite and McQueen here! No doubt they came looking for blood. No matter, either man or both would be
better than Navarre. And wait till I tell Jean about the
lead ingots and Jackson's ploy, thought Obregon.
We'll return to New Orleans and plunder Jackson's
coffers . . .

Navarre nudged a clump of dirt and sent it tumbling down on Johnny, who took up a different position below. The hole in the ground was no more than
ten feet across, but he managed to avoid the loose
earth. He knelt and scooped up a dirt clod and
launched it at his tormentor. Navarre had to quickly
duck to avoid being beaned. As it was, the clod sailed
over the edge of the pit and struck NKenai in the
neck. The African scowled and retreated out of
harm's way.

"Well done, young one." Obregon chuckled.
"Would that it had been one of my knives. With
Laffite here, we have a chance."

"And if Kit has arrived, I'll warrant Chief Iron
Hand can't be far behind," Johnny exclaimed.

"I entertained your friends and sent them on
their way," Navarre's voice drifted down to them.
"They were none the wiser." His grim visage appeared again. "Just tell me what I want to know and
I'll set you and the rest of your mates free."

"Very well, climb down here and let me whisper
it in your ear," Obregon retorted, inviting the brigand

to come within arm's length. His fists opened and closed. If he could only get his hands on the Cayman for just one brief moment . . . "You'll kill us no matter what I say. I'd sooner trust the sun not to burn than the likes of you!" A raindrop spattered against his cheek followed by several more droplets, and then a fine misting rain commenced. Obregon opened his mouth in gratitude. Nature had at least taken their side. They wouldn't die of thirst today.

"I'll have my reckoning with you, Orturo Navarre. I swear it. As God is my witness." But the news of Laffite's departure was a disheartening blow.

The Cayman only laughed. Men had threatened him before. "The Hawk screeches. But I have pulled your talons. You cannot stand against me. Before I am finished, you will welcome death." Rain formed rivulets across his shaved skull and dripped from his cheekbones. "Do you think me cruel? Mercy is for ordinary men." He fixed his stone-eyed stare at Johnny Fuller. The eight-year-old shrank back against Obregon. He was frightened. But he held another clod of hard earth and wasn't about to be taken without a fight. "Little one. Be brave. For the days to come will test your courage. I think I will cut off parts of your body and make you eat them." He glanced at Obregon. "Now do you see? You will tell me everything. Everything. In time."

Navarre straightened and issued orders for two of the guards he had stationed to remain at the pit. The brigands, neither of whom appreciated being left behind in the rain, dutifully took up their stations while four of their companions returned to the makeshift shelter they had erected out of ship's canvas, felling several saplings for support.

Navarre made his way out of the clearing and started back down the winding trail that would return him to the governor's palace. The path followed a natural incline, for Navarre had selected a site in a ravine between two hills well back of Morgan Town. The farmland was located further to the north, where broader gaps in the hills allowed longer periods of sunlight and the fertile soil coughed up fewer rocks with the passing seasons.

The pirate could have ridden a horse, but he did not trust the beasts and preferred to move along under his own power. NKenai's feet hurt, but he did not complain and fell in alongside the Cayman. Both men continued on through the misting rain. Navarre was strangely silent, wrapped in the mystery of his own thoughts, his mood darkening. He became increasingly gloomy the further from the pit they traveled. NKenai remembered earlier in the morning, when he had first brought news that Laffite was preparing to depart and had already dispatched most of his crew to the *Malice*. Even then, Navarre had appeared troubled. The African wondered if the captive Choctaw woman might be the cause, but he kept his questions to himself. Navarre was an intensely private man and did not welcome scrutiny. And yet, NKenai was worried. He glanced over his shoulder at the dozen well-armed brigands making up Navarre's personal guard. The escort was far enough behind the Cayman for NKenai to speak without them overhearing.

"Captain Navarre, *tafadhali mnisamehe,* please forgive me. But I sense you are troubled. As your loyal servant I ask if there is something I may do." NKenai lowered his gaze to the bone-handled guns jutting from Navarre's belt. The Cayman was dressed in a deep purple waistcoat that had begun to glisten with raindrops. Wet fronds whipped Navarre's black trousers and clutched at his ruffled shirt, but his guns were dry and shielded from the elements by his coat flaps. NKenai was prepared to bolt behind the nearest tree if Navarre reached for his guns.

"Troubled?" Navarre asked, as if the word were

utterly foreign to his ears. His hand drifted up to his chest and he began to subtly rub his breastbone. NKenai thought that an odd gesture, then decided to ignore it. The African did not want to press his luck. "Troubled, uh, no," repeated the Cayman.

Navarre's thoughts drifted back through the morning hours when he had woken to a woman's voice singing softly in a language he did not understand and found that Raven had not only recovered from the dream tea, but had left his bedside as the sun attempted to rise through the lowering clouds. Chanting filled the room. Orturo Navarre recognized that magic was being made and his flesh turned cold at the sound, for despite his civilized trappings he had a primitive's innate dread of things supernatural.

He found the half-breed woman crouched naked before the hearth. Her coppery flesh was streaked with a mixture of soot and blood. She had gouged the palms of her hands on a jagged outcropping of stone just above the mantle, smearing her life's fluid in snakelike designs over her chest and belly. Her rounded breasts were caked with crimson-coated ashes.

Navarre was appalled to find that Raven had marked him with the same mixture of her own blood and ashes while he slept, undisturbed by her touch, tracing the mark of the serpent from his chest to his loins. As she chanted, a look of triumph lit her features. Navarre scrambled off the bed and attempted to rub the "snake" from his chest. It was Raven's turn to laugh.

"Witch woman . . . what have you done?" Navarre blurted out.

"You will discover for yourself soon enough," she replied. "When your loins wither and courage fails and pain comes, then you will know. For you have dishonored me and there is a price to be paid." Raven stood before him, unabashed by her nakedness. She advanced on the pirate and leveled a finger at him, tracing in the air the mark of the snake. "The serpent is within you. It is your death. And you cannot escape. For I am Raven, Medicine Woman of the Choctaw, and the spirits of those who have gone before call me by name. The destroyer hears my voice and calls me by name. The soul stealer hears my voice and calls me by name."

"Conjure woman . . . this has cost you your life!" Navarre continued to paw at his flesh, smearing the design but failing to remove it from his skin.

"What will you do, strike me down? Go ahead." Raven opened her arms, leaving herself vulnerable to the brigand, even inviting his attack. "Touch me and awaken the serpent and die in agony! Cut short what life you have left." She stepped toward him. Navarre retreated toward the door, grabbing up his clothes in the process. His full-blown hatred of the woman was far outweighed by his dread of what she represented. He would have gladly struck her down, but not at the cost of his life. By the time his hand touched the door latch, his abdomen had begun to ache and he wondered if the serpent had indeed awakened.

He wondered still.

Making his way back from the pit, Navarre paused, pain returning as he stood in the center of the brush-lined trail. In his thoughts, he cursed his own weakness, the lust that had lured him to the conjure woman's bed. The sooner he was rid of her, the better. He wanted her off the island. But he wasn't prepared to sail to Cuba to sell her to some Spanish grandee. Then he thought of Artemus Callaghan. Of course. Make the slave trader a gift of the woman. Ah, but the Carolinan might suspect a ruse. Well, then, sell him all of the women, Raven among them. There would be other women for Navarre to groom for his private markets. The loss of the gold they would bring was a small price to pay to be rid of the Choctaw breed.

Tomorrow, then. Callaghan was departing and Raven with him. And until she was safely aboard the slave trader's brig, Orturo Navarre resolved to keep his distance.

"My captain," said NKenai, his ebony features glistening with moisture. "We must hurry. The rain . . ."

Navarre glanced about and wondered how long he had been standing in the middle of the path, lost in his thoughts while the rain increased in intensity. A regular cloudburst was upon them now. He tilted his head and allowed the rain to wash his leathery features, and felt the pain lessen. The serpent was sleeping. The Cayman breathed a sigh of relief and quickened his pace, forcing NKenai and his detachment of well-armed bodyguards to hurry if they wanted to keep pace with their fierce-looking captain.

A tody, a small ratlike animal indigenous to many of the islands of the Lesser Antilles, scurried out from under a canopy of fronds and darted into the underbrush, avoiding Navarre and his escort of brigands as they hurried past. The black-furred rodent remained in hiding even after the pirates had vanished from sight, for the tody's keen nostrils had picked up the scent of an oncoming party of intruders. A second pack of humans moved silently like wolves among the Caribbean pines, beneath green and gray mangroves. By a stroke of fortune, they narrowly avoided an accidental encounter with Navarre's contingent of freebooters. These newcomers were keeping well off the beaten path.

But the wise little tody wasn't fooled. It continued to cower in the emerald shadows while the gray rain fell. A boa constrictor, six feet in length, noticed the solitary rodent and decided to make a meal of the creature. The constrictor maneuvered its way underneath an outcropping of roots and slithered through a puddle of olive-colored rainwater. The tody appeared not to notice the predator, and for a moment it seemed as if the constrictor had discovered an easy dinner. But at the last minute, the second party of human intruders passed by, and in their wake, the tody scampered to safety and vanished into a thicket of yellow nightshade. The snake, rather than abandon its pursuit, slithered into the thicket after the rodent. Sooner or later it would find something to kill.

Chapter Twenty-one

"It's a poor place I've put you, lad," Obregon said, his back to the muddy wall behind him. Rainwater was seeping down the side of the pit and dripping from the boots of the hanged man; it drizzled down in a constant shower and turned the earth underfoot into slurry. "I've set one blunder atop the other, and all for a chest of lead ingots and the twinkle in a maiden's eyes." He kicked at the mud, removed his coat, and held it out to Johnny Fuller. "Fate and General Jackson have had the last laugh on me, I fear."

The boy glared at the blond-haired Spaniard and then shrugged and accepted the captain's offering. In the least, it would keep the worst of the downpour from battering him. He draped the coat over his head and held it up in front of his face like a canopy. The boy's stomach growled. He sighed and thought what he wouldn't give for a piece of Christian cheese right now. The widow LeBeouf always had cheese in her cellar and allowed the boy to eat his fill whenever he so desired. Johnny kept a stone face despite his hunger; he wasn't about to show weakness in front of Obregon. The boy had his pride, after all. He shifted his attention to the problem at hand.

"When do you think Captain Navarre will come for me?" he asked timidly, glancing up at Honeyboy Biggs. At least the gunner had died whole.

"Don't you worry," Obregon said. "I'll get us out of here. The Hawk of the Antilles has been in worse places before."

"Really," said the eight-year-old, wise beyond his years. "Name one."

Obregon cocked an eye at the lad. "Are you always so disrespectful to your elders?"

"Only when they get me killed," the boy retorted.

Obregon was at a loss for words. Thankfully he didn't have long to consider a reply when a length of knotted rope suddenly dropped into the pit and a voice from above called out, "Climb up."

Man and boy shared the same reaction. They stared at each other in surprise and then looked up through the rain. A broad grin spread across Johnny's features as Iron Hand O'Keefe peered over the edge of the pit. "Or do you aim to stay down there till you drown?"

"I told you!" Johnny exclaimed, leaping for the rope. "I told you Chief Iron Hand would come." Hand over hand he made his way up the rope, exhibiting all the agility of a monkey despite slick footing and the ordeal he had endured. Iron Hand reached out and hauled the youth up the last yard and jerked him out of sight. Obregon quickly followed, uncertain whether they meant him to be rescued or not. The climb was more difficult for him, but he gained the edge of the pit and clambered over to safety. In a glance he noted that Navarre's guards were huddled under their makeshift shelter, where no doubt they had chosen to wait out the rain. The pirates were ringed by Harry Tregoning, Strikes With Club, and Nate Russell, each of whom held a pistol on the half-dozen men Navarre had posted to guard the pit. Iron Hand O'Keefe, standing close-by, tousled Johnny's curly hair and then proceeded to scold him for running off to sea. Father Bernal abandoned the prisoners and approaching the pit drew abreast of O'Keefe.

"You have surprised me, Priest. I did not think you had the courage to act against the Cayman. I am in your debt," said Obregon with a sweeping bow.

"Not my debt," said Bernal. "But his." The priest indicated someone standing behind the Spaniard.

Obregon turned and prepared to repeat his bow. Kit's fist caught him on the tip of the jaw and sent the freebooter sprawling across the ground. Obregon struggled to his feet as Kit dove into him. Both men slammed into the ground. Father Bernal took a step forward as if to attempt to separate the two men. O'Keefe caught the priest by the arm and stopped him in his tracks.

"Hold it right there, Father," O'Keefe said with a wag of his shaggy head. "Best we let the lads get it out of their systems."

"But . . ."

O'Keefe brought his gleaming hook to his lips. "Shhh."

Obregon and Kit rolled over and over in the mud until the Castilian managed to break free of Kit's grasp. He struggled to his feet and clubbed his smaller opponent across the back of the neck, then aimed a knee at the bridge of Kit's nose. Kit deflected the blow with his forearm, caught hold of Obregon's right ankle, and twisted. The Spaniard howled with pain and fell over on his side.

Both men rose up and continued to batter one another, raining blow after blow, most of which glanced off their mud-spattered shoulders and drenched torsos. Then Obregon put everything he had into one mighty uppercut that caught Kit McQueen on the side of the head and staggered him. Obregon howled in triumph, thinking he had bested his opponent. But Kit did not go down. Instead the blacksmith's

son wiped his shirt sleeve across his square-jawed
features, spat a mouthful of blood, and sprang forward
just as Obregon attempted to finish him off. Kit drove
his head into the pit of Obregon's stomach and left the
Spaniard gasping for breath and dismayed. Red hair
plastered to his skull from the downpour, lower lip
puffed and swollen, Kit looked the worse for wear. But
appearances were deceiving. He wiped a forearm
across his face and smeared the mud and blood over his
cheek. Obregon took a step back in retreat.

"Now it's my turn," said McQueen.

"We'll see about that," said Obregon in a ragged
voice. His right arm sailed out, but Kit easily stepped
aside and landed a right fist to Obregon's side
and followed with a left to the Castilian's already-
bruised jaw. Obregon's knees buckled, and he
dropped forward but managed to catch himself, and
propped upright on his hands, managed to stand. Kit
hit him again and knocked the privateer to his knees
yet again. This time Obregon stayed put.

"Come on," said Kit. "I'm not done with you."

"Yes, you are, Lieutenant," O'Keefe said. "We
need the bastard. Father Bernal can't organize a rebellion without him." He patted Kit on the shoulder.
"Now there's a good lad."

"What rebellion?" Obregon said. He struggled
once more to his feet, but his muscles didn't thank
him for the effort. As he had done during their first
scuffle at the widow LeBeouf's party, McQueen had
taken all the Castilian had to offer and returned it
twofold. The Hawk had taken a beating and wasn't
anxious for this fight to continue. Maybe deep down
in the solitary island of Obregon's conscience, he
recognized that the punishment was well deserved.
He thrust out his hands, palm open, as McQueen
prepared to resume his attack. Cesar Obregon was
once more lowering his colors.

Father Bernal peered out from beneath the wide
brim of his hat. His arthritic fingers were folded as if

in prayer. The elements made his knees ache. My God, whither goest the bloom of youth? he thought, sighing. "I have called together all the farmers and merchants I can trust for a meeting tonight. We shall take back the island from the slavers."

"Captain Laffite has sailed for Obregon Cove to rescue your crewmen. They'll be back come sunrise," said Kit.

"And sail into a trap," said Obregon. "Laffite will run a gauntlet of fire from the twenty-four-pounders above and the twelve-pounders Navarre has hidden along the shore. They're rifled guns and shoot true. I know from experience. Laffite won't last half an hour."

"He will if we silence the twelves," said Kit, rubbing the knuckles he had bruised against the Spaniard's hard jaw. "The priest seems to think the inhabitants of Morgan Town won't rise up against these slavers unless they have you to lead them." He pulled a kerchief from his coat pocket and dabbed at the corner of his mouth; the cloth came away crimson.

"I suppose that is the reason why you didn't leave me in the hole to rot." Obregon snorted and spat another mouthful of blood and saliva. "I cannot blame you, *senor*." Obregon glared at Navarre's crewmen, who were still under the guns of Tregoning and the Choctaws. "I underestimated you, Lieutenant. That will not happen again. However, as we have a common enemy I will help you."

He tilted his features to the sky and allowed the rain to wash his battered flesh. Then he turned and drew a cutlass from O'Keefe's belt, then leaned over the edge of the pit and cut down Honeyboy Biggs, carried the old cannoneer into the underbrush, and tenderly laid the corpse beneath a canopy of broadleaf fronds. He muttered something beneath his breath that Kit took for a prayer and then patted the dead man's chest, stood, and returned to the clearing.

"Navarre shall answer for this, by all that is holy,

I swear it." Obregon met Kit's gaze and was surprised to find a glimmer of sympathy in the American's eyes. The Castilian nodded as if an unspoken understanding had been reached between him and the lieutenant. "So we are to silence the twelves, eh? Why stop there? I know of a passage on the hillside below the twenty-fours. It leads to the magazine. We could set off a charge that would bring down the wall on the battery of twenty-fours."

"That same group of men could sneak into the palace and free my daughter," O'Keefe emphatically suggested.

"And if we're lucky, we might even catch Navarre and force his brigands to surrender without a fight," Kit said. "Come along. There's work to be done." He spun on his heels and called out for Tregoning to securely bind and gag the prisoners. The priest had suggested Navarre's men could be hidden at one of the nearby farms, and Kit intended to take them to their makeshift prison without a moment's delay. He spoke with authority and his companions hurriedly complied, securing the guards with lengths of braided leather.

Obregon was accustomed to issuing orders, not taking them, and said as much to O'Keefe as he returned the cutlass to the broad-shouldered, shaggy gray-haired Irishman. O'Keefe scratched at his jaw with his hook. The sound of the iron barb scraping flesh made Obregon shudder.

"The lad does kind of take charge," O'Keefe agreed. Droplets glistened in the wiry gray bramble bush he called a beard. With a knowing chuckle to punctuate his departure, O'Keefe ambled across the muddy earth, leaving the Hawk of the Antilles to come to terms with the way things were. The Irishman's voice drifted back through the downpour, offering a final piece of advice. "Better get used to it."

Chapter Twenty-two

Kit had to give the townsmen and farmers credit, they didn't need to be talked into a fight. Once Obregon entered the dimly lit church and appeared in front of the altar, these former pirates and sea rovers hauled out their cutlasses and flintlocks and were all for charging out into the night, to avenge the wrongs inflicted upon them by Orturo Navarre and his crew of cutthroats. Kit argued for caution and patience, both of which were in short supply. Eventually with the help of Father Bernal and Cesar Obregon, McQueen managed to cool the angry words and soothe the righteous indignation that threatened to turn the gathering into a mob. Reason prevailed and the sixty-one shopkeepers, farmers, tradesmen, and fishermen agreed to hear the plan that Kit had formulated.

The shore batteries must be disabled under cover of night, each of the twelve-pounders spiked and rendered inoperable. Before sunrise, Kit and Obregon, the Choctaws, O'Keefe, and Harry Tregoning, proposed to make their way up the hillside to the narrow cave below the twenty-four-pounders. Once in the passage, the six men intended to enter the

governor's palace, free Raven, and hopefully capture
Navarre.

"And what if you're discovered?" asked a gunsmith in rolled-up sleeves, woolen breeches, and
apron. His name was Edward Pastusek, a fair-haired
Slav whose life had taken him far from the cold and
dreary villages of the Duchy of Warsaw to the sun-
drenched islands of the Cabibbean. At forty he hadn't
raised his hand in anger in over a decade. But time
had not mellowed the man; in fact, he seemed anxious for what lay ahead. Pastusek alone had brought
in over a dozen rifled muskets and as many pistols to
the church, not to mention a small crate of grenades,
iron-wrapped hand bombs with quick burning fuses.

"We intend to blow the magazine and bury the
twenty-four-pounders beneath the palace wall," Kit
interjected. "By then Laffite will have landed with
the crews of the *Malice* and the *Windthrift* and
stormed the gates."

"And if we're late reaching the walls?" one of the
farmers asked.

"Then we'll loose the dogs of war," Obregon
said. His voice sounded nonchalant in the heavy
silence that followed the question. Obviously, if Navarre's men were on the alert within the fortified
palace, then the handful of intruders accompanying
Kit and Obregon would be doomed. But with Laffite
gone, the pirates had relaxed their watch and abandoned the shore batteries for the pleasures to be
found in Morgan Town. Kit resolved to exploit such a
mistake to the fullest. These were Obregon's people,
and leaving the privateer to discuss the final details
with them, Kit stepped away from the altar and circled the gathering. Pastusek voiced a worry—
whether or not the rest of Morgan Town's inhabitants
would join the insurrection. A consensus was
reached that the remainder of the populace could be
counted upon once it became clear that Navarre was

in trouble. Human nature being what it was, Kit had his doubts, but he refrained from offering an opinion on the matter. After all, he was the stranger here and did not presume to make a judgment on the island's inhabitants.

The interior of the church had become unbearably stuffy. The windows were shuttered to avoid calling undue attention to the meeting within. O'Keefe was seated near the front door pining for a breeze, his features streaked with sweat. Johnny Fuller was lying on a pallet off to the right of the gruff-looking Irishman, who nodded in silent greeting as Kit approached. Directly behind the buckskin-clad man, a pair of moths fluttered in ever-tightening spirals around the glass chimney of an oil lamp. One of the insects, unable to resist the temptation, alighted on the chimney and died on contact with the heated glass and then dropped to the floor. The second moth continued to spiral around the flames, slowly, ever slowly, lured to its death by the brightness of the light and the beckoning warmth. Kit leaned over and extinguished the flame. The moth lost interest and fluttered away. In these final quiet moments before the violence of the day to come, all life seemed precious to him, even the most insignificant.

"Maybe you should stay here with the townsmen," Kit suggested to the Irishman.

"Not hardly."

"When was the last time you sneaked up on anything? Navarre's guards will probably have your big carcass in their sights before we ever reach the batteries," Kit protested.

"They'll be watching the road," O'Keefe said. "By my oath but I doubt there will be nary a man to watch the hillside. And you know it. So what's your point, younker? You aiming to leave Old Iron Hand out of things?" O'Keefe was a hard man to slip one past.

"I thought you might want to look after him," Kit replied, indicating Johnny Fuller asleep on a pallet near the door.

"I can take care of myself," the boy spoke up, and cracked an eyelid. He had been pretending to sleep, the better to overhear all the plans being made. He sat upright. "Besides, you'll be needing a man like Chief Iron Hand," the boy added. "Why, he routed an entire regiment of British back at New Orleans and chased them into the Mississippi, all by his lonesome."

"Well, you make a good point," Kit said, amused. He glanced at O'Keefe, who took out his hunting knife and whetstone from a deerskin pouch and began to sharpen the broad blade. "A whole regiment . . . my, my."

"Don't cut the lieutenant short, Johnny," said O'Keefe, clearing his throat. He continued to avoid Kit's gaze. "We need to give McQueen his due."

"I appreciate that," said Kit.

The front door opened, and Harry Tregoning stepped between the two men and saved O'Keefe from any further embarrassment.

Tregoning was armed to the teeth with pistols and cutlass and dagger. He wore the garb of a seaman: loose-fitting shirt and rain-spattered trousers, and he covered his thinning hair with a dark blue woolen cap whose crumpled brim seemed more an after-thought than an attempt to shade his eyes. On this moonless night, glare was the least of his worries.

"Me and your heathen brothers have something maybe you ought to see," said the man from Corn-wall. Without further explanation the man vanished through the doorway without so much as a by-your-leave. But the mystery he left in his wake propelled Kit into the night with Iron Hand O'Keefe hot on his heels.

Tregoning led his companions off to the right,
across the front of the church, and around the corner,
then down between the outside wall and a long low-
roofed storage shed where the farmers often stored
their sugar cane and other food crops at harvest time.
Tregoning entered the shed through a side door. Kit
and O'Keefe were only seconds behind him. The
interior of the shed was for the most part empty,
though the aroma of rotted cassava and bananas per-
meated the air. Nate Russell and Strikes With Club
were waiting within and they weren't alone. The
Choctaws had taken a prisoner, none other than Artemus Callaghan. The slave trader looked relieved at
the sight of Kit.

"Thank God," he exclaimed. "It's the lieutenant."

"I wouldn't count on God just yet," Kit told him.
He glanced at Nate Russell, an unspoken question in
his eyes.

"I caught him outside the church window," the
warrior said.

"He heard enough to get us all killed or I'm a
woodsprite," said Tregoning, and tugged the slaver's
oily tail of brown hair that dangled at the base of his
neck with a length of leather string.

"Mad. All of you," said Callaghan, searching
their faces for a trace of compassion. He didn't like
what he saw and shifted his attention to Kit. "See
here, you are an American soldier. Surely you have
not thrown in with this lot."

Kit leaned down in front of the slave trader and
focused his hard bronze eyes on the man. "See here,
Mr. Callaghan, *this lot* is acting on my authority. Your
friend, Captain Navarre, kidnapped an American citizen, a woman of no small authority. Under the personal directive of President Madison, I have been
assigned the task of returning this hapless lady to
New Orleans. I also have orders to apprehend or kill

the man responsible for her captivity along with any of his associates."

Callaghan gasped. "But . . . it's none of my concern. I came here to do business with Navarre. I swear I know nothing of this matter." His stubby hands began to tap nervously on his plump thighs. "Navarre means nothing to me. There are other islands and other men who know my name and would welcome my trade." He licked his dry lips and tried not to stare at Strikes With Club, who brandished a tomahawk and appeared most anxious to do the man harm.

"Where is this man's crew?" Kit asked of his companions.

"Aboard the *Homeward*," Callaghan nervously declared. "Look . . . I had no idea the government was involved. I am a law-abiding citizen, well respected in my community . . ."

"I don't have the time," Kit told Tregoning. "Keep him here until the shore guns are taken care of."

"And then what?" asked the marine.

"Put him aboard his boat," Kit replied. He put his face close to Callaghan's to ensure there would be no misunderstanding. "Jean Laffite will be arriving at sunup and things are bound to get nasty. Clear the port before sunrise or I cannot answer for your safety." He had no use for the slaver and deplored the peculiar institution that Callaghan represented. But they had enough enemies for one day. The slave ship carried no armament and posed no threat. And it was equally clear that the slave trader had no stomach for violence. Better to send the man on his way and avoid the chance of Callaghan's crew joining Navarre's forces.

"You have my word," Callaghan hastily agreed. "There's nothing to keep me here." Sweat had begun to collect in his jowls and soak the front and sides of his shirt. He scowled and shook his head and silently cursed "that damn cannibal" who'd gotten an honest merchant like Artemus Callaghan into such a terrible bind. Kidnapping a freeborn lady, a citizen no less!

"And you have my word that if you cross me or attempt to reach Navarre, I will personally hang you in Market Square," said Kit. He spun on his heels and stalked from the room with O'Keefe hurrying to catch up to him.

"A nice touch," said O'Keefe, "*by orders of President Madison.* Yes, indeed, very nice. You've a gift for the blarney." Exiting the storage building, O'Keefe caught his companion by the arm. "Hold up a minute, you headstrong Highlander." The two men faced one another in the alley. "What do you think our chances are?"

"Why? You worried?"

"Me? Hell, no!" said O'Keefe. "I can't wait to wring that cannibal's neck."

"Just take care you don't wind up his Sunday dinner," Kit said, poking the gray-haired man's girth.

"Not hardly." O'Keefe scowled, cinching his belt. He looked up and down the alley. The cloud cover worked in their favor. A moonless night was the best time for what lay ahead. "But if that pointy-toothed bastard has harmed a hair on my daughter's head . . ." His voice faded, the words caught in his throat, tears sprang to his eyes. O'Keefe was not a man given to emotion. He was grateful for the dark.

Kit patted the big Irishman's shoulder. "Come along, old friend. We have much to do. Even the darkest hour must have its dawn."

"*Una haja gani?* What can I do for you?" NKenai asked as he made his way across the night-shrouded courtyard to the lean-to barracks that ran the length of the north wall. The barracks consisted of a thatch roof jutting out from the wall to shield the men assigned to guard the governor's palace from the occasional rain showers. Word had reached Navarre's ebony-skinned lieutenant that Malachi Quince and some of the lads wished to speak to him. He found the wizened old cutthroat helping himself to a bowl of conch chowder from a black iron pot and a doughy chunk of fry bread. "You wished to speak to me?"

Quince hastily began to devour the contents of his bowl, using a wooden spoon to shovel chunks of greasy mussel, shark, rice, and pigeon peas into his mouth. Several other men in loose-fitting shirts, baggy trousers, and seven-league boots had momentarily set aside their weapons while they hurried through their dinner, wolfing down what food Quince had prepared for them. None of the men looked happy at the prospect of pulling another night of sentry duty on the walls, especially when many of their shipmates were enjoying a night of relaxation and excess fueled with near-lethal quantities of jack iron and sorrel.

"What, says you?" said the old sea rogue. "We all be worried about the captain. He don't seem his self. He's keepin' us penned up here when Laffite's gone and there be nobody to threaten us. We say it's time for us to set things back like before Laffite stuck his nose in here." Quince hitched up his trousers where they hung low around his bony hips. He wiped his mouth on his shirt sleeve, which was already stiff with grease. "And we figure maybe you'd talk to Captain Navarre for us."

Nkenai shrugged and then shook his head. "He has ordered me to the west wall to keep a harbor watch. Perhaps he does not believe that Laffite has truly left."

"A man ought to be wary of confronting the Cayman if the dark mood is upon him," another voice said from the men behind Quince. Tom Bragg limped forward to stand abreast of his old shipmate.

"What are you doing here, tavernkeeper?"
Nkenai asked.

"Why, visiting my brothers of the sea," said
Bragg. He hefted a dark brown bottle and tossed it to
the African, who caught the bottle in one hand. "I
brought up a wagonload of supplies for the governor's house." He indicated a flatbed wagon he had
left in front of the two-story stucco house that formed
the east wall of the compound. The two sentries
usually posted by the front doors were preoccupied
with unloading barrels of whale oil and crates of food
and drink, enough to stock Navarre's larder twice
over. "Let them lads work while I fire me some jack
with my former brethren." He clapped an arm around
Quince and planted a kiss on the side of the ugly little
man's cheek. The rest of the pirates broke into laughter as Quince howled and wiped his face and back-
stepped from Bragg.

"Curse your bones, you bastard. Try that again
and I'll shoot off your other leg!" Quince roared. The
angrier he became, the louder the laughter grew. Even
NKenai grinned as he abandoned the conversation
and started up the steps that led to the battlements.
The wooden walkway was slick from the rain and his
boots tended to slide on the damp path. He wasn't
alone on the wall. Half a dozen other men were
stationed around the compound. NKenai chose a spot
in the center of the north wall overlooking the bay. It
took a while for his eyes to adjust to the dark. On this
moonless night, without even a glimmer of lightning
to illuminate the hillside, posting him to harbor
watch was a waste of his time. But he wasn't about to
tell that to Navarre. NKenai leaned upon his elbows
and glanced down at the battery of twenty-four-
pounders below the walls. The dozen men Navarre
had manning those guns were resting as best they
could, curled up near sacks of powder and fuses and
pyramids of solid shot. His own eyelids began to feel

as heavy as timbers. If he could see the moon, he might be able to figure the time. No matter, it was plenty late, of that he was certain. His head drooped lower onto his forearms. He found a keg nearby and sat on it, then rose up to check the stygian expanse below. There was nothing to look at. He had to agree with Quince and the others—with Laffite and the American officer gone, things were back to normal. The only threat NKenai could see came from the Cayman himself and whatever demons were plaguing Navarre's own brooding mind.

Chapter Twenty-three

Kit McQueen, with candle in hand, stifled a sneeze as he made his way down the dusty center aisle of the powder magazine and followed Cesar Obregon over to the stone steps leading up to the palace compound. Despite his dangerous surroundings—after all, they were entering the Cayman's den—Kit was relieved to be out of the cramped confines of the tunnel. Strung out single-file, McQueen and his companions had never felt more at the mercy of the pirates in the palace.

"I'll attend the door bolt," said Obregon. He drew a dagger from his wrist sheath and trotted up the steps to the heavy-looking oak door that offered the next obstacle to bar their way. The privateer immediately began working on the outside latch, slipping his blade through a crack in the wood and easing the bolt out of its catch.

O'Keefe, Nate Russell, Strikes With Club, and Harry Tregoning made their way into the room and then closed the hinged panel of false-front shelves to once more conceal the passage that had bought them underneath the walls of Navarre's fortified palace. O'Keefe looked pale, and beads of sweat glistened on his leathery features and clung to the wiry netting of his graybeard. For one panic-filled moment he had become stuck in the passage. It had taken a concerted effort by Kit McQueen and Nate Russell to secure the burly Irishman's release. The four men found Kit McQueen hard at work on a keg of gunpowder. With his Arkansas toothpick he had whittled a hole in the top of the hogshead. Next he fit a goose-quill fuse into the gunpowder, transforming the keg into a bomb that would detonate the contents of the magazine.

A crash of steel brought everyone to attention. O'Keefe's leg had brushed against the basket hilt of a cutlass and knocked half a dozen of the weapons to the floor. Kit whirled around, his heart leaping to his throat. Silence filled the chamber as each man, fearing the worst, listened for the onrush of any guards alerted by the sound. When the worst failed to occur, the intruders breathed a collective sigh of relief.

An hour earlier, the last of the shore guns had been spiked and several prisoners taken without much ado. By the time the rebellious islanders arrived at the church, Hank Pariser, a farmer, was waiting with the welcome news that Navarre's lookouts on the point had been captured without a struggle. There would be no warning rocket lighting the night to announce Laffite's return. The liberation of the island was under way. What a shame to bring it to a halt in its infancy, thought Kit, by alerting half the brigands in the fort. Kit glared at O'Keefe, who sniffed defensively and nudged the sword blade with the toe of his boot.

"Cursed thing leaped out at me," he muttered.

"I damn near peed in my bloody pants," Tregoning said. The British marine shook his head and eased his curled finger off the trigger of his musket. He had almost fired off a shot by accident.

"Quiet!" Obregon hissed from the steps.

Kit motioned for Strikes With Club to ease past

his companions and approach the explosives. Kit handed him a tinderbox and striker. "Stay here in the magazine and watch the hacienda. If we get in trouble, fire the charge and escape through the passageway."

The warrior nodded in understanding. Sweat streaked his brown features. It was obvious he did not relish the idea of staying underground. But he was the likeliest choice, for his hair was long and unbound, his buckskin garb was that of his people, while the others, even O'Keefe and Nate Russell, were dressed for the most part as freebooters with little to give them away at a glance.

"I will remain," he said. Kit nodded, and started toward the steps. "Lieutenant . . ." Strikes With Club added. McQueen faced him again. "I think you speak straight. I think your heart is with my people, even more than you may know." The warrior was finished and stepped back to allow the others to pass.

Kit thought a moment and then replied, "I hear your words and know they are true." He clapped the warrior on the shoulder and started up the steps. Obregon was waiting for him. The Castilian had managed to work the latch free.

"Put out the candle and we'll see how things look," he said. Kit turned and gave the signal and Strikes With Club extinguished the candle, plunging the interior of the chamber into total darkness. Kit was reminded of the narrow opening in the hillside and the close confines of the passage that formed the secret entrance into the governor's palace. Josiah Morgan's escape route had not saved the life of that hapless governor, but it might end the reign of terror that had plagued Natividad since the arrival of Orturo Navarre.

Kit and Obregon eased the door open and peered out into the night-shrouded courtyard. Kit immediately noted that Tom Bragg had managed to leave his wagon in front of the hacienda. So far so good, he thought.

"Like in the bullfight, when matador and bull face one another across the cape for the last time, this, my friend, is the moment of truth," said Obregon.

"I'm not your friend," Kit retorted. "I just want to know one thing. Are you in this to the finish or do you plan to run out again like at New Orleans?"

"I have killed men for less," the Castilian said, bristling. He ran a hand across his blond mustache and twisted the tips as he stared at Kit.

"Maybe you lads can worry about this later," O'Keefe suggested. He eased his great bulk up the steps to the door. "How'd you figure we could get to the hacienda?"

"We walk across, single file, like we have nothing to hide," said Kit.

"Just like we own the place, eh, mate?" Tregoning's voice rose up from the bottom of the steps.

"We do," Kit replied. He stood and opened the door and stepped out into the courtyard and found he had to struggle to suppress the feeling of being a target for every rifled musket lining the ramparts. He lowered his head and motioned for Obregon and the others to fall into step behind him. The Spaniard emerged, followed by Nate Russell, Harry Tregoning, and, last but certainly not least, Iron Hand O'Keefe. The Irishman had divested himself of his musket and instead cradled a pair of Congreve rockets in his brawny embrace. It took a moment for him to maneuver them through the entrance. In the magazine he'd cracked off the ends and shortened the rockets by about a couple of feet. He wasn't worried about how well they'd fly. Distance wasn't an issue.

"Iron Hand?" Kit whispered.

"Never can tell, they might come in handy," he protested in a hushed tone. "Anyway, I dodged so many of these in New Orleans I'd kind of like to have a couple for my own.''

Kit shook his head in despair and quietly closed the door after the irascible graybeard. He glanced up at the north wall and could make out the dimly seen silhouettes of Navarre's sentries. Behind the powder magazine, a row of slumbering men lifted a guttural chorus of snores to the overcast sky. He couldn't see any guards by the gate, but Kit knew they must be there. And across the compound the main force of Navarre's disgruntled crewmen settled into restless sleep.

The hairs rose on the back of Kit's neck and he turned around to find a night-shrouded sentry watching him from the north wall. He couldn't make out the pirate's features, a fact that worked to Kit's advantage as well. Kit stepped aside and waved a hand in the observer's direction. The man on the wall seemed to hesitate, then returned the greeting and sat back on the barrel he'd been using for the better part of the night. Kit took his place alongside Obregon. The darkness hid the fleeting look of appreciation that flashed in his eyes. The column of men started across the compound to the hacienda where a couple of Navarre's men sat dozing in chairs outside the front door to the governor's house. Nate Russell slid a knife from his belt. Obregon still clutched his razor-sharp dagger. For the men by the door, it was time to die.

From his vantage point on the wall, NKenai had noticed the men emerging from the powder magazine and had considered challenging them; after all, he was Navarre's second-in-command. But the African dismissed such a notion. No doubt Navarre had issued more of those strange orders whose intent the entire crew had ceased trying to second-guess. Curiosity and a smidgeon of wounded pride wasn't worth the effort. So NKenai returned his attention to the bay he could not see and with weary eyes probed the obsidian night for a threat the African believed no longer existed. He never heard the muffled slap of the waves against the wooden hull of the schooner nor glimpsed a patch of sail against the moonless fathoms of night as the *Malice,* guided by the unerring seamanship of Jean Laffite, rounded the point and headed into the bay.

Chapter Twenty-four

There were other women in the governor's palace. Navarre could have had his choice of any one of the five African slaves at the rear of the house. But he was drawn to Raven's bedchamber, urged on by the turmoil that plagued him night and day. He knew she would be there; she had no choice. The door to the room could be bolted from the outside, an addition Navarre's shipwright had personally installed. The wrought-iron grating that covered the windows had been the former governor's idea. The woman within the room was Navarre's prisoner, yet through her witchery, Raven had also imprisoned the Cayman, trapping him in a device of his own creation, the half-breed's own deep-seated superstitions and primal fears.

Raven was seated by the window overlooking the courtyard when she heard the door bolt slide back. Navarre entered the room and closed the door after him. He remained with his back to the oaken panels and watched her in silence. The pirate captain wore a nut brown woolen coat and tight trousers and boots of Spanish leather that were muddy at the toes.

He unbuttoned his coat and untied his shirt lacings, then ran a thumb down his sternum.

"Conjure woman, take back your curse," he said.

Raven breathed a sigh of relief. *I still have him.* She silently uttered a prayer of thanks to her mother, the Choctaw medicine woman, who had taught her daughter the sacred rituals and insisted the young girl learn them by heart whether Raven believed in their power or not. *One day the mystery will reveal itself to you, my little one. Trust me. Trust the songs.* Raven had never really put much faith in them; still, she had foretold of a British defeat in New Orleans. And now, when confronted by her cruel captor, Orturo Navarre, the rituals and songs had become her only weapons. She had discovered a way to make him pay for what he had done to her. Nothing was going to deter her vengeance.

"It will end when the snake strikes," Raven answered. She was determined to conceal her own misgivings. She wanted to appear confident, a woman in control of her own fate despite the bars on the window and the bolted door.

"And if I said I would set you free?"

"I would call you a liar."

Navarre pursed his lips and scratched at the side of his shaved skull. It appeared solitude had not dulled the keen edge of her anger. He swaggered across the room and slumped into a high-back chair by the fireplace. The hearth was the former governor's concession to the memories of his past. Josiah Morgan had come from Danbury, Connecticut, where a winter's chill demanded a cheerful blaze in every room. No doubt he had missed the merry crackling of a fire, and despite the rarity of a truly cool night in the Caribbean, the deceased Mr. Morgan had built the hacienda to suit himself, hence the fireplace.

Minutes seemed to crawl past. Raven did not

move; rather, she kept her vigil in the seat by the window. Navarre crooked a leg over the arm of the chair. His was a crafty mind. He hadn't told Raven this was to be her last night in Natividad. Tomorrow she would be ferried out to Callaghan's boat and then good riddance. He'd see how effective her curse was from hundreds of miles at sea.

"Bring me something to drink," he ordered.

"I am not your slave," she replied. Raven reached down by her side and produced a small stoneware bowl in which there remained ashes and dried blood, a mixture she had reconstituted with rainwater. She leaned to the right and dabbed the outline of a snake upon the white clay wall beside her. She repeated the gesture on the wall to her left.

Suddenly Navarre stood and knocked the chair over as he stretched to his full height and pulled one of the pistols from his belt and advanced on her. Raven braced herself for the shot to come.

"I'll show you death, conjure woman. Your own!"

"Do not seek to threaten me," she calmly replied. "Before the echo of your gunshot fades, the snake will devour you. The beast of the hollow mountain will clean your bones." Raven gathered all her resolve and laughed in his face, knowing full well she was tempting fate to do so. But the only thing he respected was strength and she had to prove to him she was unafraid to die. The wind gusted through the window and made a moaning sigh and caught her unbound hair and set it rippling as if her long black tresses had become endowed with serpentine life. The pirate halted in his tracks and then retreated toward the door. He felt a stabbing pain in his belly. The snake had awakened. Only Navarre's pride kept him from fleeing the room. He regretted ever entering and began to wonder whether or not the Choctaw breed had lured him in the first place.

"Enough of your chatter, conjure woman," said Navarre, reaching for the door behind him. He lowered his pistol and returned it to his belt. "Soon I will be done with you. I will break your power. And you will regret the day you ever chose to anger me." He opened the door and drew himself upright, swelling with pride and bluster. "I am Orturo Navarre whom men call the Cayman, I am the master of Natividad. Who is there who can stand against me?"

"Will I do?" a voice said from the doorway. Navarre spun about and caught a faceful of Kit McQueen's iron-hard fist. The blow lifted Navarre completely off the floor and sent him sprawling into the center of the bedroom where he landed, bleeding, unconscious, and, for the moment, as much of a threat as a rag doll.

Kit held out his arms. Raven ran to fill them. They held one another, without uttering a sound, just holding one another, feeling their hearts beat as one. Their kiss was fire. The only interruption occurred when Navarre moaned and stirred and attempted to rise. Raven freed herself from Kit's hungry embrace to crack the Cayman across the skull with one of his own guns. The pirate went limp. Then she returned to the arms of the man she loved, the man she knew would never stop looking for her as long as the winds blew and stars sparkled and the sun shone.

"I love you," Raven whispered in his ear. The words returned in an instant, for man and woman had been speaking at the same time.

"I love you," said Kit McQueen.

Chapter Twenty-five

Navarre sat on the stairway, shoulders hunched forward, his hands bound at the wrists. His head felt as if it were about to split wide open. As he lifted a hand and gingerly probed his broken nose, then checked his mouth and found a couple of his pointed teeth were loose, he began to see the reality of his situation in a clearer light. True, he was at the mercy of these intruders, but they in turn were trapped within the palace compound. It made for a precarious situation all the way around.

The hours after midnight seemed interminable to all but the two guards who had been stationed outside the front door and now lay dead in the hall between the front of the hacienda and the kitchen at the rear. The guards never knew what hit them, their outcries muffled as knives were plunged home. Within moments the two had been dragged inside to expire within the governor's house.

The front of the palace was a long high-ceilinged room divided by the wide stairway. The front rooms, both sitting room and conservatory, were spacious and heavily windowed. The sitting room to the right of Navarre was appointed with several ornately carved chairs, a settee, end tables, and an armoire. An arched entrance opened into a conservatory to the Cayman's left.

The palace, such as it was, had been a comfortable place and Josiah Morgan, the former governor before Navarre had made a meal of the poor man, had frequently entertained, enjoying the conversation and fellowship of his friends from town and the outlying farms. Under Navarre, the palace had become tomblike, a place the island's inhabitants feared to visit.

The Cayman lifted his head and gazed at Kit McQueen, focusing all his hatred on the lieutenant who had orchestrated this terrible turn of events. But Navarre did not despair. He'd find a way out and kill the American officer and the conjure woman, too.

"I don't like this waiting much," Tregoning spoke up. The British marine checked the loads in his pistols for the third time. He and Nate Russell were peering out the conservatory window. From time to time he'd rub the back of his neck and look over his shoulder where a single dimly burning lamp in the hall washed the two corpses in an amber glow.

Kit had taken up a place by the door and kept vigil at the gunport, which permitted him to take in the entire compound at a glance. Iron Hand O'Keefe was in the sitting room with his daughter, enjoying a heartfelt reunion.

Obregon entered from the dining room behind the conservatory, a glass of madeira in his hand. He raised the glass in salute to Kit, gulped it down, set the glass on the floor, and continued on over to Navarre. The blond-haired Castilian glared down at the half-breed Carib and scowled.

"You are a lucky man, Orturo Navarre. I would nail your cock to a barrel and push you over backwards—if you were my prisoner." Obregon nudged the Cayman's boots. "I might do it yet."

"But he isn't your prisoner," said Kit.

"No. But you are a man of honor," said the Hawk of the Antilles. "Allow my enemy and me to settle what is between us, as men should, with cutlass in hand." Obregon trembled as he spoke, not from fear but the overwhelming need he felt for revenge. His whole being demanded such a meeting. "Navarre must answer for what he has done: have you forgotten Father Bernal's accounts of this man's unspeakable conduct?"

"He will answer for them, on a gallows in New Orleans," Kit said.

"No. He must die by my hand!" Obregon snapped.

"You'd do well to heed me," Kit said. He was nearly a decade older than Obregon and had learned the costly nature of hate. "Leave Navarre to my country's justice. Revenge can be a two-edged sword and as apt to cut both ways."

"I must be the one!" Obregon retorted.

"For one who still bears the stench of the pit, how quickly you pursue your death," Navarre said at last. He spat at the Castilian, who drew a hand back to slap Navarre.

"Cesar. Let it be!" Kit snapped. "You'll do as I say or I'll have you bound alongside him."

Obregon turned to glare at Kit. The Castilian's eyes were wild looking, like a man struggling to contain a fury that threatened to burst him at any moment. Obregon reached for the knives sheathed at his wrist.

"Haven't you caused enough problems for us?" Raven said from the entrance to the sitting room. O'Keefe was standing behind his daughter, looming over her and fixing the Castilian in a stare as warm as the iron hook he had for a hand. But it was Raven's words that hit home. Because of his rash deeds she had suffered cruel indignities and almost lost her life. She still might. The Hawk of the Antilles had much to answer for. Confronted with his own misdeeds, Obregon lowered his eyes and, with remorse for his conduct, sheathed his daggers, and glanced from Raven to Kit.

"I am not so blind that I can not see the truth. I am not so deaf that I cannot hear." He bowed to Raven and then to Kit. Navarre began to laugh, as if to taunt the Castilian and goad him into action.

"You are all going to die. All of you are my prisoners, and you don't even know it." The Cayman looked around at Tregoning and Nate Russell. "However, I will show mercy to my friends."

"I believe that fellow Tom Bragg was a friend of yours, mate, and you bloody well rewarded him for his troubles by blowing his leg off." Tregoning shook his head in disgust. "Let's gag the bastard and be done with it. Though Mr. Obregon's suggestion about the barrel has merit, if you ask me."

"Something's going on!" Nate Russell called out, his face inches from the partly shuttered window.

Kit returned his attention to the gunport. Sure enough, the compound had instantly transformed itself into a scene of frantic activity. Men were awake and hurrying to the walls. Listening, he could hear what sounded like a rumble of distant thunder and assumed a melee had broken out in town. Laffite must have arrived. Kit refused to contemplate otherwise.

The lieutenant turned to his companions. "Navarre's men are on the walls. Their backs are to us. We'll make a try for the main gate. If these brigands notice us, I don't think they'll open fire for fear of hitting their captain." In these early predawn hours, the darkness had brightened enough for the front gate to be visible. Kit looked at Navarre. "If we're stopped, tell your guards that you are taking a small detachment of men to find out what's happening in town." The ruse might work, as even Raven was dressed in breeches and a shirt and looked like a young man at first glance. If trickery failed, they still had Navarre, and despite the Carib's air of unconcern, Kit doubted the man would risk a bullet just to spoil their escape.

"He'll do as you say or I'll carve my name in his side," Obregon said. "With your permission, of course."

"You have it." Kit grinned. He glanced at O'Keefe and Raven, then Nate Russell and Harry Tregoning. They had come a far piece together. Each of them was someone to ride the river with. "Let's go."

Kit opened the door and stepped outside. A warm moist breeze brushed across his face carrying the smell of rain and smoke. He looked toward the powder magazine and raised a hand to wave toward the shadowy entrance and the unseen figure of Strikes With Club watching from across the compound. The Choctaw knew what to do: set a fuse burning and escape back down the passage.

McQueen had considered all of them trying for the magazine passage, but if they attracted attention and were discovered, it might jeopardize silencing the battery on the other side of the palace walls. No, the front gate offered the only escape for the rest of them.

Raven and her father were right on McQueen's heels, followed by Obregon and Navarre, Nate Russell, and Harry Tregoning. The marine glanced back through the open door and saw that the African women who had shared captivity with Raven had congregated on the stairs. Now there was a waste of some comely lasses, the man from Cornwall thought with regret, and he wondered if he should have volunteered to remain behind, sort of as their protector. There was no room for these ebony lovelies in the wagon, and besides, the women's presence would have attracted undue attention.

Kit climbed aboard the wagon and took the reins in hand and trained one of his pistols at Orturo Navarre as the pirate chieftain joined him on the seat. Cesar Obregon sat behind the Cayman, the point of his dagger nudging the prisoner's side. O'Keefe, Raven, Tregoning, and the Choctaw, armed to the teeth with pistols and muskets, swords and a pair of Congreve rockets, climbed aboard and settled down in the wagon bed. With a flick of the reins, Kit started the mares toward the main gate. So far so good, he told himself. His optimism lasted all of a couple of minutes, just before all hell broke loose.

NKenai had rounded the wall and was standing on the ramparts above the front gate. He stared at the blossoming muzzle blasts, deeply perplexed by the conflict that had erupted in town. The exchange of gunfire was impossible to mistake. He had heard it many times before.

"*Sifahamu.* I do not understand this," he said beneath his breath. Men lined the walls now, all of them with muskets. The swivel guns were trained on the road leading up from town; the palace defenders were ready. The African's keen eyes searched the harbor as the sky began to slowly brighten despite the gloomy canopy of morning clouds ripe with moisture. His brows arched and he cursed beneath his breath when he realized Laffite's schooner, the *Malice,* had anchored alongside Navarre's brig. The ship was dimly seen at first, but NKenai recognized the cut of the sails and the lay of the ship in the bay. One thing more made it eminently clear that the schooner meant trouble. The vessel loosed a broadside with its sixty-four-pound carronades into Navarre's *Scourge.*

The brig was manned by a skeleton crew jolted from their sleep as the carronades continued to maul the vessel, crushing the hull with solid shot and raking the decks with chain and grapeshot.

The battery of twenty-four-pounders below the palace walls opened up with a single cannon trying to establish the range. Malachi Quince was exhorting his gun crews to sink Laffite's ship before the brig went under. The wiry little brigand had a tongue that bit like a cat-o'-nine-tails, and he blasted the tardy crewmen for their lack of speed and erring aim. An unanswered question lingered in the air like trailing gunsmoke . . . Where were the shore guns? Why hadn't they opened up and riddled Laffite's ship? Why no warning rocket from the point? NKenai could only surmise someone had silenced the lookouts as well as the twelve-pounders and their crews.

Indeed, anything could have happened under the cover of such a bleak and moonless night as this had been, NKenai told himself. There but for fortune, Captain Laffite and his crew might have marched right up to the walls. Under cover of darkness, who could distinguish friend from enemy? At night all cats are gray.

Nkenai froze and remembered the half-dozen men who had emerged from the powder magazine, a couple of hours past. Their faces had been indistinguishable. But who were they? How much trust had hinged on one man's casual wave of a hand? Too much, came the answer. He stared at Morgan Town. The cries of men carried to him now, and the clash of cutlass punctuated by pistol shot and musket fire. Some of the buildings were ablaze, and against the flames, the silhouettes of men locked in a life-and-death struggle were made strikingly visible.

"What do we do?" said one of the pirates, worry in his voice. The *Scourge* had lost a mast and was beginning to list to starboard.

NKenai had seen enough. He spun around and took up one of the torches that had been set in brackets along the wall providing enough light for men to load by. With every intention of heading for the governor's palace and alerting Captain Navarre, the African drew up sharply as he spied the wagon approaching from the governor's hacienda. NKenai noticed the Cayman sitting on the seat and heard the pirate captain call out to the guards at the gate to unbolt the iron-fitted oaken doors while the wagon was still some distance from the main entrance. NKenai frowned and hurried to the steps that led down to the entrance gate, and gave orders along the way for silver-haired Rico Amidei, the shipwright, and several of the cutthroats close at hand to follow him.

"Captain Navarre! It is not right for you to leave us. There is fighting in town!" NKenai shouted. Who were the men with the Cayman? NKenai threw his torch to the ground in front of the team of mares pulling the wagon. The startled animals pawed the earth and whinnied and fought the reins and refused to proceed further. The wagon was about fifty feet from the gate. NKenai was determined to halt its progress until he learned the identity of its human cargo. He snapped another order that sent four more brands spinning through the night to land to either side of the wagon. The wet ground caused the flames to sputter, but they continued to burn and bathe the wagon in firelight.

In the glare of the torches the faces of Navarre's escort were at last revealed. Kit McQueen stood in the wagon box so that NKenai and his cohorts could see the American officer had the reins in his left hand and, in the other, one of his fifty-caliber Quakers jabbed against Navarre's neck. Kit swept the walls in a single glance. It seemed just about every musket lining the battlements was suddenly trained on them. Kit's accomplices in the wagon leveled their rifled muskets at the surrounding cutthroats. Raven checked the loads on the bone-handled pistols she had taken from Navarre. If there was to be a fight, she was determined to prove herself the equal of any man.

"What now?" O'Keefe muttered, eyeing the overwhelming force that threatened to riddle them with lead. He wondered how many slugs it would take to bring him down. He didn't aim to go gentle.

"We wait," said Kit.

"Throw down your guns," NKenai shouted. His voice carried a trace of anxiety. The sporadic gunfire by the water signaled the battle for Morgan Town had just about ended. The twenty-four-pounders outside the walls continued to boom defiance. "*Husikilizi*. You are not listening. Throw down your guns or we will kill you."

"You are a clever man, Lieutenant McQueen. I offered mercy once. I will not offer it again," said Navarre. Sweat had begun to trickle down his shaved skull. "Put down your guns. Leave this island. I give you your freedom. Take the girl. And her father. I give you this last chance."

"And what about Obregon and Father Bernal and the rest of the people on the island?" asked Kit, buying every precious minute he could.

"What happens to them will happen whether I kill you or not," said Navarre. He stood, braving the pistol at his throat. "I see something in your eyes, eh. Defiance. We are much alike, you and I, Lieutenant. We are not afraid of death." Navarre smiled and raised his hand to the pistol. "What will you do?"

"Wait," Kit replied. *Any second now. Please, God, any second now.*

"For what!" Navarre snapped. An instant later, he found out. The earth buckled and heaved; explosions followed one upon the other; a cloud of debris, some of it fist-sized chunks of stone, showered the compound. The wagon was thrown over on its side, spilling Kit and his companions onto the trembling ground. The singletree shattered and the startled mares raced off toward the makeshift barracks. One of the mares lost its footing and went down, whinnying in agony. Men toppled from the walls to suffer broken limbs as the magazine continued to rock the compound with one explosion after another. A tremendous fireball erupted into the night sky. The wall overlooking the bay crumpled outward to bury the four-gun battery and its crew beneath tons of rubble. One final blast shook the compound, and black smoke erupted from the pit that had once been the powder magazine.

Kit rose up on his hands and knees and, steadying himself against the wagon, scrambled to his feet and stumbled over to Raven, who had suffered a bruised forehead but was none the worse for the experience. Kit didn't try to speak. His ears were ringing and he doubted either of them would be able to hear. A bullet clipped the wooden wagon bed and another glanced off an iron wheel rim. Kit ducked, and swung around. Finding his pistol in the dust, he immediately primed the weapon with a sprinkle of gunpowder from his brass flask. The pirates were upon them, materializing out of the smoke. Kit fired and saw a man in a ragged shirt drop his cutlass and clutch at his face. Raven, kneeling, her eyes streaming tears from the grit, searched in vain among the debris for Navarre's pistols.

Other guns came to the couple's defense as Iron Hand O'Keefe led Nate Russell and Harry Tregoning into the fray. Cesar Obregon limped along after the others; he had broken an ankle falling from the wagon and was using his musket as a crutch. Even injured, the Hawk of the Antilles proved himself a formidable foe. He managed to brace himself against the side of the wagon and fire his musket one-handed. The musket's recoil nearly toppled him. He cheered as one of

Navarre's henchmen stumbled and fell back into the dust, clutching his side. Obregon tossed the musket aside and drew his cutlass as Rico Amidei tried to bring him down with a quick thrust. Cesar Obregon parried the shipwright's blade and buried his own length of steel in the pirate's abdomen, dispatching him to perdition. Harry Tregoning sang hymns while he loaded and fired, loaded and fired. Nate Russell stood abreast of his English companion and matched him shot for shot.

Navarre's crewmen staggered out of the settling dust, stumbled, clutched their wounds, some returned fire, while others sank to the ground and died or turned tail and ran for cover. Musket balls and pistol shot gouged holes in the earth around the wagon and thwacked into the wooden bed and siding. Suddenly Nate Russell rose up on his toes and clutched at his chest, then sagged against Tregoning, who lowered the Choctaw to the ground. O'Keefe noticed his friend was hurt and knelt at the warrior's side. Nate was trying to speak, but the noise was too great. He shook his head and sighed and then settled into death. It was over in a matter of seconds; one moment the Choctaw was alive and defiant, the next, dead.

"You poor bastard," said O'Keefe. "Come all this way to die." He squeezed Nate's shoulder until he felt the warrior go limp. Then Iron Hand O'Keefe rose up in his fury and charged into the smoke, scattering pirates before him like so many leaves in a hurricane. The hook rose and fell and soon was drenched with blood. Harry Tregoning took his stand by Obregon and began to calmly load and fire his rifled musket with uncanny accuracy.

The gates . . . we need to open the gates, Kit thought as he rammed a powder charge down the barrel of his flintlock. Suddenly, NKenai loomed out of the sooty gray smoke that drifted over the compound from the burning ruins of the magazine. The African lunged straight toward Kit and swung a scimitar in a vicious arc that McQueen barely avoided by ducking beneath the flashing steel. The blade clanged off a wheel rim. Kit dropped his unprimed pistols and reached for his Arkansas toothpick. NKenai tried to back away to give himself the advantage with his longer blade, but Kit stayed with him.

NKenai slashed with his curved blade and carved a chunk of flesh from Kit's shoulder. The American lieutenant entangled his legs with the African's and both men went down. Kit landed on NKenai's chest and drove his knife into his enemy's torso once, twice, a third time, while the African clawed at the lieutenant's throat.

"Enough. You have killed me," NKenai moaned. His ebony features were a mask of hatred as his hand fell from Kit's neck, tearing his shirt in the process.

"Where's Navarre?" Kit asked, glancing around for the Cayman, gritting his teeth against the pain of his shoulder wound.

NKenai tried to laugh, but only managed to choke on his own blood. He no longer saw the smoke or McQueen's face. Instead he was standing in his village on the coast of East Africa and he was a child seated before his grandmother's lodge. He held the *udi* his father had made for him, a small wooden boxlike instrument strung with gut strings. NKenai coaxed a discordant tune from the instrument and watched for the old woman who had raised him. He thought he saw her stirring in the shadows of the lodge. *"Nyanya,"* he called out. Was she inviting him into the cool shadows? Of course. He was always welcome. The boy, NKenai, stood and entered the darkness.

Kit crawled to his feet and searched the acrid smoke for some sign of Navarre. He shouted the Cayman's name and heard laughter in reply. The flesh-eating son of a bitch was taunting him, daring Kit to follow him into the black mist. The front gate was somewhere ahead. Kit heard gunfire and instinctively ducked before realizing the shots weren't meant for him. Several of the pirates had returned to the walls. The swivel guns began to blast away, wreaking havoc with their grapeshot on a force of men approaching up the town road. Navarre or the front gate, Kit resolved to reach one or the other. He charged through the screening black smoke toward the entrance.

"No," Raven called to him from the overturned wagon. The medicine woman held the Quakers primed and loaded in her hands. She stamped her foot and mentally decried all such brave and foolish men who were so awfully quick to sacrifice their lives. She and Kit had just found one another, for heaven's sake. Raven was not about to lose him again.

The young woman not only realized the front gate must be opened, she had just the key—one of the Congreve rockets her father had pilfered from the magazine. Harry Tregoning noticed her struggling to dig the rocket out from underneath the wagon.

"I think I can help you with this, missy."

"Do you know much about these rockets?" she asked him.

"English rockets, missy. And I'm an Englishman. Me and Lord Congreve here be old chums." Harry put his back against the wagon, Obregon helped as best he could, but the wagon bed was too heavy for them. Then all of a sudden, a third back was added to the effort. Strikes With Club had rejoined his beleaguered companions. The Choctaw had risked life and limb to fight alongside his comrades at arms. His had been a grueling climb over a treacherous mound of rocks and timber and the grisly broken bodies of the wall's former defenders.

Together the three men raised the wagon bed

enough for Raven to drag the six-foot-long rocket free. Strikes With Club spied Nate Russell's body in the dust and a flicker of emotion crossed the Choctaw's stoic features. He looked away, wiping the tattered bloody sleeve of his buckskin shirt across his soot-streaked face. The young warrior had come to respect Russell and he vowed there would be time for grieving. Strikes With Club shouldered his rifle and loosed a shot in the direction of several wounded pirates who had taken to sniping at anyone who moved in the vicinity of the wrecked wagon.

"Bloody hell! The fuse is damaged," Tregoning muttered. "But I can fix it. I need a small blade."

"Will this do?" asked Obregon. He slipped one of the daggers from his wrist sheath and tossed it to the ground at the marine's feet. A musket ball glanced off a wheel spoke and dusted the privateer with splinters. Obregon cursed and answered with a pistol shot. "Whatever you're about, you had better hurry. They'll be on us again any second."

A sudden increase in musket fire preceded Iron Hand O'Keefe's arrival back behind the wagon. The big man slumped against the wood and tried to catch his breath. His pistols were gone, as were his cutlass and tomahawk. But his iron hook was sticky and crimson. O'Keefe was bleeding from half a dozen wounds, none of which appeared to be fatal. He saw what Raven was up to and grinned.

"No man ever had a better daughter. Smart as a whip, too. She takes after her pa."

"Talk yourself blue in the face, for all I care, but if you ever run off like that and try and get yourself killed, best you don't come back or I'll shoot you myself!" Raven scolded. She glared at the silver-haired war chief and then, despite her anger, knelt at his side and hugged his burly neck. She grabbed his whiskers and gave a gentle tug. "You hear me?"

He heard.

"There you be, missy. Lord Congreve is at your service," said Tregoning. He had balanced the rocket on a wheel and pointed the weapon in the direction of the front gate.

Raven took up one of the Quakers and, pointing the pistol at the dirt, held the flash pan near the fuse, and slowly squeezed the trigger . . .

The rage was upon Kit McQueen. Armed with his broad-blade hunting knife, he stalked his victims amid the swirling smoke, rising from a crouch to knock a man senseless with the heavy iron embossed grip, darting away and catching another pirate attempting to reload and slipping the razor-sharp blade beneath the brigand's ribs and finding the heart, his left arm encircling his prey's throat to cut off any cry.

This was the Highland rage, the black anger, the fire whose flames could only be doused with the blood of his enemies. A pirate with a patch over his right eye charged from underneath the wall. He was fair-haired and lithe of limb and fearless as he tried to crush McQueen's skull with the butt of his musket. Kit's powerful left arm shot up and stopped the musket in midswing and then straightened, stiff-arming the freebooter square in the face. "Patch" went reeling backward and crashed into the stewpot, spilling the contents over himself and scalding his legs in the process. He shrieked in pain and stumbled off through the smoke.

Another pair of swarthy-looking reivers brandishing muskets fitted with bayonets charged Kit, who overturned a long oaken table and met his attackers head-on. Both men buried their bayonets into Kit's wooden shield. He slammed the table into the men and drove the pirates back against the stone wall with enough force to knock the wind out of his attackers. Gasping, they grabbed for their pistols. Kit grabbed the ruffian on his left and slashed his knuckles, tore the flintlock from his grasp, and emptied the pistol into the second brigand at close range. The first man howled in agony and cradled his ravaged hand. Kit silenced him with a slap across the skull, using the pirate's own pistol for a club.

"Navarre!"

Kit heard the Cayman's name called out, somewhere near the front gate, followed by a roar of pistols fired almost simultaneously. McQueen sprang like a cat in the direction of the gunshots and tracked the sound through the smoke and rubble until he stumbled over a body lying prone on the ground. It was Tom Bragg. The tavernkeeper had a hole between his eyes, a smoking pistol clutched in his outstretched hand.

"Tom was never the forgiving kind," a voice said from behind Kit. It was Orturo Navarre. "I thought the Sea Spray an ample reward for a leg."

Kit leaped to his feet, turning as he lunged. He gambled that Navarre only had one pistol . . . and lost. Navarre shot him at close range with the second bone-handled flintlock he had retrieved from the debris. Kit groaned as a slug seared his side and flung him backward toward the front gate. The damn door was bolted. Kit ignored the white-hot burst of pain in his side and started to crawl toward the entrance to the compound. Navarre realized what his adversary was up to and hurried over to block his progress. The Cayman placed himself between McQueen and the gate and calmly reloaded. He shoved the lieutenant back with a well-placed bootheel. Kit groaned and tried to collect his strength for one last try. He would reach the gate or die.

"You are a dead man, Lieutenant. And for what? An island that means nothing to you." Navarre rammed a charge down the gun barrel and followed it with wadding and shot. "Your woman said I would die by the snake. But I do not see any snakes, eh? But you will die by the Cayman." He threw back his head and laughed, enjoying his moment.

It was at this precise moment Kit heard a familiar high-pitched swooshing sound he remembered all too well from the battle of New Orleans and the bombardment the American defenders had endured at the hands of the British. He instinctively hugged the earth.

For Orturo Navarre, the oncoming rocket was something out of a nightmare. Launched from the wagon, the projectile first skimmed along the earth, then bounded into the air where it spiraled through the drifting smoke like some hellish snake, leaving a serpentine trail of fire and smoke in its wake. Navarre shrieked and held up his hands as if to ward off a demon. The Congreve rocket struck the Cayman square in the chest, lifting him off the ground and impaling him like a bug on a needle. The rocket carried its victim across the remaining few yards and pinned him to the gate.

Navarre writhed in agony as the rocket continued to spew smoke and embers.

"No!" he screamed, struggling to pull free of the skewer. "No!" as the propulsion dissipated, signaling the inner fuse was burning down to the explosive charge. *"Noooo!"* His voice no longer sounded human, but animalistic, and thick with terror, confronted at last with his own mortality and the conjure woman's revenge. *The snake. The destroyer of souls. The snake.*

Kit could have reached the pirate captain and freed him from the rocket. After all, there was a time to temper justice with mercy. But not today.

"Nooo!" wailed Orturo Navarre.

"Yes," said Kit, and curling tight, he pressed himself against the hard-packed earth. The world was about to become a better place.

The explosion blew the gate to bits, and with it,

Captain Orturo Navarre. The last thing that went through the Cayman's mind . . . was an iron hinge.

Kit had the best berth in the place to watch Jean Laffite, his crew, Obregon's men, and the townspeople, led by none other than Father Bernal, storm through the gaping hole in the wall where once the gate had stood. Laffite looked as if he had been through his own battle. His coat was powder-burned, his cheek gashed, and the side of his neck was stained crimson. He halted for a moment, but Kit waved him on. There was still work to be done.

Raven hurried to Kit's side, sank to her knees, and held him in a tender embrace. O'Keefe lumbered forward as a familiar figure raced through the ruined wall to stand alongside the Irishman. Johnny Fuller seemed wholly offended that he had missed all the excitement.

"I knew you'd make it, Chief Iron Hand," the boy exclaimed. "I bet you chased those pirates off the walls all by your lonesome."

"I had a little help," O'Keefe magnanimously admitted.

Harry Tregoning and Strikes With Club joined their companions at the entrance as the remainder of Navarre's crewmen, with no one to lead them, began to surrender by the dozen to Laffite and the islanders. The rebellion was ended. Natividad was free again.

Obregon limped forward and stood over Kit and Raven. The Hawk of the Antilles saluted Kit and bowed to Raven. "I shall do everything in my power to make the last days of your visit here more pleasant than the first." Cesar Obregon started down the road toward Morgan Town. He hoped he could find a cask of jack iron that hadn't been smashed. His ankle slowed him down quite a bit; however, he wasn't worried. The Hawk knew where he was going. At last.

"I say, Captain Obregon. You wouldn't be needing a chief gunner, would you?" Tregoning called out. He glanced at Kit. "That is, if you no longer require my services."

"Good luck and Godspeed, Englishman. No man had a better enemy or truer friend," said Kit.

"Ah, yes, then. I wish you both every happiness," Tregoning replied. "Wait up there, I say, Captain Obregon! And if there is no one to run the Sea Spray, well, I warrant I'm your man. What Harry Tregoning doesn't know about women hasn't been writ." The thickset, flat-nosed little man from Cornwall fell in step with Obregon and the two men descended the road toward town.

Kit grinned and then looked up into Raven's emerald gaze.

"I'm hurt," he said, wincing.

"You'll heal," she replied, and brought her lips to his. Kit closed his eyes. There wasn't a better way to lose consciousness. And when he came to, McQueen knew she would still be with him.

"Well," O'Keefe sighed, taking in the ruined fortress with its scenes of terrible carnage. "Maybe we better bring the lad home."

Raven cradled her beloved, feeling his heartbeat against her breasts, his breath even and steady and warm upon her neck.

"He *is* home."

ABOUT THE AUTHOR

Kerry Newcomb is the bestselling author of several major frontier novels, including *Morning Star* and *Sacred Is the Wind*. He lives with his family in Fort Worth, Texas.